"Is this some kind of joke?" Vinnie asked, directing his question to Jake.

"What? I don't know what you're talking about."

"You don't, huh? Well, The Silver Moon took in a hundred grand and change Saturday. Barney's had some high rollers that stayed all night Friday and half the day Saturday, so their take was twice that much, and Maury booked ten g's on Saturday night."

"Yeah," Jake said, feeling the sweat beginning to drip down into his shoes.

"How much is missing?" Marko asked before Jake could say anything else.

"All of it."

"That's impossible. It was all there when I put it in the safe yesterday."

Vinnie took the duffel bag and turned it upside down on the desk. Scraps of newspaper fell out.

"Beth." Jake spat out her name like it was a morsel of spoiled food. "Beth took it."

Marko moved next to Jake. "Beth?"

"She disappeared yesterday, a few hours after I put the bag in the safe."

"I just asked you about her and you said she was fine," Marko said as he reached under his jacket and removed a shiny black gun.

CAROL COSTA

WHEN NOTHING ELSE WAS RIGHT

W RLDWIDE®

TORONTO • NEW YORK • LONDON
AMSTERDAM • PARIS • SYDNEY • HAMBURG
STOCKHOLM • ATHENS • TOKYO • MILAN
MADRID • WARSAW • BUDAPEST • AUCKLAND

For the Gecko Gals,
friends who never fail to support and inspire me.

Recycling programs
for this product may
not exist in your area.

WHEN NOTHING ELSE WAS RIGHT

A Worldwide Mystery/February 2014

First published by Open Books Press

ISBN-13: 978-0-373-26884-9

ONE

JAKE SLAMMED OUT of the truck and marched towards the convenience store. The door closed silently behind him as he stood in the entrance scanning the store for a sign of Beth.

An older man with a bald head and rimless glasses stood behind the counter. "Can I help you, sir?" he asked.

"I'm looking for my wife," Jake told him. "Where the hell is she?"

"I don't know, sir. Did she come in here?"

"Hell, yes, she came in here," Jake replied. Without waiting for the clerk to say anything else, Jake began searching the store for Beth, muttering obscenities to himself as he walked up and down the narrow aisles.

In a few minutes, Jake was back at the checkout counter. His face was flushed with anger.

"I take it you didn't find her," the man behind the counter said. "Are you sure she came in here?"

Jake was about to grab the guy by his stupid bow tie and throttle the grin off his chubby face, when another customer approached the counter. She was a middle-aged woman, as wide as she was tall. Jake had seen her enter the store right behind Beth.

Jake stepped back and waited while the clerk rang up the woman's purchases. Then, the door opened and a group of teenagers came bursting in, laughing and shouting at one another.

The older woman left with Jake right behind her. "Excuse me, ma'am," Jake said, falling into step next to her. "My wife went into that store just before you did. Do you recall seeing her?"

"The pregnant girl?"

"Yeah."

"Never saw her," the woman said letting out a breath that smelled like she had recently consumed a clove of garlic.

"Then how did you know she was pregnant?" Jake yelled.

The woman shrugged. "Lucky guess."

"You stupid old bag," Jake whispered. "I should knock you on your fat ass."

The woman shoved Jake away with such force that his head bounced up against the store window. Surprised by her attack, Jake shook his head to clear it as the woman wobbled away down the street. Jake was about to chase after her when another car drove into the parking lot and pulled up directly in front of him.

Jake recognized the car and the couple inside of it. It was that newspaper reporter, Dana Sloan, and the big cop she dated. Dana lived in the nice apartment building across the street from Jake and Beth. They had all met at a block party a few months back.

Dana smiled and waved at him as she got out of the car. "Hi, how are you?"

"Not so good," Jake told her. "My wife went into this store a half hour ago and never came out."

"Women often get lost in stores," Detective Al Bruno said. "You have to go in with them."

"Maybe she's in the bathroom," Dana said.

"I didn't think they had one in this place," Jake replied.

"It's in the back by the canned goods," Dana told him. Jake nodded and walked into the store with Dana and

Bruno. Maybe Beth was in the bathroom. Now that she was pregnant she spent a lot of time in the bathroom.

The counter area was crowded with the kids who were still laughing and teasing each other as they paid for their sodas and candy bars.

Jake ignored them and strode to the back of the store. Sure enough, there was a door with a sign that said, "Restroom." Jake knocked on the door. "Beth, you in there?"

When there was no answer, Jake tried the doorknob and the door opened to reveal a room the size of a small closet with a sink and a commode. There was no place to hide in that room and no window to climb out of either. Jake pulled the door closed again and returned to the front of the store.

The teenagers were gone, but now Dana and Bruno were at the counter paying for a big bag of chips, a six-pack of beer and a few large bottles of soda. Jake didn't like cops. He'd had enough trouble with the law to last him the rest of his life and given his current profession, he had to be exceptionally cautious.

As the clerk was ringing up the sale, he looked past his customers and spoke to Jake. "You find your wife?" the old man asked.

Everyone looked at Jake as he shook his head in a negative reply. "Is there a back door to this place?"

"Sure, but it's locked. No one can get out that way. An alarm sounds if it's opened."

"I want to see it."

"Sorry, no one's allowed back there."

Jake's face turned red. "Listen, jerk. My wife came in here and never came out again. I'm going to look in your back room."

The clerk backed away from the counter as if he thought Jake was going to leap over it and attack him. Bruno held up his hands and stepped between them.

"No need to get excited here," Bruno said calmly.

"I'm sorry," Jake babbled quickly. "I'm worried sick about my wife. She's pregnant for God's sake. I just want to look in the back room for her."

Bruno looked at the clerk. "Did you see his wife come in here?"

"No, I didn't," the man said moving forward again. "But there were a lot of people in and out so I could have just missed her."

Bruno nodded and pulled his badge out of his pocket and showed it to the clerk. "Is it okay if I look in your back room?"

"Yeah, sure officer," the clerk stammered.

"Okay, come on," Bruno motioned for Jake to follow him. "We'll take a look in the back room."

"Thanks," Jake said without a trace of gratitude in his voice.

Dana collected Bruno's change while Jake followed Bruno to the back of the store and through a door marked private. It led into a room piled high with boxes of all sizes and shapes. They walked past them to the back door. It was indeed padlocked with a heavy metal bar across it. Jake didn't think Beth was strong enough to lift the bar much less get the padlock opened.

He turned around and surveyed the boxes stacked everywhere. "Maybe she's hiding among these boxes," Jake said.

"Why would she do that?" Bruno asked pointedly. "Is there some reason she might want to get away from you?"

Jake forced a laugh. "Hell, no. Beth's just a joker that's all. Likes to give me a hard time."

Bruno took Jake's arm and led him out of the storage room. "I'll tell you what. Why don't you go home and look for your wife? If there were a lot of people in and out of here, she could have come out and slipped past you while you were daydreaming or something. If she doesn't turn up there, call the police and file a missing persons report."

Dana was at the car waiting for Bruno when he escorted Jake out of the store. "Your wife's name is Beth," she said. "Pretty blond girl, right?"

"Yeah. Right," Jake said.

"I'm sorry, I've forgotten your name."

"Jake. Jake Carlson."

"I'm Dana Sloan. I work at The Globe. This is Detective Al Bruno. Please let us know if there's anything we can do to help."

"I told him if he didn't find her, he should file a report," Bruno said. "Ask for Harrison in Missing Persons."

"Thanks. I'm sure you're right and she slipped past me while I was listening to the sports' news. She's pregnant and a little daffy sometimes. Probably forgot I drove her here and walked on home."

"I'm sure that's it," Dana agreed.

Jake opened the door to his truck and climbed inside. He started it up, and drove out of the parking lot. Not knowing what else to do, Jake headed for home. Maybe Beth was there. He didn't see how she could have gotten past him. She was supposed to go into the store, buy the beer he wanted and the candy bar she said she was craving and come right out again. Where the hell did she go? She knew better than to play games with him. If she was at home, he was going to teach her a lesson. Pregnant or not, she was going to pay for what she had just put him through.

Jake opened the door to the apartment and yelled for Beth. No answer. He slammed the door shut and began going from room to room looking for her. Since the apartment only had four rooms counting the bathroom, Jake's search didn't take long. Jake went into the kitchen and retrieved a beer from the refrigerator. He carried it into the living room, flopped down on the sofa and turned on the television set. The Bears were playing the San Diego Chargers and the game had just started.

Although Jake wasn't really a football fan, he did some of his best thinking in front of the television set. He drank his beer slowly trying to figure out what had happened to his wife. He had been sitting in the truck the whole time watching people come and go from the convenience store. The clerk had been right. It had been busy during the time Beth was inside. Several people came and went while he was waiting for her. Still, how could he miss his own wife? Her stomach was sticking out a mile now. She couldn't have gotten past him.

"I'll bet she was hiding in the back room," Jake said aloud. "Damn cop should have let me look through those boxes." Beth was probably still there hiding like her scruffy old cat.

Suddenly, Jake jumped to his feet. Beth's cat. Where was he? Jake began to move around the apartment again.

"Hey, Spenser, where are you? Want a treat?" Jake called softly. He looked under the bed, in the cabinet under the kitchen sink and the one under the bathroom sink. Spenser was also missing.

Jake hurried back to the bedroom and opened the closet. Beth's meager wardrobe of maternity clothes was hanging there, pushed to the center in front of the regular clothes she could no longer fit into. He went to her dresser and opened the drawers. Everything was there, at least as far as he could tell.

Back in the kitchen he looked for her vitamins. They were there on the shelf where they always were. He shook the bottle and looked inside of it. It was half empty. There should have been more pills he thought, but he couldn't remember how long ago she had refilled her prescription.

Once again, Jake settled himself in front of the television set. Spenser was gone. Beth loved that cat. Jake often accused her of loving the cat more than she loved her husband. Maybe some of Beth's prenatal vitamins were gone too. Just maybe, Beth had left him.

"She'll be back," Jake said, talking aloud to himself again. "Where's she going to go?" The answer was obvious.

Jake grabbed the phone and punched in his mother-in-law's number. Greta answered on the third ring.

"Hello."

"Put Beth on," Jake said curtly.

"Beth's not here, Jake," Greta answered sharply.

"Don't lie to me, Greta. Put her on the phone now."

"Go to hell," Greta replied as she slammed down the phone.

She's lying, Jake thought sullenly. Beth's there all right, crying on mama's shoulder again. Well, let her stay there tonight. I'll go get her in the morning. Her and that damn cat both.

TWO

WHILE JAKE CARLSON was contemplating the disappearance of his wife, Dana and Bruno were watching the Bears game at Bob and Cynthia Farrell's house. Bob worked with Dana at the newspaper as one of her investigative staff. Cynthia's brother, Greg, was there with Marianne who also worked at the newspaper.

Bob had acted as a matchmaker between his wife's brother and his gorgeous red-haired co-worker. That had been over a year ago and although it was not yet official, Bob was sure Greg and Marianne would soon be engaged.

As Dana had told Jake earlier, she worked for *The Globe,* but she was not a regular staff reporter. Dana Sloan headed a division of the newspaper, called Globe Investigations. It had been established a few years back by The Globe's editor, Sam McGowan, who believed a city's newspaper should do more than report the news. Sam believed that the newspaper should reach out into the community and be of service to people in need of advice or help with problems. The city of Crescent Hills, Illinois, was fifty miles south of Chicago and was a growing, thriving metropolis. With the growth and prosperity had come more crime and other problems so Globe Investigations had plenty of work to handle.

Requests for assistance came into Dana's office on a daily basis, by mail, telephone, and e-mail. Over the years, Dana and her staff had investigated thousands of cases. Fraud, missing pets, petty thefts, complaints about business practices, politicians, the school board and other matters were handled by Globe Investigations.

Dana tried to stay out of more serious police cases but there had been times when that was impossible. It was those times that caused problems in her relationship with Bruno. It was those times that had come close to ending her relationship with Bruno.

Detective Al Bruno thought that Dana should be attending PTA meetings and Little League games, not chasing down thieves and murderers.

While Dana admitted that she loved Bruno and would probably marry him someday, she was not quite ready to give up her career for him. Some men might have walked away from the relationship by now, but Bruno was as stubborn as he was tall and broad. He was determined to marry the girl with golden brown curls and hazel eyes who had captured his heart the first moment she had stuck her dainty nose into one of his cases.

At half-time, the game was tied. Bruno, Bob, and Greg were rehashing the plays and discussing the way the coaches should handle the second half of the game.

Cynthia was in the kitchen replenishing the snack bowls. Dana and Marianne both escaped the armchair quarterback session to join her.

"Where are the kids?" Dana asked Cynthia.

"At my mom's house. She'll bring them home when the game is over. I thought Casey was coming, has anyone heard from her?"

Casey Jordan was the other investigator on Dana's staff. Casey was putting her life back together after a marriage to a man who had become a murder victim shortly after their wedding. Her friends were still concerned about her mental state.

"Oh, sorry," Dana said quickly. "She called my cell

phone and said she feels like she's catching a cold and decided to stay home and rest."

"I hope it's not just an excuse to avoid another social event with couples," Marianne said.

"Please don't repeat that in front of my husband," Cynthia warned. "He's been driving me crazy trying to get me to think of someone wonderful to fix her up with."

Dana laughed. "His success with Greg and Marianne has gone to his head."

Cynthia nodded. "One good match out of hundreds of attempts is not a good track record, but he's a hopeless romantic."

"What about his mechanic friend?" Marianne asked. "I thought he was interested in Casey."

"He was, but Casey refused to go out with him."

"Casey needs more time to heal," Dana said. "That whole business with Tony was a tragedy. Anyway, I'm sorry I forgot to tell you she wasn't coming. She called right before Bruno and I got to the convenience store and ran into my neighbor who was looking for his wife."

"I think that sounds a little weird," Marianne said. "Maybe his wife was deliberately trying to ditch him. How well do you know them?"

Dana had related the incident to everyone when she and Bruno had arrived at the house, but then the game started and they hadn't really discussed it.

"We sat with them at a block party last summer. She was very nice. Her name is Beth and she works at the law firm that handles a lot of The Globe's legal matters. Her husband is one of those tough guys with an attitude. He might have jumped the counter and punched the clerk at the convenience store if Bruno hadn't been there and intervened."

Bruno entered the kitchen in time to hear Dana's remark. "The guy's a punk and I'm pretty sure he's a bag man for Marko Senese."

"What's a bag man?" Cynthia asked.

"The guy that goes around and picks up the money from the various enterprises Marko runs for his father. All of them are strictly cash operations. Jake picks up the cash several times a week and delivers it to Marko."

Marianne raised her perfectly formed eyebrows. "Nice job."

"How interesting," Dana said, looking at Bruno with a frown. "Why didn't you tell me that earlier?"

"I just thought of it now. I knew his name rang a bell, but I wasn't sure why. Jack's been keeping a file on all the guys that work for Senese and company and now I remember seeing Carlson's name in it."

"Do you think his wife knows what he does for a living?"

"Yes."

"Can you look him up tomorrow and see if he's got a record?"

"Why?"

"Because I like his wife and now I'm worried about her."

Bruno shook his full head of black curly hair that women itched to run their fingers through. "The game is starting again." He reached for a bowl of chips and hurried out of the kitchen.

Dana turned back to Cynthia and Marianne. "He always makes me beg for information."

"Don't do it during the game," Marianne warned.

"Hey, girls," Bob yelled from the living room. "What happened to the rest of the snacks? I'm wasting away in here."

The truth was that Bob could stop eating for a week and still be as plump as the Pillsbury Dough Boy.

"I wish!" Cynthia yelled back, picking up the pretzels and tortilla chips. "He's starting another diet tomorrow," she said. "I'm counting on you two to monitor him at work."

Dana and Marianne exchanged glances as Cynthia left the room.

"Is she kidding?" Marianne whispered. "We'd have to tie him up and gag him to keep him from snacking."

"We'll give the assignment to Casey," Dana replied as they gathered up bowls of salsa, dips, and a plate of homemade fudge. "That'll give her a new goal to focus on."

On the way home that evening, Dana decided not to broach the subject of Jake Carlson again. Bruno was already in a bad mood over the Bear's loss to San Diego.

As they pulled into the parking lot of Dana's apartment building, Bruno's cell phone rang.

"Detective Bruno," he said into the phone that looked like a toy in his large hand. He listened and nodded as the station relayed information to him. "Okay. I'll be there in five minutes." He clicked off the phone and turned to Dana. "Give me a kiss that'll last all night. Someone just called in an apparent homicide."

"Is it a woman?" Dana asked, thinking about Beth Carlson.

Bruno nodded. "I'll call you when I have some details."

Dana kissed Bruno and got out of the car to enter her building and climb the stairs to her apartment unescorted. Once upstairs, she made herself a cup of tea and drank it standing in the alcove of windows in her living room. Her easel with a partially finished painting occupied one end of the alcove along with a small table that held her paints and brushes. Dana's dreams of being an artist someday were buried behind the excitement and challenges of her investigative work, but they were not forgotten.

The painting she was currently working on was the trees

she could see from her window, their leaves now turning beautiful shades of red and gold from the early unexpected chill of September.

The phone rang and Dana rushed to answer it. It was Bruno reporting that the dead woman was not Beth Carlson. "Who is it?" Dana asked.

"We don't know. No identification on her, but it's definitely not your friend, so you can stop worrying."

"Thanks for calling. I was worried."

"I know. I have to run. The lab boys just arrived. I'll call you in the morning."

Dana hung up the phone and went back to stand at the windows again. She looked past the trees she had been trying to capture on her canvas to the parking lot of the building across the street. The lights in the lot allowed her to see the truck that belonged to Jake Carlson. Apparently, he was home. The big question in Dana's mind was whether Beth Carlson was there with him.

THREE

THE NEXT MORNING, Jake awoke half-expecting to find Beth in bed next to him, or crashed on the living room sofa. Now that she was pregnant, she claimed the sofa was more comfortable than the bed. When Beth was still missing, Jake showered and left the apartment. He stopped and got himself a cup of coffee.

He arrived at his mother-in-law's modest ranch style home before eight and banged on the front door. He had to knock three more times before Greta finally came to the door.

She opened it with the chain in place and glared at him through the small opening. "What do you want, Jake?"

"I want my wife. Tell her to get her ass out here now."

"I told you last night. Beth isn't here."

"Then where the hell is she?"

Concern appeared in Greta's eyes. "What happened, Jake? Did you hit her again?"

"No. I haven't laid a hand on her in months. That's all over. She's carrying my son for Pete's sake."

Greta undid the chain and opened the door all the way. Jake walked into the house. It smelled like rotten eggs. Greta wasn't much of a housekeeper.

"Tell me what happened." Greta said softly with fear in her eyes. "Did you have a fight?"

"No. Nothing like that. Beth said she had a craving for a chocolate bar so I drove her down to the convenience store. She went inside and never came out again."

"That's crazy," Greta shouted. "Did you look for her?"

"Of course I looked for her. I went inside and searched the john and even got a cop to take me in the back room and check the back door and stuff. There were boxes piled all over the place, but the cop wouldn't let me look through them. I think she was hiding in one of them."

"Why would she do that?"

"That's the same question the cop asked me. I don't know. Maybe because she's nuts."

"Or maybe because she was afraid to face you," Greta shouted. "I'm calling the police."

Greta turned to go to the phone, but Jake grabbed her arm. "Wait. Spenser's missing too." Greta stared at him. "You know Beth wouldn't leave that mangy cat. He's got to be with her. And I think you know where they are."

Greta wrenched her arm free and ran to the telephone.

Jake stood there silently while she dialed 911 and told the dispatcher that her daughter had disappeared.

Greta looked up at Jake. "He wants to know how long she's been gone."

"Since yesterday afternoon when she went into the store," Jake answered sullenly.

Greta repeated the information to the 911 operator and then nodded and hung up. "He said we should file a missing persons report," she told Jake.

"That's the same thing the cop at the store told me."

"Have you called her friends?" Greta asked anxiously. "Talked to the neighbors? How about that girl that Beth pals around with, the blond upstairs from you?"

"I ain't talked to no one but you," Jake said, clenching his fists into a tight ball. "I figured if Beth left me again, this would be the first place she'd run to."

"Well, she's not here."

"So you say."

"You don't believe me," Greta replied. "Fine. Search the house. See for yourself she's not here."

Jake thought maybe Greta was bluffing, so he decided to call her on it. He walked out of the living room and began looking through the house. His search uncovered nothing but dirty laundry, dust and clutter. When he got back to the living room, Greta was on the phone again.

"Thanks, Marsha, I'll call you as soon as I hear anything." Greta quickly dialed another number to inquire about her daughter's whereabouts. After the fourth call, Greta burst into tears. "No one's heard from her," she croaked. "What happened, Jake? Tell me the truth."

"I swear to God, I told you the truth. She went into the convenience store to get a candy bar and a six-pack for me and never came out again."

"What store was it? I'm going over there myself."

"The one on Ashland, near our apartment. You go and look for your nutty daughter and her stupid cat. I'm going over to the pool hall. Call me there when you find her."

Greta's eyes filled with anger. She moved menacingly towards him. "You go to the pool hall, Jake. I'm going to find my daughter. And when I do, you'll be the last person I tell. Now get out of here."

"With pleasure," Jake shouted back.

Jake got into his truck and started the engine. His special cell phone rang. "Damn it," Jake muttered as he opened the small phone and pushed the button. He knew who was calling.

"Where the hell are you?" Marko Senese demanded. No hello, just the question shouted into the phone.

"Sorry, Marko," Jake said quickly. "I got delayed."

"How long are you going to be?"

"I'll be there in thirty minutes."

The phone clicked in Jake's ear as Marko disconnected without any further discussion.

Jake closed the phone and dropped it back into his pocket. Now thanks to Beth, Jake was in trouble with Marko. He put the truck in gear and sped back to the apartment. Jake wasn't supposed to be at the pool hall until ten, but Marko often called him and told him to get there earlier.

Jake was letting himself into the apartment when Beth's friend came clomping down the stairs in her thick-soled shoes. She was dressed in her waitress' uniform.

"Hey, Millie," Jake said. "You seen Beth today?"

"No. Why?" Millie was a bleached blond who always wore her hair in a ponytail. Today it was pulled back so tight, her eyes looked slanted. She was in her forties with a good figure and a face that was always caked with too much makeup. Millie and Beth were friends, two dizzy blonds, Jake always said, only Beth's hair was natural and fell in soft waves around a face that was pretty with or without makeup.

"No reason. Just thought maybe you two were going to hang out today."

"I have to work."

"Right. Okay. See you later then."

Millie shrugged and hurried out of the building. Jake pushed the door open to the apartment and looked around again. Still no sign of Beth or the cat. Well, he didn't have time to worry about that now. Marko would be freaking out as it was.

Jake went into the bathroom and knelt on the floor next to the toilet. He removed one of the floor tiles. Built into the floor was a safe, the same size as the tile that covered it. He put his key into the lock and opened the door. Inside was a small duffel bag. Jake pulled out the bag, locked the safe, and replaced the floor tile.

The pool hall was a ten-minute drive from the apartment. Jake walked in exactly thirty-five minutes after his phone call from Marko.

The pool hall didn't officially open until noon, but some of the regulars were already there drinking at the bar. Jake ignored the few people who called out to him and hurried to the back where the office was located.

Marko opened the door and gave Jake a little shove as he came into the room. "About time," Marko whispered.

"Hey, I'm not late. I'm not supposed to be here until ten. You're just spoiled because I show up early most of the time."

"Give me the bag. Vinnie's waiting to verify the take."

Jake handed the bag to Marko and watched him walk through another door to the official counting room. Marko was back in a minute and nodded for Jake to have a seat in one of the two chairs in front of his desk.

"Where's everyone at?" Jake asked.

"Harry's got a cold and Turk went out to get some breakfast."

Harry and Turk were Marko's enforcers, big and ugly as bulls and twice as mean. Marko needed every ounce of muscle they provided because Beth could have decked Marko with one punch. Of course that didn't make Marko any less dangerous. He had worked his way up in the Chicago organization with his wits and total lack of conscience and patience. Everyone knew that Marko would shoot you for passing wind in his presence.

Jake smiled and nodded, trying not to show his impatience. He wanted to get out of there and have a beer and shoot some pool with the guys out front, but the delivery procedure had to be done Marko's way.

"So, how's that pretty little wife of yours?" Marko said. His voice always got softer when he asked about Beth. Marko liked Beth. Of course Beth had the kind of looks that most men liked. She wasn't movie-star gorgeous, but

Beth had a real sweet face and before she was pregnant a figure to match.

Jake considered telling Marko that Beth had disappeared and that's why he had been late, but decided against it. "She's okay. The pregnancy has her pretty tired out these days."

"Is she still working for that lawyer?"

"No."

"Why not?"

"They wouldn't let her work past six months. She's on a leave of absence now."

"Makes sense."

The door to the back office was suddenly flung open and all three hundred pounds of Vinnie, the accountant, filled the doorway. "Marko, Jake, come in here."

Jake rose from his chair. He didn't like the sound of Vinnie's voice and his fat face was all flushed like he was upset over something.

"What's wrong?" Jake asked, trying to sound casual.

"Just get in here," Vinnie said.

Marko stood at the door and motioned for Jake to enter Vinnie's office in front of him. Jake shrugged and walked through the door ignoring the prickles of fear that were racing down his spine.

Marko closed the door quietly behind them and looked at Vinnie who had moved back behind his massive metal desk.

"Is this some kind of joke?" Vinnie asked, directing his question to Jake.

"What? I don't know what you're talking about."

"You don't, huh? Well, The Silver Moon took in a hundred grand and change Saturday. Barney's had some high rollers that stayed all night Friday and half the day Saturday, so their take was twice that much and Maury booked ten g's on Saturday night."

"Yeah," Jake said, feeling the sweat beginning to drip down into his shoes.

"How much is missing?" Marko asked before Jake could say anything else.

"All of it."

"Shit!" Jake shouted moving forward to the desk. "That's impossible. It was all there when I put it in the safe yesterday."

Vinnie took the duffel bag and turned it upside down on the desk. Scraps of newspaper fell out.

"Beth." Jake spat out her name like it was a morsel of spoiled food. "Beth took it."

Marko moved next to Jake. "Beth?"

"She disappeared yesterday, a few hours after I put the bag in the safe."

"I just asked you about her and you said she was fine," Marko said as he reached under his jacket and removed a shiny black gun.

"I know. I didn't want to burden you with my trouble. But the truth is she went into a convenience store and never came out again. I've been going crazy looking for her."

"You knock her around again?" Vinnie asked.

"No. Honest to God. I haven't laid a hand on her. She's pregnant for God's sake. I wouldn't take a chance on hurting my kid."

"Too bad the kid's going to grow up without a father," Marko said softly, leveling his gun at Jake.

FOUR

Monday mornings at the paper were always busy. Marianne usually came in before nine to pick up the mail that had been delivered on Saturday when Globe Investigations was closed. She went through that first, opening and sorting it so it would be ready for Dana to look through when she arrived. Then, Marianne booted up her computer and went through the e-mail.

"Good morning," Dana called out as she came through the office door dressed in a pale green dress that hung loose from her shoulders to her knees. It was a soft, silky fabric and looked very comfortable.

"New dress?" Marianne asked.

"No. I found it in the back of my closet when I was packing my summer things away. It's one of those in-between outfits you can only wear for a few weeks before it gets really cold. Although I was thinking I could buy some type of sweater or jacket to go with it to prolong its wear. What do you think?"

"One of those cute half-sweaters we saw at Logan's last week would do it."

"Hmm." Dana smiled. "I just may run over there at lunch time. Want to come along?"

"Don't I always?" Marianne gathered up the mail she had put aside for Dana to review and held it out to her.

"Did you get the messages from the answering service?" Dana asked.

"Not yet. I decided to look through the e-mail first."

"Okay. You do that and I'll check the service." Dana walked through the door into her private office and put her purse and the mail on her desk.

Dana's office was large enough to hold a big oak desk set in front of windows that looked down on Main Street. When she was so inclined, Dana could position her desk chair so that she had a view of police headquarters across the street from the newspaper. Sometimes, she saw Bruno going in or out of the station.

To the right of the desk, there was a small conference table in the office with straight-backed chairs around it, but it didn't get used much. For staff meetings, Dana sat behind her desk where she could access the computer if necessary. Bob, Casey and Marianne usually settled in three of the four comfortable leather chairs with rounded backs and wide arms.

Across the room from Dana's desk was a matching credenza with a television set on one side of the top of it and a coffee pot and serving items on the other. As usual, Marianne had made a pot of coffee and Dana helped herself to a cup before settling herself behind the desk to check the phone messages.

There were only two messages. One was from Bruno left at two a.m. when he had returned home from the call he had gotten the night before. "Hi sweets. I'm going to sleep in this morning, but thought maybe we could have lunch today. I'll be in the office by noon and I'll call you then. Don't run off shopping with Marianne."

Dana laughed and erased the message. The next message was from a woman and had come in a few minutes before nine that morning.

"Hello, this is Greta Malone for Dana Sloan. My daughter has been missing since yesterday afternoon. I'm afraid her husband did something to her. I called the police and am going to file a report, but I'm hoping you can help me.

Her name is Beth Carlson and she told me she met you last summer and you were very nice and you help people. Please call me."

Dana felt a jolt of worry as she wrote down Greta's phone number. Apparently, Beth Carlson had not shown up last night after all. She erased the message and dialed the number Greta Malone had left for her.

"Hello," the woman's voice was anxious.

"Greta Malone?"

"Yes. Do you have news about Beth?"

"No. I'm afraid not. This is Dana Sloan of Globe Investigations returning your call."

"Oh, yes. Thank you. Beth said she met you at some type of neighborhood party. Do you remember her?"

"Yes, of course I do. And yesterday afternoon, my friend and I were at the convenience store on Ashland Avenue and ran into Beth's husband. He was frantically looking for her."

"That's what he says, but I don't believe him. It's all an act. I think he did something to Beth. He's a gangster. I'm not supposed to know that, but I do. And he's hurt Beth before."

"I see. I'm so sorry. How can I help you?"

"Help me find Beth. My friends say the police are overworked and may not spend much time looking for her. I really think Jake may have done something to her. Please, please, help me." Greta's voice broke and she started to sob.

"Okay, Mrs. Malone. Give me your address. I'll come right over to talk to you."

Greta took a deep breath and gave Dana her address.

IN THE BACK office of the pool hall, Jake was trying to reason with Marko. "Hey, Marko, Vinnie, how long have I worked for you guys? Years now without a dollar missing. You know I'd never steal from you. And if I did why the hell would I bring you a bag full of paper instead of just taking off. I'm telling you it had to be Beth."

"You're saying Beth took money she didn't know was there and ran off with it?" Vinnie asked.

"It had to be her. No one else could have done it."

"How'd she know about it? No one is supposed to know about your job." Marko's voice was cold as ice.

"I don't know. She's always at work when I get done with my pick ups." Jake stopped as Beth's actions over the last week or so began to replay in his head. "Oh shit. Listen to me. I told you that the law firm made her take a maternity leave, so she's been home when I get there. She must have seen me stash the bag in the safe. She pretended like she didn't know, but she had to know. The little bitch had it all planned."

"How'd she know the combination to the safe?"

"There is no combination. It's a lock and the only key is on my key…" Jake stopped talking as he suddenly remembered that his keys had been misplaced the week before. He had screamed at Beth and accused her of taking them, but then they turned up on the floor behind his dresser. And last week it had been okay. Last week everything was fine, but this week she took the money and replaced it with newspaper and now he was going to get his head blown off because of her.

"I can't believe Beth would do something like this," Marko said.

"That's because you like her. I see the way you look at her all the time," Jake replied desperately.

Marko nodded and lowered the gun a bit. "Too bad. I hate to waste a woman."

"Hey, where's everyone at?" Turk shouted from the outer office.

Marko backed over to the door and opened it. "Get in here, Turk," he ordered.

Turk eased his bulky frame into the back office, closed the door and leaned against it. It was getting awfully crowded in the small room.

Marko turned back to Jake. "Okay, Jake. Here's how it's going to go. You and Turk are going to find Beth and the money and bring both of them here. I'll give you twenty-four hours."

"Listen, Marko. With all that cash, she could me miles from here by now."

"So you want me to just shoot you now?"

Jake's stomach did a flip. "No. I'll find her. I got a real good idea of where she is."

"Turk will be with you every minute. By noon tomorrow, you bring me the money and I'll let you live."

"But…"

"No buts, Jake. You were responsible for the money. If your pretty little wife took off with it, she'll be on my hit list until we get it back, but if you and Turk don't find her and return the cash in twenty-four hours, you're dead. Understand?"

"Yeah. Sure. Don't worry, Marko. I know where she is. I'll find her and get your money back. I promise."

Marko nodded and turned to Turk. "You got any questions?"

Turk shook his head in a negative reply.

Marko smiled and put his gun back into the holster under his jacket. "Don't let Jake out of your sight. He goes to the can, you go with him. You go to the can, he goes with you."

"Right," Turk nodded his head and reached out and grabbed Jake's arm. "Jake and me are going to be like Siamese Twins."

Turk kept Jake's arm in his iron grip and opened the door. Jake's face was wet with relief as Turk led him out of the office. He had twenty-four hours to find Beth and the money or think of some other way to avoid a bullet from Marko's gun.

FIVE

GRETA OPENED THE door to her house before Dana had a chance to ring the doorbell. Dana handed the middle-aged woman her business card. Greta took the card and stuck it in the pocket of the slacks she was wearing without looking at it.

Dana followed her into a sparsely furnished living room and took a seat on the sofa. Greta perched herself on the edge of the chair next to the sofa. Both pieces of furniture were worn and lumpy. The small tables scattered around the room were piled with magazines and newspapers. One table held a lamp with a china base that was cracked down the middle.

Greta Malone's hair was more gray than blond and her face showed the lines and wrinkles accumulated from years of hard work and worry.

"Thank you for coming so quickly," she said breathlessly. "I'm out of my mind with worry. Did I tell you that Beth is six months pregnant?"

"Her husband told us that last night. I assume you've checked with her friends to see if any of them have seen her."

"Yes. She only has two girlfriends she still sees on a regular basis. Jake doesn't like her going out without him and her friends don't like him."

"You said that Jake had hurt Beth in the past?"

"Right. She left him once because of that but somehow he talked her into coming back. Then, she got pregnant so

I guess she felt trapped. As you can see, I don't have much and couldn't support her and a baby."

Dana nodded sympathetically. "What about the law firm where Beth worked? Have you contacted them?"

"No. They made her take a leave of absence because of the baby. She hasn't been there for almost three weeks now. I doubt if anyone there knows anything."

"You said her husband is a gangster. Why do you think that?"

"Because Jake never talks about what he does for a living, like most men do. It's like a big secret. But last winter before she got pregnant, Beth told me about having dinner at a fancy restaurant. I was surprised because Jake is a cheapskate and I asked her why they went to such an expensive place. She said they were guests of Jake's boss, Marko Senese. Well, I asked around and found out he's a gangster, so if Jake works for him, Jake's one too."

"I see. Do you have a recent photograph of Beth I could have?"

"I have some that were taken before she married Jake, but she hasn't changed any. I'll get them."

Greta got up and hurried down a hallway that separated the living room from what Dana assumed was the kitchen area. The woman was back in a few minutes with a large manila envelope. She opened it and withdrew several 8 x 10 photos and handed them to Dana.

The photos were professional studio pictures, head shots used by actors and models. Dana recognized Beth Carlson from the block party and from the few other times they had seen each other in the neighborhood.

"Beth is a very pretty girl. I assume she did some acting or modeling."

"Acting. She was too short to be a model, but she's a real good actress. She worked at a theater in Chicago for almost two years when she got out of school. That's where she met Jake."

"At the theater?"

"No. He worked at some bar the actors used to go to after the shows. She met him there. He promised that he was going to take her to New York City so she could be on Broadway. Instead she ended up back here in Crescent Hills, married to Jake and working at the law firm."

"I'll take three of these photos. Two for myself and one for the police. I'm going to talk to someone I know at the station and see if I can get them to start searching for Beth right away."

"I'm so afraid he killed her," Greta said softly as tears began to slide down her face.

"We don't know that," Dana said firmly. "Let's keep good thoughts. I'll get started on this right away and I'll be in touch. Try not to worry and if you hear from Beth call me immediately. My cell phone number is on the card I gave you."

Dana rose to her feet and Greta did the same. Silently, Greta led Dana back to the front door.

"Thank you," she whispered as Dana went out the door.

When Dana got back to the office, Bob was there waiting for her. Marianne had already filled him in on the case. She handed Bob the photo of Beth Carlson.

"Start checking the bus station and train station and see if anyone recognizes this woman." she instructed Bob.

"Pretty girl," he said looking at the photo.

"Yes, oh and she's pregnant."

"Good, that'll make it easier for people to remember her. I'll check the car rental places too. She could have driven to Chicago and got on a plane."

Without any further conversation, Bob hurried out of the office. Dana turned to Marianne. "Have you heard from Casey?"

"Yes and she sounds awful. The cold wasn't just an excuse, she's really sick."

"I'm going to look through the mail now. Was there anything urgent in it?"

"I don't think so," Marianne said. "But there's some e-mails that need your attention. I printed them out and put them on your desk. Oh, and Bruno called. The message is on your desk too."

"Good. I'll call him first. I was worried that I'd have to wake him to ask for a favor."

BETH STUDIED THE photo on her new California driver's license and smiled. It had been easier than she thought possible.

Her next stop was the bank. She hailed a cab outside of the motor vehicle office and told the driver where she wanted to go. "World Savings Bank on Cuyamacha and Third," she said sweetly.

The driver nodded and pulled out into traffic. Beth looked at the driver's license photo again. Her shoulder length blond hair had been dyed a reddish brown and although the cut was a little uneven, she thought it looked short and sassy. Now all Beth had to do was get rid of the baby she was carrying and she could buy some new clothes.

At the bank, a young woman with spiked blond hair that contrasted with her business attire took Beth's information and accepted her new driver's license for identification. She also asked for her social security number and Beth recited it for her.

"When's your baby due?" she asked Beth.

"In a few months," Beth replied.

"Boy or girl?"

"It's supposed to be a boy."

"Did you want to open a checking or savings account?"

"Not today." Beth smiled. "I just need the safety deposit box for some jewelry and papers."

"Of course," the clerk smiled back. "Come with me and I'll get you into the vault."

A few minutes later, Beth was sitting in a private room with an empty safety deposit box on the table in front of her. She removed her rings and dropped them into the box. Her wedding ring made a clunk as it hit the metal bottom of the box and Beth laughed. "Good-bye Jake," she whispered.

Then, Beth stood up and lifted up her favorite lime green maternity top. It went well with the black pants she had changed into in the bathroom of the convenience store, where she had hidden the disguise she had worn to get past Jake. The black wig and funky hat had already been ditched in a bathroom at Chicago's Midway Airport along with the oversized trench coat. Beth rather liked the coat, and it had looked fine in Chicago, but it was much too warm for Los Angeles.

During the two years she had spent working in theater Beth had learned how to change her appearance in a variety of clever ways. Last night at the motel she had cut her hair and used an over-the-counter hair dye on it.

She looked down at her bulging stomach. "Good-bye, baby," Beth whispered. She undid the prosthesis she had worn and padded more and more the last few months. Her "pregnancy" had accomplished all Beth had wanted it to do. Jake had been thrilled when she told him she was expecting his baby. Then, when Beth had shown him the note she had written on the doctor's letterhead that instructed them to refrain from all sexual activities, Jake had sullenly complied. After all, the baby was a boy, and Jake really wanted a son. In his mind, a son was evidence of Jake's manhood, something he could be proud of.

Fortunately, Jake was only interested in the birth of his

boy and didn't want to inconvenience himself by going along on Beth's doctor's visits or child birthing classes. It had been easy to fool him.

Carefully, Beth opened the ties and began taking out the money. She stacked the bills neatly into the safe deposit box. She wasn't sure how much was there, as she had not yet counted it, but she knew it was enough for her to start a new life.

Beth put several hundred dollars into the purse she had bought that morning. It was a nice black shoulder bag, roomy and stylish. It had come with a sleek thin wallet into which she had slipped her new driver's license.

The last items Beth put into the safe deposit box were the social security card and birth certificate that verified her new identity and had allowed her to get the passport she had used to purchase the airline ticket and get through security at Midway.

The photo on the passport had been taken before she altered her appearance so she could no longer use it for identification. She put the passport in the box with the other items.

The fact that the name she was now using belonged to a real person was sad and a little risky, but Beth refused to think about that now. She had a new wardrobe to buy.

SIX

DANA SAT BEHIND her desk for the second time that morning and dialed Bruno's cell phone number. It was answered on the third ring.

"Detective Bruno."

"Where are you, Detective Bruno?" Dana asked.

"I'm in the squad room. Where are you?"

"In my office. I just got back from seeing Beth Carlson's mother. Beth never showed up and she's worried sick. I promised I'd look for her. In fact, I already have Bob out doing just that. What did you find out about Jake Carlson?"

"What are you talking about?"

"You promised to check and see if he had a record?"

"You asked me to do that. I didn't say I would."

Dana sighed loudly. "Greta's mother is afraid he killed her. I think he needs to be questioned right away."

"Are you going to have lunch with me today?"

"Are you going to send someone out to question Jake and look for his wife?"

"Dana, I thought we agreed you'd stay out of police business."

"Whenever possible I will. In this case, it's not possible, but you can limit my involvement by considering this case a possible homicide and starting the search for Beth Carlson immediately."

"You're already doing that."

"Are you going to help me or not?" she asked, her voice rising slightly.

"I'll ask Harrison to get on it right away. and that will include questioning the husband. Will that make you happy?"

"Yes. Thank you. I'll let you know if Bob comes up with anything."

"Great. I'll meet you at Big Lou's at noon."

"I'll see you there."

The call ended and Dana hung up the phone. Bruno had given in a little too easily and that concerned her. She wondered if he had checked out Jake Carlson and come up with information that had made him worry about Beth Carlson's welfare.

Dana glanced at the stack of papers Marianne had put on her desk. She would get to them in a minute, but first she wanted to make another call.

"Good morning, Stratton and Cauthorne," the receptionist at the law firm Dana had called said cheerfully.

"This is Dana Sloan from Globe Investigations. Is Mr. Stratton available?"

"He's in court this morning."

"What about Mr. Cauthorne?"

"He's with a client. Can I take a message?"

"Maybe you can help me," Dana said slowly. "I'm trying to locate one of your employees, Beth Carlson. Do you know her?"

"Beth? Sure I know her, but she doesn't work here any longer."

"Is there someone there that she was close to that could talk to me about her?"

"Who did you say you were again?"

"Dana Sloan with *The Globe*. Your firm handles a lot of our legal work."

"Right. Well, maybe Lena can help you. Hold on, please."

Dana waited through a few clicks and four rings before another female voice spoke. "This is Lena. Can I help you?"

"I hope so," Dana replied and then explained who she was and what she wanted.

"I haven't seen Beth since her farewell party," Lena said. "Is she okay?"

"She's missing and her family is concerned," Dana said. "Do you know if there is any place or anyone Beth would go to if she were in trouble."

"Beth's troubles are in her own house with that jerk she's married to and the people he associates with."

"Yes, I understand that. What can you tell me about Beth's situation?"

"Look, Miss Sloan. This isn't something I should talk about on the phone, especially here at the office. I'm sorry."

"You're right. You should not give information to a voice on the telephone. May I come over there with my identification and speak to you in person?"

"When?"

"Right away. I'm at the newspaper, just down the street from your office."

"Oh, I don't think."

"Please. I understand your reluctance, but Beth hasn't been seen since yesterday afternoon and her mother has asked me to look for her. I think you may be able to help me." Lena didn't answer, so Dana forged ahead. "Both of your bosses know me, just ask one or both of them if it's okay for you to talk to me. I'll be there in ten minutes."

Before Lena could protest, Dana hung up the phone and got to her feet.

"Where are you going?" Marianne asked as Dana came into the reception area.

"To the law firm where Beth Carlson worked to talk to one of her co-workers."

TURK HAD INSISTED that they take Jake's truck. Jake was driving while Turk sat next to him with a gun laid across his lap.

"Come on, Turk," Jake said. "Put the gun away. You're not going to shoot me, are you?"

"Only if you try something stupid," Turk replied.

"Look, I'm telling the truth. Beth took off with the money. We've got to find her."

"Right," Turk agreed. "Just keep driving."

"Where to?"

"How the hell should I know? She's your wife."

"Maybe we should go by my place and pick up a photo of her," Jake said.

"Fine."

At the apartment, nothing had changed. Turk positioned himself in front of the door, while Jake looked for a photo of Beth. He found several taken at the beach last summer before Beth's pregnancy had started to show. One of the photos was a good close-up of her face. Jake stuck it in his shirt pocket and went to the refrigerator to look for some food. All this tension was making him hungry.

"You want a sandwich and a beer?" Jake shouted.

"No, but I'll take a soft drink."

Jake removed a beer for himself and a can of cola for Turk. If only Jake had a way of putting some knock-out drops in the big man's drink, but he didn't.

Jake delivered the cola to Turk and went back into the kitchen and made himself a ham and cheese sandwich. He carried his beer and his food back to the living room and settled on the sofa. He flipped on the television set. There was nothing on but soap operas and talk shows. Jake settled on a local talk show.

"Today we have some guests from the local animal shelter," the hostess said. She was tall and slender with breasts that had to be fake, lots of bushy dark hair and capped teeth. "Please welcome, Donna Meadows and Spenser, the cat."

Jake almost choked on his sandwich. There on the television screen was Beth's cat. "Holy Shit!" Jake yelled.

Turk came across the room. "What?"

"The cat," Jake said. "That's Beth's cat."

Turk stared at the white and black cat that was sitting on a uniformed woman's lap and looking into the camera.

"Tell us about Spenser," the buxom hostess asked the animal shelter employee.

"Spenser was brought to the shelter two days ago. He was found in an alley, obviously abandoned there by his owner."

"How sad."

"Yes. He had a collar with his name on it, but no other information."

"Does this happen often?" the hostess asked.

"More often than you'd think," the employee replied.

"That proves it," Jake shouted, jumping to his feet. "I knew Beth wouldn't just up and leave Spenser."

"But she did," Turk told him. "The lady just said she abandoned him."

"No. I'll bet that was just a story she made up so the shelter would take the cat. She knew if she left him with me I'd kill him."

Turk looked at him sternly. "You'd hurt a defenseless animal?"

"No," Jake said nervously. "Of course I wouldn't."

"Good. I hate people who abuse animals."

"Me too," Jake agreed. "Look, Turk, don't you see? This proves Beth had planned on disappearing or she never would have left her cat."

"Okay," Turk nodded. "But how does this help us find her?"

Jake sat down and turned off the television. "I don't

know, but I'm going to that shelter and see if I can get some more information."

Turk shrugged. "Okay. It's your gas."

BACK AT THE pool hall, Marko and Vinnie were staring at each other across Vinnie's desk. "You know we're going to have to give Angelo the cut he's expecting," Vinnie said softly.

Marko nodded. "You got a figure?"

"Yeah."

"Then take it out of the money we have and I'll take it over."

Vinnie opened a drawer and began placing stacks of cash onto the desk in neat piles. "You think Jake's story is on the level?"

"No. I find it hard to believe that Beth would do something like this."

Vinnie chuckled. "That's cause you got the hots for her."

Marko looked at him sharply. "Beth's a classy girl. I don't know how she ended up with a pig like Jake."

"Jake's a little rough, but a lot of ladies like that kind of guy."

"And a lot of ladies end up dead hooking up with guys like him."

Vinnie sat back quickly, causing his chair to creak with the sudden shift in weight. "What are you saying?"

"It's no secret Jake abused Beth. You know I warned him about it not too long ago."

Vinnie sat up straight again. "You think he did something to her?"

"Yes. And I think he made sure she couldn't come to me again. Think about it. Jake kills his wife and steals our money. Then, he makes up a story saying Beth disappeared with it."

"Why didn't he just take off?"

"Because Jake knows I would hunt him down and kill him. He also knows how I feel about Beth. He knows that I'd be glad to let her have the money, especially if it enabled her to get away from him."

Vinnie nodded. "Listen, Marko, Beth is a smart girl. I think she did take off with the money. Jake is too stupid to think up a complicated plan like that."

"Maybe."

"Okay, so now what?"

"Jake's a dead man."

"What if he finds Beth and the missing money?"

"I'll listen to Beth's side of the story."

Vinnie began packing Angelo's share of the gambling funds into Marko's briefcase. He didn't say anything else to Marko. It wasn't necessary. No matter what happened in the next twenty-four hours, Jake was a dead man.

SEVEN

LENA PACED THE floor of her office waiting for Dana Sloan to arrive. As soon as she hung up the phone, Lena had gone into Mr. Cauthorne's office and told him that Beth was missing and Dana Sloan wanted to talk to her about it.

"Lena?" Dana asked as she appeared in the doorway.

"Yes."

Dana walked in and held out her hand. "I'm Dana Sloan. Thank you for seeing me."

Lena shook hands and invited Dana to have a seat in a chair in front of her desk. "I asked Mr. Cauthorne about speaking with you and he wants to sit in on our meeting."

"Fine," Dana replied.

Lena called her boss on the inter-office line and within a few seconds he came into Lena's office and closed the door behind him. He and Dana exchanged greetings and he sat down in a chair that matched the one Dana occupied.

Donald Cauthorne was tall and slender with a long face, a receding hairline and light blue eyes. Dana had met him and Mr. Stratton at a number of meetings held at the newspaper and a few social events.

Lena settled herself behind her desk. She was very petite, with short black hair and a round pretty face. Her dark eyes looked darker behind a pair of tinted glasses.

Cauthorne began by explaining that he had just learned that Beth's husband worked for Marko Senese and wanted to make sure that Dana understood that the law firm did not know Senese. "I didn't know that Beth had any connection to the man or I would have had to discharge her. Our clients include many wealthy and influential people who would not be happy to know that someone connected with the mob worked in our office and had access to their files." He turned and looked at Lena who squirmed uncomfortably in her chair.

"I'm sorry I didn't tell you sooner," Lena exclaimed. "But Beth only confided that to me, a few days before she left. I didn't know before that, honestly."

"So you told me," her boss said curtly.

Dana was annoyed by the situation and the conversation that excluded her. She also felt a twinge of guilt for suggesting that Lena ask her boss for permission to talk to her.

"Mr. Cauthorne," Dana said, touching his arm to divert his attention back to her. "I think you're over reacting here. And to be honest, I think the fact that Beth Carlson is missing should be more important to you than the remote possibility that her connection to Senese would reflect badly on your law firm."

Lena pushed her chair back from her desk distancing herself from her boss and Dana, expecting Cauthorne to order the impudent young woman from the office.

Silently, Cauthorne rose to his feet. Dana stared up at him, her hazel eyes turning gray with annoyance.

"I'm sorry, Dana. You're right. I'll leave you and Lena to talk privately. I know that I can rely on your good sense and discretion. Please give my best regards to Sam." He looked back at his employee. "Lena, please tell Dana anything she wants to know."

Then, out the door he went closing it quietly behind him. "Oh, my God," Lena whispered. "No one talks to him like that and gets away with it. For a minute there, I thought he would throw you out of the office and fire me."

"You're not going to get fired. My newspaper is one of this firm's major clients and my editor has probably sent a number of those wealthy and influential clients here. If Cauthorne gives you any trouble, let me know. What do you do here anyway?"

"Research and file management. I was Beth's supervisor."

"Okay. What can you tell me about her?"

Lena took a deep breath. "Beth was already married to Jake when she started working here. Apparently, she had been an actress appearing in productions in Chicago when she met him. He promised to help her get to New York and Broadway, but then dragged her back here to Crescent Hills. Beth's aunt on her father's side is Mr. Stratton's mother-in-law and she got Beth the job here two years ago. So I doubt if Mr. Cauthorne would have fired Beth even if he knew about her connection to Marko Senese. Mr. Stratton is really the brains of this firm, Cauthorne just follows his lead."

"Were you aware that Jake Carlson abused Beth?"

"I suspected it, but for a long time, Beth never talked about her husband or their marriage. The times she displayed bruises she lied and said that she fell or bumped into something."

"Pretty typical of abused women," Dana said.

"Yes, but Beth wasn't the typical abused woman. She was very pretty, very bright and very outgoing. It wasn't until Marko Senese started romancing her that she confided her problems to me."

"Whoa," Dana blurted unable to hide her surprise. "Marko Senese was romancing Beth."

"He was sending her flowers here almost every day and calling her on the phone. I think it freaked her out. She kept saying the flowers and calls were from her husband, but I could see how upset she was. Finally, she told me the truth about the flowers and once she started talking, the whole story about Jake and the abuse and the fact that he worked for Senese came out."

"Marko Senese is married," Dana said. "If I remember correctly his wife's family owns one of the big casinos in Las Vegas."

Lena shrugged. "I don't know about that, but one day when Beth and I were going out to lunch, he was waiting outside the building for her. She told me to go on without her and went to talk to him." Lena stopped talking and shrugged again.

"What happened after that?" Dana asked.

"He stopped sending flowers and calling the office, so I guess Beth told him she wasn't interested. A month or so later, Beth announced that she was pregnant."

"Was Beth happy about her pregnancy?"

"Not really. She said it was going to make leaving Jake more difficult. Beth is an only child and her mom is a widow without much money."

"Do you know the name of Beth's doctor?"

"No, but she was going to someone across the street in the medical clinic."

"What about the aunt who got Beth the job here?"

"She moved to Connecticut a few months ago when she remarried. I don't think Beth has had much contact with her recently."

"Do you know the aunt's name? It's possible that Beth ran away and went to her for help."

Lena's face brightened. "Yes. That's possible. But I don't know her name or where she is now. I'm sure Mr. Stratton would know but he's going to be in court all day."

"What about her daughter, Mrs. Stratton?"

"She's on an extended holiday in Europe. I don't know how to reach her. Mr. Stratton is your best bet," Lena said.

Dana stood up. "I think you're right. I'll leave a mes-

sage for him at the front desk. He does call in for messages, doesn't he?"

"Yes. He always calls in at lunch time when court is in
recess. Sometimes, he even comes back here for awhile."

"Good. Thank you for talking to me Lena."

"I hope you find Beth. Will you let me know if you do?"

Dana promised to do that and left Lena's office. She
stopped in the reception area and left an urgent message
for Richard Stratton to call her as soon as possible.

It was after eleven a.m., and Dana hurried back to her
office to go through the stack of work on her desk. As
she walked back to the newspaper building she turned on
her cell phone. She had turned it off before her interview
with Lena and now wanted to see if Bob had called to report on his search for anyone who might have seen Beth
Carlson after her disappearance yesterday. There were
no messages.

Dana sighed. While the information about Marko Senese romancing Beth was interesting, it seemed that it was
just a fleeting thing and Dana didn't see how it would help
her find Beth.

IN LOS ANGELES, Beth had finished her business at the bank
and was shopping at a department store a few blocks away.
She had purchased underwear, a nightgown, a lovely long
robe and several new outfits. It was nice to be able to shop
for regular clothes again.

In the luggage department, Beth bought a suitcase and
packed her new clothes inside of it. Then, she left the store
and hailed a cab and directed the driver to take her to the
La Maison Hotel in West Hollywood. Beth had heard of the
hotel when she had watched the Academy Awards telecast
earlier that year. Several people mentioned the gala post
Oscar celebration being held at that hotel. All the movie

people were expected to make an appearance at that party as it was one of the most prestigious.

Now that her escape plan seemed to be working smoothly, Beth felt more relaxed and decided to pamper herself at least for a day or so. Although she didn't have a reservation, she was able to get a nice room on the fifth floor. Beth unpacked and took a shower. She slipped into the long terry-cloth robe she had purchased. She was tired, but she was also hungry, so she called room service and ordered breakfast, coffee, a bottle of mineral water and a copy of the Hollywood trade paper, *Daily Variety*.

"I could get used to this," Beth whispered as she tipped the waiter who delivered the tray to her room.

Beth ate and looked through the newspaper. She was too tired to check out any of the casting ads or other opportunities the movie industry's newspaper contained, so she put the paper aside and poured herself another cup of coffee from the insulated pot. Gazing out the window Beth reflected on all she had done over the last few months. First and foremost, she had escaped from Jake. That was a good thing, a blessed relief. However, in the process of freeing herself from her abusive husband, she had done several bad things, some were illegal, some were just hurtful to other people like her mother.

Beth and her mother had never had a close, loving relationship, but Beth's father had died when Beth was two and Greta had worked hard and gave Beth the best she could afford.

The best had been a shabby house in a rundown neighborhood. Welfare checks and food stamps allowed them to eat and wear second-hand clothes.

Beth knew that living on the edge of poverty was what drove her to the drama department in high school. On the stage, Beth could become a different person. Her natural beauty and talent were appreciated by her teachers and classmates, and more importantly by an audience of strangers who cheered for her and made her feel special.

Beth won a scholarship for drama and continued to act her way through college. Although she had found some success at the Chicago theater, her goal was to travel to New York and try to make a real name for herself as an actress. That goal fell by the wayside when she met Jake.

Jake was good looking and funny and knocked himself out trying to please Beth. He professed his love for her everyday and convinced Beth that he would cherish her forever and help her attain all her goals. Those promises died two months after the wedding when Beth found herself back in Crescent Hills. Jake said he was being transferred there by his company. She soon realized that Jake was not the person he had pretended to be.

First, she discovered that Jake's job as a deliveryman was not what he told her it was. He was a deliveryman all right, but he didn't work for a legitimate company like UPS or Federal Express. Jake worked for mobsters. When she begged him to quit, Jake admitted that he couldn't quit. He was in too deep. That was the first time Beth threatened to leave him and the first time Jake had beat her up and warned her he would kill her before he'd let her go. Jake also told Beth that it was time she stopped wasting her time with auditions and get a real job. That was how Beth had ended up working at the law firm.

Beth knew that stealing from Marko wasn't right, but that money was all from illegal activities like gambling, prostitution and drugs and in a few days Marko would make up what she had taken and more. Even so, Marko had been nice to her and he was the one person who realized that Jake was abusive and tried to help her.

Beth remembered the first time she had met Marko. She and Jake were having dinner downtown at Berghoff's when Marko came in and stopped at their table.

He greeted Jake and then slid into the booth next to Beth. "Who's this pretty lady?" Marko asked.

"This is my wife, Beth," Jake replied, putting an emphasis on the word, wife. "Beth, this is Marko."

Marko had put out his hand and Beth had offered hers to him. Marko had held onto Beth's hand, ignoring Jake. "I'm happy to meet you, Beth. Jake is a very lucky man."

"Thank you," Beth said softly. She tried to withdraw her hand, but Marko held it fast. She glanced over at Jake and could see the anger in his eyes, but then Marko turned his head and looked at Jake.

"Something wrong, Jake?"

The anger in Jake's eyes disappeared instantly and was replaced by a glimmer of fear. "No. I'm just surprised to see you here alone."

Marko laughed and motioned for Jake to look behind him. Two of the biggest men Beth had ever seen were standing near the bar watching the three of them. "I have a meeting in the back room. Turk and Harry are going to have a drink while they wait for me."

"Oh yeah, sure," Jake stammered. He waved at Turk and Harry. They didn't wave back.

"I hope I see you again," Marko told Beth as he let go of her hand and slid out of the booth.

Beth just smiled and nodded. Marko turned to Jake again. "Take good care of this lady. I can see she's special."

They had finished their dinner and left the restaurant. On the way home, Jake had been livid. He accused Beth of flirting with Marko. When she protested, he slapped her so hard it bruised her cheek.

The next day, Beth received a huge bouquet of flowers. They were delivered to the law firm. When she saw they were from Marko she quickly slipped the card into her pocket and told everyone they were from Jake.

Beth hoped that would be the end of it, but it was not.

More flowers arrived the next day and then Marko called and invited Beth to lunch. She refused, but when she got home from work that day, Jake said Marko was taking them to dinner.

"I don't want to go to dinner with Marko," Beth had said.

"You don't have a choice," Jake had answered nervously. "Go put some of your stage makeup on to cover that bruise."

That was when Beth had decided that meeting Marko might work to her advantage. Jake was obviously afraid of the man.

Marko picked them up in a limousine and took them to his country club for dinner. Unfortunately for Jake, Beth had not hidden her bruise under stage makeup.

Just before dessert, Marko told Jake to go to the men's room. Jake didn't argue. He got up and left the table.

"Jake give you that bruise on your cheek?" Marko asked as soon as Jake was gone.

Beth nodded. "He thought I was flirting with you, the other night."

Marko smiled. "Were you?"

Beth shook her head. "I take my marriage vows seriously."

"Too bad." Marko said. He reached in his pocket and pulled out a business card. "You keep that card. It's got my private number on it. If you decide not to take those vows so seriously, you call me. Okay?"

"Okay." Beth whispered.

Jake came back to the table and nothing more was said until the three of them were in the limousine on the way back to Jake and Beth's apartment.

"How did your wife get that bruise on her cheek?" Marko asked Jake.

Jake tried to cover. "She bumped into the door frame."

Marko turned to Beth and touched her face gently. "Is that so?"

"Yeah. Tell him Beth," Jake said.

Before Beth could say anything else. Marko pulled out a gun and put it to the side of Jake's head. "Beth better not bump into any more door frames. You understand what I'm telling you?"

Jake's eyes were wide with fright as he nodded. Marko grunted and put the gun away.

When they got to the apartment, Jake jumped out of the limo so fast that he tripped and fell. Turk picked him up. Marko got out and held out his hand to Beth.

"Thank you for a lovely evening," she said.

"You're welcome," Marko replied as he kissed her bruised cheek. "I'll see you again soon." Then, Marko turned to Jake who was brushing the dirt from the street off his clothes. "You know I don't make idle threats," he said softly. "You hurt this girl again and I'll make you sorry you were born."

Jake nodded silently and reached out for Beth's hand.

"You don't have to worry," he replied in a hoarse voice. "I'll take good care of her."

Beth ignored her husband's outstretched hand and walked into the building. Although she was pretty sure that Jake would be afraid to hit her again, she worried that this was the beginning of a more serious problem. She was right.

Apparently, Marko didn't take his own marriage vows too seriously because the next day, more flowers arrived at her office. The flowers kept coming and then one day, Marko was waiting outside the building when she went out at lunch. As soon as she saw him, Beth knew that the plan she had been working out to leave Jake and start a new life was in danger of falling apart.

"I was in the neighborhood," Marko said. "I thought maybe I could take you to lunch."

"That would be nice," Beth said. "But I have a doctor's appointment."

"Are you all right?" Marko asked pointedly.

"Sure. I'm fine. It's just that…" she paused and lowered her head. "I shouldn't say anything until after I see the doctor."

"What's wrong?" Marko asked with concern. "Did Jake do something to you?"

Beth looked up and gave him a radiant smile. "Yes, but not what you think. Look, I haven't said anything to him yet, so if I tell you, you have to promise to keep it a secret."

Marko's face showed his disappointment as he guessed what Beth was going to say next. "Of course," he said.

"I think I'm pregnant."

"That's what I was afraid you were going to say."

"I'm sorry, Marko, but I have to go. I'll be late for my appointment."

"I'll drive you," Marko said.

"Oh, that's not necessary," Beth told him brightly. "It's just across the street." She pointed to the medical clinic across the street.

Marko grabbed her hand. "It seems my timing with you is a little off. Still, if you need anything, anything at all, call me."

"I will. Thank you," Beth told him.

Beth had hurried across the street and into the building. She got on the elevator and rode it up to the tenth floor. From a window in the lobby there, she saw Marko's car drive off.

Beth leaned against the wall and shook her head. Telling Marko she was pregnant had been a spur of the moment thing, not part of her escape plan. It was the first thing that came to mind when she saw him standing outside waiting for her. It was the only way she could think of to discourage his obvious interest in her.

Beth remembered how she had sat down on the floor in the lobby and spent the rest of her lunch hour revising her original plan to incorporate her pregnancy into it.

EIGHT

"I COULDN'T FIND anyone at the bus or train station that re-membered seeing Beth Carlson." Bob told Dana.

They were sitting in Dana's office. She was going through the new cases on her desk and Bob was making his report while munching on a stalk of celery.

Dana smiled at him. "Is that part of your new diet?"

Bob nodded his curly blond head. "Did you know that celery has minus calories?"

"No."

"Well, it does. The story is that it burns more calories to digest it than it supplies to the body. I figure if I cheat on my diet, I can just eat a few stalks of celery and get rid of the extra calories I eat."

"I don't think it works that way," Dana said. "What about the car rental places?"

"No luck there either, but then I remembered there's a cab stand a block or so from that convenience store so I went over there and asked around. One of the cabbies said he picked up a fare there yesterday about the time the girl disappeared. He said she was wearing a big funky hat and a trench coat.

Dana nodded and smiled. "Beth Carlson is an actress, she could have been using those clothes to alter her ap-pearance and get past her husband." She made a notation to call Jake Carlson and see if he remembered anyone dressed like that coming out of the store.

"Where did the cab driver take her?"

"Midway airport," Bob said with a note of disappointment in his voice. "If it was Beth Carlson, she could be almost anywhere now."

"I think you're right," Dana agreed. "See if you can find out what flights left Midway late yesterday afternoon. She has an aunt that just moved to Connecticut. Maybe she went there.

"You have to show a photo I.D. to get through security." Bob said.

"True. I wonder if I can get Bruno to ask the Chicago police to show Beth's photo to the people who were on duty at the security checkpoints yesterday afternoon and evening."

"You're going to coerce Bruno into a missing persons case?"

"I already have. He met Beth Carlson at the same time I did and he thinks her husband is a punk, so I think he's as concerned about her as I am."

"Do you think her husband did something to her?"

"I know that he used to abuse her, which would give her a good reason to run away from him. Check those airline flights at Midway, please."

"Okay. What about those cases you're piling up there?" Bob indicated the stack of requests for help that Dana was sorting through.

"None of these are urgent. They can wait for a day or so." Dana glanced at her watch and was glad to see that she still had forty-five minutes before she had to meet Bruno for lunch.

TURK ACCOMPANIED JAKE to the animal shelter to claim Beth's cat. Of course Jake didn't want the animal but he was hoping that going to the shelter would distract Turk. It seemed that the big lout had a soft spot for animals.

"So why are we here?" Turk asked as Jake parked his truck in front of the shelter.

"To get my wife's cat back," Jake told him. "And to find out if anyone here saw her or talked to her."

"Right."

The shelter was located in a long narrow building that had recently been painted a bright shade of green. The walls inside the building were painted the same as the outside and glowed like neon from the sun that came in from the unshaded windows. Dogs began barking frantically from the kennels behind the office as Jake and Turk walked through the door.

"Geez," Jake whispered. "This place looks like a huge lime Popsicle."

"Yeah," Turk agreed. "It makes me dizzy." He pulled his sunglasses from his shirt pocket and put them on again.

A girl who looked like a teenager was on duty. She smiled and greeted them. "Can I help you?"

"I saw my wife's cat on television and I want to claim him."

"The big black and white cat?"

"That's him. His name is Spenser."

"Right. Spenser with an "s" instead of a "c". That's why I remember it."

"That's Beth's cat. I want him back."

"I'm afraid you're too late. He's already been adopted."

"How can that be? He was just on TV a few minutes ago."

"I know, but the show you were watching was taped earlier this morning. One of the TV crew fell in love with Spenser and took him home after the taping."

"Damn!"

"I'm sorry," the girl said quickly. "But we have lots of other cats and dogs you can choose from."

"Listen, that was my wife's cat and she's disappeared.

I'm afraid something may have happened to her. Is there someone here that can give me some information about who dropped the cat off and when?"

The girl looked stricken. "I guess that would be me. I was on duty when she brought him in."

"When was that?"

"On Saturday, about one o'clock."

"Did she say why she was giving up the cat?" Turk asked.

"She said she found the cat on the street, but had to leave town and couldn't take him with her. Just like you heard on the television show. She made me promise to find him a good home."

Jake pulled Beth's photo out of his pocket and showed it to the girl. "Is that the girl?"

"No."

"No?" Jake's voice rose an octave. "Look at her face again. I know she probably looked different when you saw her. She's six months pregnant now."

"I'm sorry. It's not the girl that brought the cat in here."

"How can you be so sure?" Turk asked.

"Because the girl in this picture is white and the girl who brought the cat in was a black girl with long dread-locks and a gold ring in her bottom lip. The dreadlocks were really cool. I wish I could get my hair braided like that." She smiled and touched the thin brown hair that hung straight to her shoulders.

Jake staggered back away from the counter. "That bitch," he shouted. Jake was about to let off a string of obscenities, but Turk grabbed his shoulder making him wince in pain.

"Watch your mouth, Jake. That's no way to talk in front of a young girl. Maybe that wasn't Beth's cat you saw on TV. Maybe you just dragged me down here to make me think you're worried about Beth."

"It was Beth's cat," Jake insisted. "This little girl just told us the cat's name was Spenser. How many big black and white cats do you think there are in this area named, Spenser, with an "s" after Beth's favorite detective."

"Beth knows a detective?"

"It's a fictional character in the mystery books she's always reading." Jake turned back to the young girl. "What was the woman's name who brought him in here?"

"She didn't say."

"And you didn't ask?" Jake shouted.

The girl shook her head. "I'm sorry. I'm just a volunteer here."

"What about his tags? I think he had tags with our name and address on them." Jake seemed to remember that there was a jangling noise associated with the cat.

"He had a collar with his name on it, but no other information," the girl replied.

Turk was losing patience. "Okay, thanks sweetie," he said to the girl. "Come on, Jake. Let's go."

Turk grabbed Jake's arm and led him out the door and back to the truck. He didn't say anything until they had driven away from the shelter.

"You know what I think, Jake?" Turk said softly. "I think you got rid of your wife and then threw her cat out in the street for some stranger to find and take to the shelter."

"Are you nuts?" Jake cried. "If I got rid of Beth and her cat, do you think I would have taken that bag full of newspaper to Marko today? Hell, no. I would have been on another continent by now."

Turk shrugged his massive shoulders. "People do all kinds of stupid things when they're scared. Maybe you didn't mean to hurt Beth. Maybe it was an accident. Maybe Beth did take the money and hide it from you. Maybe that's why you killed her."

"I didn't do anything to Beth," Jake said evenly. "She's

carrying my kid and I wouldn't do anything to hurt my kid. And for the last time, I didn't know the bag was full of newspaper or I would have never showed up with it today. Use your head, Turk. You know I'm smarter than that."

"Maybe. Maybe not," Turk replied. "You know what's funny? I don't think Marko cares as much about the money as he does about Beth gone missing. He likes her a lot. I think you'd better find Beth or you're a dead man."

Jake didn't answer. He couldn't. He had broken out into a cold sweat. There was a police car in front of the apartment building and there were no parking spaces, so Jake drove around through the alley and parked.

Turk grabbed his arm and dragged him across the seat out the passenger door of the truck. Jake walked silently in front of Turk down the narrow cement path that led to the front of the building.

What the hell was he going to do? Beth had taken off with Marko's cash and left him to pay the consequences. There was no way he was going to find her. His only chance was to get away from Turk, but then what? He didn't have enough money to run very far. Marko would track him down and kill him. Turk was right; he was a dead man.

Jake pushed open the door to the lobby to find two uniformed police officers standing there. The cops looked at Jake and Turk.

"One of you guys, Jake Carlson?" one of the cops asked.

"I'm Carlson," Jake told him.

"We got a report of a missing person, the daughter of a Greta Malone. Girl's name is Beth Carlson. Is that your wife?"

"Yes. Have you found her?"

"No, sir. We're just here to ask you some questions."

"Wait a minute," Jake said. "I thought you wouldn't do anything for twenty-four hours."

"We got orders from our boss to begin the investigation immediately."

"I see," Jake said slowly. A way out of Turk's iron grasp flashed across his mind.

"Rather than discuss this here in the lobby, we should go to your apartment and fill out the forms," the other cop suggested. "Do you want your friend here to come along?"

"No," Jake said softly. "I think you'd better take me down to the station to talk."

"Why is that, sir?"

"Because I don't want to do it here in the lobby or up in my apartment."

Turk grabbed his arm. "Take it easy, Jake. You don't have to go to the station. This is just what they call preliminary talk."

"And who are you, sir?" the cop asked Turk.

"Like you said, I'm his friend. Theodore Smith. We've been out looking for Beth."

Jake had never heard Turk's real name and he wasn't sure if he had heard it now, but that didn't matter. Getting away from Turk did.

The officer turned back to Jake. "Mr. Smith is right. We're just beginning the investigation and just need to ask you a few questions."

"I want to go to the station," Jake said. He didn't have to fake the emotion that filled his voice. He was very upset and going for the only thing he could think of that would save his life and give him time to find a way out of this mess.

The other cop stepped forward and looked Jake up and down. "And why is that, sir?"

"I have information about my wife's disappearance that you'll want to hear," Jake replied, avoiding a direct answer.

Turk took hold of Jake's arm again. His hand was like a vise squeezing so hard Jake could feel a bruise forming. "My friend is just very upset about his wife," Turk told the cops in a calm voice. "He doesn't know what he's saying. Do you, Jake?"

Jake looked into Turk's dark eyes and saw the danger reflected there. If Jake didn't convince the cops to take him away, Turk would drag him back to Marko and tell him that Jake was stalling, that he knew where Beth and the money were.

Jake said the only thing he could think of that would get him away from Turk and buy him some time.

DANA WALKED INTO Big Lou's at 12:15 p.m. and looked around for Bruno.

"Hi Dana," Big Lou, who was a lovely tall woman named Lucille, said from behind the cashier's counter. "You looking for lover boy?"

Dana grinned. "I'm late. Is he upset?"

"He called and reserved the back booth, but he's not here yet either. Come on, I'll get you settled. You want some coffee?"

"Yes, please."

Lou grabbed a coffee pot and Dana followed her back to the booth that was nestled into the corner of the small café. Dana slid into the booth and Lou turned over one of the cups and filled it with coffee. Cream and sugar were already on the table and Dana added a little of both to her coffee and took a sip.

"Sorry, I'm late," Bruno said, bending to brush his lips across her cheek. "Been here long?"

"Since noon," Dana replied.

"Right. I saw you walk out of the newspaper building two minutes ago."

"So you were just standing in your office looking out the window?"

"Actually, I was talking to Detective Harrison. He sent

two uniforms out to talk to Jake Carlson and he is now under arrest. After lunch I get to interrogate him."

"Oh, no."

"Oh, yes. But here's the weird part. The officers met up with him in the lobby of his apartment building. All they wanted to do was ask a few questions and get the paperwork going. Carlson was with one of Marko Senese's goons. When the uniforms suggested they go up to Carlson's apartment to talk, Carlson suddenly insisted that the cops arrest him because he killed his wife. Something's going on that we don't know about. The arresting officers said it was more like Carlson was desperate to get away from the goon. Guys like Carlson don't just break down and confess."

"It sounds like someone should talk to Marko Senese."

"Dana, don't get any ideas. That guy is poison."

"That guy was romancing Beth Carlson."

"What? How do you know that?"

"I talked to Beth's friend at the law firm she worked at. She told me that Senese had been chasing after Beth for weeks, sending flowers, calling her on the phone."

"How long ago was that?"

"Before Beth announced her pregnancy, so a little over six months ago."

A waitress came over and filled Bruno's coffee cup and asked if they were ready to order. Dana ordered a cup of soup and half a tuna salad sandwich. Bruno ordered the special that was meatloaf and mashed potatoes.

"I've seen photos of Mrs. Senese. She's very attractive, but guys like Senese make up the rules to suit themselves," Bruno said. "I doubt if his alleged romance with Beth Carlson has any bearing on the girl's disappearance. So you promise me you'll stay away from that guy."

"I will if you let me listen in on Carlson's interrogation."

Bruno laughed. "You know that's not going to happen. What do you really want?"

"Bob found a cab driver at the taxi stand near the convenience store that said he picked up a fare there yesterday afternoon. It was a woman wearing a big hat and a trench coat and he took her to Midway Airport. I think it was Beth Carlson."

"Okay, so what does that have to do with me?"

"I want you to call one of your contacts in Chicago and have them take Beth's photo to the airport and show it to the security personnel there. If someone remembers her, we can find out what airline she used and maybe even where she went."

"Do you know how many people go through Midway Airport on a Sunday?"

"Yes. That's why we need the Chicago police to help us."

"Us, as in you and me?"

"We are a couple," Dana said with a smile.

"Especially when you want one of your favors," Bruno replied. "Although if we can get a positive I.D. on the woman, we may be able to wind up this case sooner than later."

"Then you think there's a possibility Beth is still alive?"

Bruno nodded. "I haven't ruled out that possibility."

Dana suddenly realized that despite the fact that Jake confessed, she hadn't ruled it out either. "Jake could be in trouble with Senese. Why else would Senese assign one of his enforcers to watch him? And why else would Jake confess to something he didn't do?"

"We don't know that he didn't do it," Bruno replied. "Let's wait and see what he says this afternoon. He may tell me where to find her body."

"No." Dana had decided to trust her instincts and her instincts told her Beth Carlson was alive. She told Bruno about Beth's aunt in Connecticut. "She may be there with her."

"Let's hope so."

Their lunch was delivered and since Bruno and Dana had agreed not to discuss crimes and criminals while they ate, they both fell silent. Dana thought back to the incident at the convenience store the day before and suddenly dropped her soup spoon.

"What's wrong?" Bruno asked.

"I just remembered something else. When we drove into the parking lot yesterday, Jake was having some type of confrontation with a heavy-set woman. She shoved him so hard he bounced against the window. I think he was going to go after her, but we pulled up to the curb and he thought better of it."

"I remember seeing the woman. She was hard to miss."

"I'm going to try to track her down."

"Why?"

"Because she obviously came out of the convenience store and may have seen Beth Carlson in there. The guy behind the counter was busy, but she could have seen her."

"What is that going to prove?"

"That Jake was telling the truth about her going in there."

"Dana, if the woman in the cab was not Beth Carlson, her husband could have caught up with her at home. Don't get your hopes up too high."

"Promise you'll call me as soon as you finish questioning Jake."

"I will."

"In the meantime, I'm going to work on the premise that Beth is alive and try to reach her aunt in Connecticut and the woman from the convenience store."

"It may be a waste of time and effort," Bruno warned.

"Maybe." Dana agreed.

MARKO WAS PACING back and forth in front of his desk. Vinnie had gone to lunch and Marko was alone in the office when Turk burst through the door.

"Guess what?" the big man said.

"I don't like guessing games," Marko told him. "Where's Jake?"

"In jail."

"Jail?"

"Yeah."

"What happened?"

"Jake saw his wife's cat on TV and dragged me down to the animal shelter saying he wanted to claim it. Someone had already adopted the cat but he questioned the girl who had accepted the cat yesterday afternoon. She said it wasn't Beth who brought the cat in, but some black babe who said she found it. Jake was really upset, or he pretended to be. I think it was all an act."

"Get to the jail part," Marko ordered.

"Oh, right. Anyway we went back to Jake's apartment and there were two cops in the lobby. They wanted to question Jake about his wife's disappearance."

"Okay, then what?"

"The cops just wanted to ask him some questions, and Jake went nuts and said he killed Beth and they should arrest him. So they did. There was nothing I could do to stop them."

"So Jake is in jail?"

"Yeah. I'm real sorry, boss. I know you thought a lot of Beth."

Marko sat down hard in his chair. He felt as if the wind had been knocked out of him, but he couldn't show any signs of weakness in front of Turk. "Go out and get yourself a beer," he said softly. "We have a dinner appointment at seven. I was going to take Charlie with me, but since Jake is in jail, you can go."

"Sure thing."

Marko waited until Turk had left the office again. Then he reached for the telephone and dialed a number. "I need you to go to the police station. One of my guys was arrested. His name is Jake Carlson. He needs a lawyer. If they gave him a public defender get rid of the jerk and you take over. And if for some reason, the cops decide to release Jake you bring him to me immediately. Got that?" Marko paused to listen, then nodded. "That's right. Call me when you know what's going on."

NINE

JAKE HAD BEEN in the interrogation room for almost two hours before Bruno walked in and sat down. One of the uniformed cops who'd brought him in had taken his statement. Bruno had a copy of it in his hand.

"Hey, Detective. How's it going?" Jake asked going for the friendly, casual approach.

"This report says the arresting officers read you your rights and you waived your right to legal counsel. Is that correct?"

"Yes, sir."

"Do you understand that this interview is being videotaped?"

"Yes, sir."

"I'm going to read you your rights again and you tell me if you understand." Jake nodded and listened to Bruno recite the Miranda warning again. When asked if he understood, he said he did. "Do you want an attorney?"

"No. I don't need one. Look, I was in a bind earlier. That big brute was going to bash my brains in. The cops showed up and I said what I had to say to get away from the guy."

"Who was the guy?" Bruno asked casually.

"I don't know. He jumped in my truck when I stopped at a red light. I think he wanted to rob me."

"According to this report, his name is Theodore Smith. Theodore Smith is also known as Turk and he works for Marko Senese. Do you know Senese?"

"Not personally," Jake replied.

"Rumor has it that you work for Senese."

"I don't know how that rumor got started."

"Okay, let's drop that for now. This report also says you confessed to killing your wife but when you got here you said your wife was missing, but you didn't kill her."

"Right. Like I said I was trying to get away from that big guy and the cops showed up at an opportune time so I took advantage of it."

"They were there to ask you some questions about your wife's disappearance."

"Yeah. Remember you and your girlfriend were there yesterday when I was looking for her. Well, she's still missing and I'm crazy with worry. I don't know what I'm saying or doing right now. Beth is my life. She's carrying my baby. I would never do anything to harm her."

"What did you do with your wife's body?" Bruno asked softly.

"I told you. I didn't do anything. She ran off on her own."

"Why would she do that?"

"I don't know. She's pregnant. Everyone says pregnant women do nutty things. Why would I have been causing that ruckus at the convenience store yesterday if Beth hadn't disappeared from there?"

Bruno shrugged his massive shoulders. "I don't know, Jake. You tell me."

Jake ran his hands through his hair. He had gotten away from Turk but now he was in a worse mess. "I changed my mind. I do want a lawyer."

Bruno immediately got to his feet. Once a suspect asked for a lawyer the interview was over. "I'll see that you get to make a call."

There was a knock on the interview room door. Bruno

opened it and found Detective Harrison standing there. "Mr. Carlson's lawyer is here."

Bruno looked at the man standing behind Harrison. He recognized him immediately. "Perfect timing, your client was just asking for you."

Bruno stepped aside and Michael Dominic walked into the room. Jake Carlson's face turned ashen. "This isn't my lawyer," Jake said.

"Of course I'm your lawyer," Dominic said firmly. He turned to Bruno. "I'd like to speak to my client alone, Detective. Will you excuse us?"

"Certainly." Bruno was enjoying the look on Jake Carlson's face. Marko Senese had sent one of the slick lawyers on his payroll to talk to Jake and that could mean only one thing. Jake was in very deep trouble.

WHILE JAKE WAS conferring with his lawyer, Dana was knocking on the door of a tiny house around the corner from the convenience store. The door was flung open and the doorway was filled with yellow and green stripes. Dana looked up into the face of the large woman with the frizzy red hair she remembered from yesterday.

"Who are you?" the woman asked in a loud voice.

"I'm with Globe Investigations. I'm looking into the disappearance of a young woman. I'm hoping you can help me." Dana held out her business card, but the woman ignored it.

"You looking for that pregnant girl?"

"Yes. Her name is Beth Carlson. She lives across the street from me and her mother asked me to try and locate her."

"How'd you locate me?"

"I saw you leaving the convenience store yesterday shortly after Beth disappeared. I went over there this afternoon and asked the clerk on duty about you and she told me your name and where you lived."

The woman made a face. "I guess everyone in there knows Big Bertha. That's what they call me behind my back."

"I wouldn't know about that. Can I come in and speak to you for a few minutes?"

"Maybe. You got any cigarettes?"

"No, but I have a Snickers Bar. The clerk said it was your favorite."

Bertha laughed and invited Dana inside. The door opened into a small living room, nicely decorated and furnished.

"What a lovely room," Dana said.

"I used to be an antique dealer before I got too old and fat to work. Have a seat."

Dana perched on the edge of a chair that looked like it had come from the set of a Victorian movie. "The man I saw you talking to outside the store was the missing girl's husband. He and her mother are very worried about Beth."

"That guy is a sleaze ball," Bertha said. "I wouldn't give him the time of day if he paid me."

"You know Jake Carlson?"

"I've seen him around the neighborhood. How he got that pretty little girl to marry him and carry his kid is beyond me."

"You were in the store at the same time Beth was. Did you see her?"

"Sure I did. I even spoke to her."

"What did you say?"

"I was standing by the bathroom door and she asked me to move so she could get in there. As you can see, I take up a lot of space and I guess I was blocking the door." Bertha rolled her eyes. "So I moved out of the way and told her I hoped everything came out all right. It's an old joke, but I don't think the kid got it. She thanked me and went into the bathroom."

"And did you see her come out of the bathroom?"

"Nope. I went over to the other side of the store to look for a jar of spaghetti sauce and a bottle of wine. They were out of the wine I usually buy so I was there a long time trying to decide on another brand."

"So you didn't see Beth come out of the bathroom or leave the store."

"Nope."

"What did Jake Carlson say to you that made you shove him into the window?"

"He asked me if I saw his wife in the store and I didn't like the tone of voice he used. So I said, the pregnant girl? He said yes, and just to bust his chops I said I hadn't seen her. He didn't get the joke. If I hadn't seen her how would I know she was pregnant. Anyway he called me a name so I shoved him out of my way and left."

"That's when my boyfriend and I drove up," Dana told her. "Well, thank you very much for your time, Bertha." Dana held out the Snickers bar to her as she stood up.

Bertha took the candy and walked Dana to the door. "You and your boyfriend serious?" Bertha asked.

"I guess you could say that," Dana replied.

"You engaged?"

"Not officially."

"Well, you're a pretty girl. You probably have your pick of guys. So, don't get married unless you're sure, really sure. I wasn't totally sure the three times I got married and I got three sets of divorce papers to show for my lack of certainty. Remember that."

Dana grinned and held out her hand to Bertha. "Thank you. I'll remember. And if you think of anything else about Beth Carlson, please call me." Dana held out her card to Bertha again and this time she took it.

By the time Dana got back to the office, it was after three. Marianne was doing research on two of the cases that had come into the office over the weekend. Some of the requests Globe Investigations received were handled by Marianne who was a whiz at finding information on the Internet and other places.

"Richard Stratton called and left the address and phone number of his mother-in-law in Connecticut. Any luck with the convenience store lady?"

"Yes. She not only saw Beth Carlson in the store yesterday, she actually spoke to her briefly."

"That means her husband wasn't lying about her going into the store."

"Right. Were you able to locate Beth Carlson's doctor?"

"No. I called the three offices located in that medical clinic and none of them had a record of a patient by that name."

"I'm going to call the aunt in Connecticut and then I'll report back to Greta Malone. She isn't on great terms with her husband's family so when I talked to her earlier she couldn't help me with her sister-in-law's address or phone number."

Dana went into her office and closed the door. Beth's aunt's name was Dorothy Summerfield. She answered the phone on the first ring. Dana explained who she was and why she was calling. Dorothy was upset to hear that her niece was missing, but said that she had not seen or heard from Beth in several months.

"We promised to keep in touch, but then I remarried and moved to another state and we didn't."

"Does Beth have your new address and phone number?"

"She should have. I sent her one of those, Hello, I moved cards, but never heard from her. Do you think something bad has happened to Beth?"

"I don't know, Mrs. Summerfield," Dana said honestly.

"She was seen in a convenience store yesterday and was all right then. I don't know what happened to her when she left the store."

"Her husband is a violent man. Do you think he did something to Beth?"

"Again, I don't know. I'm sorry."

"Please let me know if you hear anything."

"I will and please call me if she should contact you."

The call ended and Dana called Greta Malone and told her what she had found out from Big Bertha. "It's possible that Beth slipped out of the store without Jake seeing her and ran away."

"How would she do that? She doesn't have any money. Jake took her paycheck and wouldn't even let her have a credit card."

"She could have gotten a credit card without his knowledge based on her employment history," Dana told her. "If she did that we'll be able to trace her movements."

"Have the police talked to Jake?" she asked.

"I believe so, but I don't have any information about that."

"What about showing Beth's photo to the security people at the airport?" Greta asked. Dana had shared the information about the taxi driver with Beth's mother the last time she talked to her.

"That hasn't happened yet. I'll let you know as soon as I find out anything else. In the meantime, can you give me the name of Beth's doctor? I was told that she was seeing someone at the medical clinic across the street from the law office, but so far, we haven't been able to get the name of her doctor."

After a short silence, Greta sighed. "I have no idea. Beth never told me who she was seeing. You'll have to ask Jake."

Greta's voice broke. "I bet you think I'm a terrible mother, and you're right. I should have asked about the doctor, but Beth never wanted to talk about her pregnancy or the baby. I assumed it was because she didn't want to have a baby with a man like Jake so I didn't press her. I'm sorry."

"It's okay, Mrs. Malone. We'll find out some other way. Good-bye."

Dana hung up feeling very sorry for the woman again. If Beth had run off to get away from her husband, she should have told her mother. Dana couldn't imagine ever breaking ties with her own mother. Even though she had grown up and left the farm in downstate Illinois, she and her mom kept in close contact.

Dana's intercom buzzed. "Dana, there's a gentleman here to see you?"

"Bruno?"

"No. His name is Marko Senese."

"Thank you," Dana said slowly.

Dana hung up the phone and stared at her office door, not sure if she should open it and greet Senese or hide under her desk.

TEN

DANA WENT TO the door and pulled it open. Marko Senese and one of the biggest men she had ever seen stood in the reception area. The big man was looking at Marianne like she was a hot fudge sundae and he had a sweet tooth.

"Mr. Senese," Dana said cordially. "Won't you and your associate come into my office?"

Senese turned to Turk. "Wait here."

Turk immediately sat down in one of the two chairs near the door across from Marianne's desk. He continued to stare at Marianne who nodded at him and then turned her attention back to her computer. If she were unnerved by his obvious interest in her she didn't show it. Marianne was used to men staring at her and even one as big as Turk didn't seem to phase her.

Dana walked into her office and Marko followed her. She closed the door and invited Marko to sit in one of the comfortable leather chairs.

He was a strikingly handsome man of medium height and slight build. His hair was black, cut short and slicked back into a style that suited him well. He was impeccably dressed in a black suit, a white shirt and a black tie with subtle red lines running through it. He remained standing until Dana settled herself behind the desk. A gentleman, Dana thought, smiling at him. Marko's eyes were dark as night and although his lips turned up into a smile, his eyes showed no trace of humor or friendliness.

"What can I do for you, Mr. Senese?" Dana asked, thinking that Bruno was going to have a fit over this meeting.

"I'm interested in hiring you to locate Beth Carlson."

"I'm already looking for Mrs. Carlson. Her mother requested my help. And Globe Investigations does not charge for its services."

"What have you found out about Beth?"

"I've confirmed her husband's claim that she went into a convenience store yesterday afternoon. I talked to a witness who saw her in the store."

"And?"

"And unfortunately, the witness didn't see her leave the store."

"What else have you done to locate her?"

"May I ask why you are interested in finding Beth?"

"It's a personal matter."

"I see. Well, since I am already looking for her, it would seem that you've wasted your time coming here, unless you have some information that can help me find Beth."

The dark eyes studied Dana for a few minutes and then Marko Senese broke into a genuine smile, one that brought some light to the sinister eyes. "I heard you were a gutsy lady. I also hear you're dating a cop and he helps you with your cases."

"Sometimes our investigations overlap."

"Does that mean you share all the information you gather with him?"

"If I receive confidential information, I don't share it with Detective Bruno unless the information involves a crime that could be prevented."

Marko nodded. "What if the crime has already occurred?"

"Then it would depend on the crime." Dana felt like Senese was playing a game with her. She wanted to cut to the real reason behind his visit. "I know that Jake Carlson works for you. I also know that you were fond of his wife and I assume that you are concerned about her or you wouldn't be here testing my integrity. So, I ask you again. Do you have information that may help me find Beth Carlson?"

"Gutsy and smart." Marko nodded his head. "From your tone, can I assume that you think Beth is alive?"

"Yes, I do."

Marko lowered his eyes and was silent for a few seconds. When he looked up again, Dana saw the raw emotion he couldn't hide, and she knew that his feelings for Beth Carlson were a lot stronger and deeper than casual concern and affection. "I hope you're right, Miss Sloan, but knowing Jake and his abusive nature, I'm afraid you're wrong."

Dana nodded slightly. "I could be," she admitted. "But I must operate on the assumption that she ran off on her own in order to conduct a proper investigation."

"Okay, Miss Sloan, I'm going to give you some information and it does involve a crime of sorts. Jake claims that the money he collected over the weekend from the various business enterprises I oversee disappeared at the same time Beth went missing. He says Beth ran off with the money."

"How much money are we talking about?" Dana asked.

"Enough that if she is alive, she could be in another country by now. While I don't personally want to report this incident to the police, I am giving you permission to share the information with Detective Bruno. I want Beth Carlson found alive and well or I want Jake Carlson punished for killing her. Sources tell me that he has already confessed to doing that."

"So the missing money is the reason one of your men, presumably the one in my reception area ogling my secretary, was with Jake when the police came to question him about Beth's disappearance."

"That's right."

"What's more important to you, Mr. Senese, getting your money back or Beth Carlson's well-being?"

"If Beth is alive and has the money, she can keep it. However, I think that Jake has the money stashed somewhere. He told me that Beth took off with it because he knows, as you put it, I am fond of Beth and would overlook the loss."

"I'm sorry," Dana said. "That doesn't really compute. If Jake has the money why didn't he just run off before you found out it was missing?"

"Because Jake is not very bright, but he thinks he is. Jake has a girlfriend in Chicago. He keeps her in an apartment there and she's been bugging him to leave his wife and go away with her. So, Jake comes up with this elaborate plan to convince everyone that Beth ran away. He tells me that she took the money knowing that I would be glad to let her have anything she needed to get away from him."

"But wouldn't Jake realize that you'd be watching him and he wouldn't be able to use the money?"

"As I said before, Jake isn't too bright. Also, there is a reason Jake thinks he can get away with taking my money."

"What is that?"

"In a few weeks this will be public knowledge. In the meantime, I need you to agree not to share this information with anyone."

For a split second, Dana thought of refusing and asking Marko Senese to leave her office, but she was too intrigued by the man and his story to do that. "I agree," she said quietly.

"My father is in charge of all the business enterprises in the Chicago area. Unfortunately, my father is in poor health and will soon be turning over all the Chicago area businesses to another boss. The new boss thinks Crescent Hills is small potatoes and is closing down the business enterprises here. Within a few weeks, I'll be relocating to another city and Jake Carlson's services will no longer be needed. I'm sure Jake thinks there won't be anyone here to keep an eye on him and he and his girlfriend will be able to get away with my money."

"Have you considered the possibility that his wife may be in on it with him?"

"No. It's possible that Beth found out about the girl in Chicago and Jake was afraid she'd tell me. Stupid guy doesn't realize that I already know about the affair. Not too long ago, I told Jake if he hurt Beth in any way I'd make him sorry he was born."

"Let me see if I understand this," Dana said. "Jake's got a girlfriend. He's killed his wife and his claim that Beth disappeared is his way of getting away with murder and your money."

"Unfortunately, that's a good possibility."

"But now he's confessed to killing his wife and he's in jail."

"And I want him to stay there. It'll make my life less complicated if I don't have to watch him and his girl-friend too."

"Where can I find Jake's girlfriend?"

"I thought you'd never ask."

THE AZTEC CLUB was a mile or so from the downtown area. On a Monday night it wasn't too crowded so Dana was able to find a parking space right next to Bruno's unmarked squad car. The fact that he had driven the official vehicle to the Aztec Club probably meant he was only taking a dinner break and was still on duty.

Dana had called Bruno as soon as Marko Senese and friend had left her office and asked him to meet her. Bruno told her it would be after seven before he could get away and they agreed to meet for dinner.

Since Marianne had brought in the paperwork on the additional cases that had arrived in that day's mail and some more e-mailed requests for help to add to the weekend requests, Dana decided to stay in her office and sort through it until it was time to meet Bruno.

Bob had called Dana on her cell phone to report on the flights that had left Midway Airport on Sunday. Dana had Bob fax the list to her at the office and she now had it in her purse.

Bruno waved to Dana as she came through the door of the Aztec Club and she walked back to join him in a booth with leather bench seats and high backs.

"You must have stayed at the office," Bruno commented when he saw she was wearing the same dress she had on at lunch time.

"I had a stack of new cases to sort through. Thankfully, Casey called and said she felt better and would be in tomorrow. What happened with Carlson?"

Bruno laughed. "How about we order dinner before you start interrogating me. I'm starved."

"Is he still in custody?" Dana persisted.

"Yes. How about a pizza?"

"Fine. Whatever you want."

Bruno signaled for the waitress and ordered a large pizza with pepperoni and extra cheese and two soft drinks. "I'd rather have a beer, but I'm still on duty," Bruno said after the waitress left.

"I know," Dana said impatiently. "I parked next to your car. Tell me what happened with Carlson."

"He confessed to the officers at his apartment building. When he got to the station, he took back the confession and when I tried to ask him some questions he yelled for a lawyer." Bruno grinned.

"Ordinarily that would make you angry," Dana observed. "Why are you smiling?"

"I was about to get him a phone when Jake's lawyer showed up. The lawyer was none other than Michael Dominic."

Dana sat forward and grabbed Bruno's hand. "Marko Senese must have sent him there to find out what was going on with Jake."

"That's pretty obvious because after ten minutes with Dominic, Jake confessed again. So, Dominic left and Jake stayed."

"I don't think he killed his wife," Dana said as the waitress delivered their soft drinks to the table.

"Me neither, but since he confessed again, he's staying in jail."

"With Dominic as his attorney?"

"For the moment. Jake must have done something to upset Senese. That's why he's willing to stay in jail rather than face his boss."

"He did and I know what it is."

"You do?"

Dana nodded her head vigorously causing her curls to bounce in various directions. "I'm going to tell you, but first you have to promise to remain calm."

"Why?" The edge in his voice warned Dana that he was not going to be calm at all. She gripped his hand a little tighter.

"Because of the person who gave me the information."

"A reliable person?"

"In this case, yes, very reliable."

"I asked you not to go to Marko Senese."

Dana squeezed his hand. "I didn't break my promise. Senese and some guy as big as a building came to my office this afternoon."

"Good Lord. Here we go again. If you don't go looking for trouble, it comes to your doorstep."

Dana decided not to argue the point. "Do you want to hear what he told me or not?"

"How much did Jake steal from him?"

"He didn't give me an exact amount, but that's why the big guy was with Jake at his apartment. And to be clear here, the reason Marko came to me was because he knows that you and I are a couple and he wanted me to pass the information he gave me along to you."

Bruno called out for the waitress to bring him some ice water. "Did he threaten you in any way?"

Dana shook her head. "Of course not. He was a gentleman. He even had his bodyguard stay in the reception area with Marianne so we could speak privately."

"Is that supposed to make me feel better?"

"Do you want the rest of the information he gave me or not?"

"Tell me everything he said."

Dana told Bruno everything Marko Senese had told her except for the part about the new boss shutting down the Crescent Hills operation. Of course, Bruno wanted to know why Jake thought he could get away with taking the mob's money.

"He was counting on Marko believing that Beth took the money and ran off with it. It all fits, Bruno. The girl at the law firm was right about Marko romancing Beth because when I asked him about his feelings for her, he admitted that he was very fond of her. And he also said he warned Jake not to hurt her in any way or he'd make Jake sorry that he was born."

"Well, it does explain Jake's actions today," Bruno admitted. "The big question is did Jake really kill his wife?"

"I don't think so. I talked to the heavy-set woman we saw at the convenience store yesterday and she saw Beth in the store, even talked to her briefly. And don't forget the cab driver who said he took a girl to Midway Airport about the time Beth disappeared."

"Do you think she actually ran off with Senese's money?"

"Her mother said Beth didn't have any money of her own. So, yes, I think that's entirely possible."

"Did Senese give you the girlfriend's address in Chicago?"

"Yes. Do you want to come with me to question her tomorrow?" Dana asked as the waitress delivered the ice water to the table.

Bruno picked up the glass and took a long slow drink. Dana waited patiently, knowing that this was Bruno's way of cooling down. Her meeting with Senese had ignited a fire inside of him that he was trying to extinguish.

"You don't think I'm going to let you go there alone, do you?"

"I hoped not." Dana smiled. "I also want to go to the theater Beth was connected with there. Beth is an actress and I'm betting she went to Los Angeles to try to break into the movies or television."

"I thought she was six months pregnant."

"That's what she told everyone, but I'm beginning to have my doubts about that." Dana told him about calling the clinic where Lena said Beth was being treated and coming up blank. "Her mother doesn't even know the doctor's name."

"Are you saying she faked the pregnancy?"

"I don't know, but it would be a way to discourage the unwanted attentions of Marko Senese and even keep Jake from mistreating her."

The waitress brought their pizza to the table and served them each a slice of it. It smelled wonderful and Dana dug right into hers. Bruno ignored his, pulling out his cell phone and quickly dialing a number. When the station

answered, he requested that one of the officers go to Jake
Carlson's cell and ask him for the name of his wife's doctor.

"Call me back on my cell," Bruno instructed. He picked
up his pizza and took a bite. "If Jake doesn't know the
name either, your theory may be correct."

"I have a list of the flights that left Midway Sunday,"
Dana told him. "One of them was a direct flight to Los
Angeles. We need to get the passenger list and we need
to show Beth's photo to the security people and the airline people."

"I'll call Chicago and try to get that started tonight,"
Bruno promised. "I can fax them a copy of the photo and
your list. Hand it over."

"Thank you," Dana said brightly. "It's nice to be on the
same page for once." She opened her purse and handed him
the list of flights that Bob had gotten for her.

"I'm going to stick to you like glue until this case is
settled," Bruno said. "And if Marko Senese shows up at
your office again, you call me immediately."

"I don't think he's going to be back, Bruno. He was just
using me to pass information along to you."

"Have you passed along everything he told you?"

Dana smiled and crossed her fingers. "Of course," she
lied.

They discussed the various possibilities regarding Beth
Carlson's disappearance while they finished the pizza. As
the waitress came up to clear the table, Bruno's cell phone
rang. He answered it and listened to the information the
caller gave him.

"Was that the station?"

Bruno nodded. "Jake Carlson says he doesn't know the
name of his wife's doctor either."

"I guess it's possible that Beth gave him the name and
he just wasn't interested enough to remember it. Is his
apartment being searched?"

"Not until tomorrow morning."

"Maybe Beth left something there with the name of her doctor on it."

"Maybe. I have to get back to work. I've got this screwy case to write a report on and we're still trying to determine the identity of the woman we found in the motel last night."

"How was she killed?" Dana asked.

"She was shot in the head and the hotel room was stripped of anything that would identify the woman. Sounds like something your new friend, Marko Senese, might orchestrate."

"What time do you want to leave in the morning?" Dana asked ignoring Bruno's last remark.

"Not too early. I'll have to check in before we leave."

"That's good. I'll have to go into the office first and meet with Bob and Casey so I can make the case assignments. I should be ready to go by ten."

Bruno got up and offered his hand to Dana. She took it and slid out of the booth. "Don't you have a jacket?" he asked. "It's probably getting chilly outside."

"I was going to buy a sweater to wear with this dress today, but I met you for lunch instead."

"Sometimes you make excellent decisions."

Bruno paid the bill and they walked out to the parking lot. Standing between their two cars, Dana unlocked her door. She turned and kissed Bruno lightly on the mouth. "Two nights in a row, that I go home alone," she said.

"Gives me one more reason to dislike Jake Carlson." Bruno pulled her into his arms and kissed her again. "Call me at the station when you're ready to go tomorrow," he said as he released her.

Dana nodded and got into her car. Bruno waited for her to start her engine and drive out of the parking lot before he got into the car he was using. As soon as Bruno got back to his office, he called Chicago and requested their help. He faxed Beth Carlson's photo and the list of airline flights Dana had given him and was assured that someone would go to Midway Airport and report back to Bruno.

While Bruno was reading the autopsy report on the woman that was murdered in the motel on Sunday evening Dana was approaching the door of her apartment.

A note was taped to her door. It said, "Dana, I took a delivery for you this evening. I'll be up until 10, so please come by and get it. Lucy Walters."

Dana's building was three stories high with two apartments on each floor. Lucy Walters' lived in the other third floor apartment down the hall from Dana. She was a sweet old woman in her eighties. Dana glanced at her watch. It was nine o'clock, still early enough to retrieve her package. As she walked down the hallway, Dana was thinking that her mom must have sent her something. She knocked on Lucy's door and it was opened almost immediately.

"I saw you through the peephole," Lucy said. "My son had it installed. He says I open the door too quickly to anyone who knocks and I guess he's right. At my age, I don't get many visitors so I'm always happy when someone comes to my door."

"Your son is right," Dana told her. "You should always check before you open the door."

"Do you?"

"Yes. I have a chain on my door so it only opens enough for me to see who it is."

"I have a chain too and I told my son that, but he says someone could stick a gun into the crack and shoot me. Speaking of guns. How's that big good looking cop of yours?"

"He's fine. He's working tonight."

"Oh, that must be why he sent the flowers." Lucy Walters pulled Dana inside and motioned towards a huge vase of long stem roses of various colors.

Dana was puzzled. Bruno only sent flowers on special occasions like her birthday or Valentine's Day and he had never sent anything so large and extravagant.

Dana crossed the room to the coffee table where Lucy had set the flowers. Lucy was saying how beautiful they were and how lovely they smelled and how she hated to give them up. Dana snatched up the envelope from the plastic holder in the midst of the bouquet and tore it open.

"For a beautiful and gracious lady. Yours, Marko."

Dana felt a cold chill run down her spine. She quickly folded the note in half as if to hide its message.

"I hate to have you take them away," Lucy was saying. "I've enjoyed them so much."

Dana forced a smile. She thought of telling Lucy to keep the flowers, but realized that would just prompt a multitude of questions from her neighbor. "What time were these delivered?" Dana asked.

"Oh, about six-thirty. Yes, that's right. I was just about to sit down and watch Wheel of Fortune. Do you watch Wheel of Fortune?"

"Not often. Well, I'll just take these to my apartment. Thank you for keeping them for me."

"My pleasure. You tell Bruno that if I was fifty years younger, I'd marry him in a minute."

Dana smiled and nodded as she picked up the vase. It was heavy. She thanked Lucy again and carried the roses down to her own door where she had to set them on the floor in order to get into her apartment. Once inside Dana used her foot to close the door and carried the flowers into her dining room and set them on the table. She hurried back and locked the door and then went to her bedroom to kick off her shoes and deposit her purse on the dresser.

Returning to the dining room in her stocking feet, Dana sat down at the table and stared at the flowers. They were absolutely gorgeous and the fragrance filled the room, but unlike her neighbor, Dana was not enjoying them.

Apparently, Marko Senese made a practice of sending flowers to the women he met. The girl at the law firm said that Beth Carlson had been receiving flowers from him on a daily basis.

Dana thought how lucky she was that Bruno had to work and hadn't come home with her tonight. He would have a stroke if he found out that Marko Senese had sent her flowers.

"Oh, please," Dana whispered. "Let this be a one-time thing."

ELEVEN

THE NEXT MORNING, Bruno picked Dana up in the newspaper parking lot. Bruno had recently gotten a new car. It was a big black SUV with four wheel drive and tires that were guaranteed to move through the ice and snow that Midwest winters always brought. Whenever they went anywhere together they took Bruno's car. Mainly because Bruno didn't fit too well into the sporty Mustang that Dana owned.

As they headed towards the freeway that would take them to Chicago, Bruno handed Dana a sheet containing the passenger lists from the airline flights that had left Midway on Sunday evening.

"What about the photo?" Dana asked. "Did anyone recognize her?"

"A few people said they thought they might have seen her, but no one could make a positive I.D. It's not surprising when you consider how many people go through there every day."

"You're right," Dana said. "But Beth Carlson is a very pretty girl. I thought one of the men would remember her. Any news on Jake?"

"No. He's not talking to anyone right now. I've got the lab people at the apartment this morning trying to find some evidence that he killed his wife."

"I don't think he did," Dana said again. "I think Beth Carlson ran away with the money Jake was supposed to deliver to Senese."

"That's pretty cold. She must know that Senese will make Jake suffer for it."

"Everyone I've talked to says Jake deserves whatever he gets."

"So, you don't feel sorry for him?"

"I don't think he should be tried for a crime he didn't commit."

"And I shouldn't have to waste my time chasing down leads and witnesses for a homicide that never happened. By the way, I talked to mama this morning. She wants us to stick around and have dinner with her tonight."

"I'd love it," Dana said. "Is she cooking for us?"

"No. Today is her day to volunteer at the hospital. We're going to pick her up there and go to a restaurant she likes near there."

"Too bad. I was hoping she'd make eggplant."

"She asked me when we were getting married."

"She always asks that," Dana replied quietly. "But she knows I'm not quite ready yet."

Angelina Bruno was a warm, vibrant person who always said what she was thinking. Dana had been slightly intimidated by Angie until last February when the two of them stumbled into the path of a killer and had to work together to survive.

"You know she likes you more than she likes me now," Bruno said.

"That's because I'm sweeter than you are." Dana had been studying the passenger list from the American Airlines direct flight to Los Angeles that had left Midway at seven o'clock on Sunday evening. "Oh wow," she exclaimed as a name on the list struck her like a bolt of lightning.

"What?"

"One of the passengers on this flight is named, Elizabeth Stratton."

"So?"

"Beth Carlson worked for Richard Stratton and women named Elizabeth are often called Beth."

"I thought her given name was Bethany."

"It is, but this needs to be checked out. How can we find out more about this passenger?" Dana asked. "I think it could be her."

"I guess we can go back to the airline and find out how the ticket was purchased."

"And whether it was a round trip or one way," Dana added.

"What's this girlfriend's address again?" Bruno asked. They had merged onto the Dan Ryan Expressway in Chicago and Bruno was thinking about what exit he needed.

Dana got out the slip of paper with the girlfriend's name and address on it. Victoria Romero had an address on Lake Shore Drive, near Chicago's famous Museum of Science and Industry. This was an area of expensive high-rise buildings. If Jake Carlson was keeping this girl, it was costing him plenty.

Twenty minutes later, Bruno parked the car in the lot of a restaurant near Romero's apartment building. He showed the lot attendant his badge and said they'd be back to have lunch in the restaurant in an hour or so.

They entered the building and spoke to the doorman on duty in the lobby of the building. "We're looking for Victoria Romero in Apartment 10 A," Bruno said.

"You and ten other people," the man said. "She went away for the weekend and hasn't returned."

"Do you know where she went?" Dana asked.

"No, miss. The tenants just advise us of when they're leaving and when they're coming back. They don't provide their travel itinerary."

"Don't be a smart ass," Bruno said losing patience with

the guy's attitude. "Where's the manager of this building?" he asked showing his badge again.

"I apologize," the guard replied stiffly. "I'll call the manager for you."

Dana and Bruno waited for the manager to appear. When he did Bruno explained that Miss Romero was wanted for questioning in a police matter. The manager checked a clipboard he was carrying and told them she had signed out of the building on Friday afternoon and was supposed to be back on Sunday evening but had not yet shown up.

"Several people have been inquiring after her, but she didn't leave a number where she could be reached."

"Do you have a key to her apartment?" Bruno asked.

"Well, yes, but I don't think…"

Bruno interrupted him. "Get it. I think we should check and make sure she's not there."

The three of them rode the elevator to the tenth floor and the manager opened the door to 10A with his pass-key. Bruno walked through the living room, tiny kitchen and bedroom. He opened the closet doors and checked the bathroom. The apartment was clean and empty.

Dana was standing in the living room with the manager looking out at Lake Michigan through the sliding glass doors that led to a balcony. On a small table near the doors there was a silver frame with a photo of a man and woman. She picked it up and looked at it.

"Is this Miss Romero?" Dana asked the manager.

"Yes. That's her," he replied.

Bruno came back in the room. "Bruno, look at this." Dana held out the photo for him to see. "My informant could have been telling the truth. Here's a photo of her with Carlson."

Bruno took the photo and his face registered his surprise. He turned to the manager. "Is this Victoria Romero?"

"Yes. I just told the young lady that it was."

"Do you know the man in the photo with her?"

The manager looked at Jake Carlson and shook his head. "Never saw him before."

"Okay," Bruno said slipping the photo out of the frame and into his pocket. "Thanks for your help."

"Hey, wait a minute," the manager protested. "You can't take that."

"Yes, I can. If this woman in the photo is Victoria Romero, I have some bad news for you. She was found dead in Crescent Hills on Sunday night."

Bruno and Dana skipped lunch and drove to the nearest police station where Bruno met with a homicide detective and reported the murder of Victoria Romero.

Dana waited in the coffee shop next door to the station where she had a bagel and a cup of tea and used her cell phone to call her office and talk to Marianne.

"That's pretty bizarre," Marianne said. "Do you think she was in Crescent Hills to meet Jake Carlson?"

"Probably. And now he'll be suspected of her murder as well as his wife's."

After determining that she had no urgent phone messages and that Bob and Casey were working on the cases she had assigned them that morning, Dana asked Marianne to transfer her to Sam McGowan's office.

Sam and Dana had talked early that morning and she had filled him in on her investigation into the disappearance of Beth Carlson and explained why she and Bruno were going to Chicago for the day.

When she got her editor on the phone, Dana told him how they had inadvertently discovered the identity of the woman that was found murdered at the Riverside Motel on Sunday night.

"Does Bruno know you're reporting this?"

"Yes. It's going to be a joint investigation between him

and the Chicago police and you can report that too. However, don't report the connection between her and Jake Carlson. He's become the prime suspect and Bruno wants to question him about her first."

"Absolutely. I understand," Sam said. "Anything else?"

"Yes. We got the passenger lists for the flights that left Midway on Sunday evening. Because of her acting background, I thought Beth Carlson might have gone to Los Angeles and there was a direct flight to LA from Midway on Sunday night."

"Was her name on the passenger list?"

"No, but the name Elizabeth Stratton was on it." There was such a long silence, Dana thought they had lost their connection. "Sam? Are you still there?"

"Beth Carlson worked in Richard's office, didn't she?"

"Yes, that's why I took notice of the name, plus the fact that Beth is often short for Elizabeth. I want Bruno to get more information on this passenger, but in light of finding that photo of the dead woman, he's probably forgotten about it."

"Don't mention this to anyone else for the moment. I want to talk to Richard first."

The alarm in Sam's voice was disturbing. "Why? Is that his wife's name?"

"No. What time are you coming back to Crescent Hills?"

"I'm not sure. I want to talk to the people at the theater where Beth Carlson performed and we're supposed to have dinner with Bruno's mother."

"All right. Let's plan on meeting first thing in the morning."

"What's going on, Sam?"

"It may be nothing, but remind Bruno or the Chicago people to see if they can find out more about the passenger named, Elizabeth Stratton. I'll explain everything to you in the morning."

The call ended and Dana slipped the phone back into the pocket of her purse. She felt off-balance by the distress she had heard in her editor's voice. Elizabeth Stratton was obviously a name that meant something to Sam McGowan and Dana was now convinced that the name on the passenger list was no coincidence. It was the name that Beth Carlson had used to purchase an airline ticket and escape from Crescent Hills.

TWELVE

"DETECTIVE WATERS IS going to send a lab crew over to Victoria Romero's apartment and start questioning her friends and neighbors. I called Jack and faxed the photo to him, but I told him I want to question Carlson myself."

"Do you think Jack will comply?" Dana asked. Detective Jack O'Brien was not one of Dana's favorite people. He had caused some problems between Dana and Bruno and had tried to arrest Casey when her husband was murdered.

"On Carlson, yes, but he's dying to haul Marko Senese in and question him."

"That seems a little reckless even for Jack. Does he have a reason to do it?"

"Waters ran Victoria Romero through the computer and she's got a rap sheet which we also faxed to Jack. Romero was a topless dancer in one of the clubs here that is owned by Senese and company. She was arrested in a raid there two years ago and at the time, Marko Senese was managing the place."

"That was before Marko took over the Crescent Hills enterprises?"

"Right. Jake Carlson was also arrested in the raid, so apparently he was already working for Senese and that's how he met Romero."

"Beth's mother said her daughter met Jake when she was performing at the theater here. Is this club near the theater?"

"From the addresses, I'd say it's right across the street."

"Did the police close the place down?"

"No, just interrupted the fun for a few hours."

"Why was the place raided?"

"One of the losers probably called in an anonymous tip about the gambling and drug dealing that was going on there."

"I don't think Jack should question Marko without you or Detective Waters there too."

"That's exactly what I told him."

Dana wanted to tell Bruno what a jerk she thought Detective O'Brien was, but he had heard it all before. She almost wished O'Brien would try to question Marko Senese on his own. She didn't think Jack would last five minutes in a room with Senese and his lawyer.

Bruno turned right on Archer Avenue, a street that ran on an angle. Center Stage Playhouse was on the next corner.

"The guy I talked to said to park in the lot and go around the back to the office," Dana said.

A few minutes later, Bruno and Dana were standing in the midst of a room with some battered desks and shelving units piled high with papers and play scripts. A young blond girl with a long braid greeted them and directed them to a smaller room that served as the office of the theater's artistic director.

"Hi. I'm Aidan Kellogg." A middle-aged man dressed in jeans and a T-shirt that had the name of the theater printed across it, rose to shake hands with Dana and Bruno. He had long dark hair pulled back into a ponytail. "Have a seat." Bruno and Dana sat down on the two metal folding chairs against the office wall. "Is there any news on Beth?"

When Dana called and arranged the appointment with Kellogg she had told him why she wanted to talk to him. Now she shook her head in a negative reply. "Not really, but I'm working on the assumption that Beth may have gone to Los Angeles. Do you know if there's anyone in that area she could contact for help or for a job?"

"No. All my theater contacts are in New York City, which is where Beth always said she wanted to go."

"Her mother told me that," Dana replied. "But so far, it looks like she may have gone in the opposite direction."

Bruno spoke up. "Was Beth good at make-up and changing her appearance in general?"

"Most actresses are," Kellogg said. "Especially girls who work in small theaters like this one, where budget constraints limit makeup and wardrobe help for the players."

"How talented is Beth?" Dana asked.

"Extremely talented." Kellogg nodded his head several times as if to give extra weight to his opinion. "In fact, she may be one of the most talented girls who performed here. Beth could do everything. We did a few musicals while she was part of our ensemble here and she always got the female lead. She has a beautiful and unique singing voice and she's a good dancer too. Despite her talent she was not at all temperamental. She took direction well and got along with everyone in the company."

"It sounds like you wish she were still here," Bruno said.

"I do. And I curse the day she met up with Jake Carlson. I knew he was trouble from the moment I met him. He worked at the club across the street. It's owned by mobsters and Jake worked for them."

"How did she meet Jake?" Dana asked.

"He wandered over here one night and saw Beth on stage. We were doing a show called *The Last Decent Crooks*. The title is probably what attracted Jake. It's a musical-comedy-mystery. It's set during prohibition and it's about a gangster who uses a funeral parlor as a front for a speakeasy. Beth had one of the leads. Jake saw her perform and fell in love."

"And she fell for him," Bruno added.

"Right. I tried to warn Beth that he was involved with some dangerous people, and maybe that made it all the more exciting for her. Anyway, Jake promised to make her dream of going to New York to live a reality and she believed him. The next thing I know, she's married and he's taking her back to Crescent Hills."

"Have you talked to Beth since she left here?"

"No, not a word."

"What about other members of your company. Has she kept in touch with any of them?"

"I think she did at first, but no one I know has heard anything from her for over a year."

"So, you think if she ran off, she would go to New York, not Los Angeles?" Bruno asked.

Kellogg shrugged. "That would be my guess, but maybe she thought that would be the first place Jake would look for her."

"Los Angeles doesn't have the theater opportunities that New York has, but there's television and movies," Dana said.

"Do you think she could get work with one of the studios?"

"There's a lot of competition on the West Coast, but Beth is probably more talented than 90% of the people I see on television. As a matter of fact, when we were doing *The Last Decent Crooks,* we did a CD of the songs in the show that we sold to the public. I still have some copies. Would you like one?"

"Yes. I would," Dana said quickly.

Although Kellogg protested, Dana insisted on purchasing the recording from him. Then, she thanked him for his time and she and Bruno left the theater. It was after five and Chicago's rush hour traffic was in full swing. Bruno slowly maneuvered his way through the congested streets to the expressway and headed for North West Hospital where Angelina volunteered on Tuesdays.

"I'm starving," Dana said. "That bagel I had in place of lunch was not enough to sustain me."

"At least you had a fresh bagel. I had a stale doughnut and coffee that will keep me awake for a week."

Since Angie's apartment was only a few blocks from the hospital and her son said he would pick her up, she had walked there that morning instead of driving her car. Today she had been stationed in the surgical waiting room. It was always a difficult assignment. The phone rang constantly with people calling to check on patients. The families of patients who sat in the room, waiting for word of their loved ones, never seemed to understand that the people who manned the desk had no control over how long the surgeries lasted.

Angie waited at the main entrance to the hospital and was happy the day was over. She was happier still to know that she was having dinner with Alphonso and Dana. She had decided not to make any comments or ask any questions about their future plans. They would just have a nice leisurely dinner and talk about other things.

A black SUV stopped and Bruno got out and walked towards her. "When did you get that monstrosity?" Angie asked. "I'll need a ladder to get into it."

Bruno hugged her. "You won't need a ladder. I brought a step stool for you."

Angie and Bruno's sisters were petite women. Bruno got his size from his father's side of the family. While Bruno's late father had not been a big man, his brothers were all over six feet and broad like her son, the ex-football player.

Dana slid down from the passenger seat of the SUV and greeted Angie with a hug while Bruno got the little step stool from the back seat.

"You sit in the front," Dana told Angie. "The front seat is easier to get into."

Bruno helped his mother into the car and then gave Dana a hand getting into the back seat and handed her the stool.

"And why black?" Angie asked as they drove out of the hospital grounds. "All the gangsters drive black cars."

"That's why," Bruno told her. "So they'll think I'm one of them and make it easier to follow them."

Dolce Vita restaurant was only a few blocks from the hospital. Dana was glad because her empty stomach was about to start growling for food.

Angie had made a reservation so they were seated immediately. They ordered wine and a basket of warm Italian bread was brought to the table.

Dana and Bruno both reached for the bread. "We didn't get lunch," Dana explained.

"Why not?" Angie asked.

"We went to question a witness and discovered that she was a murder victim from another case I'm working on," Bruno told her.

"She was killed in Crescent Hills?"

"Yes."

"But she lived here in Chicago?"

"Right."

"Crescent Hills used to be such a nice safe town. Now the gangsters have set up shop there and it's getting more dangerous than Chicago."

Bruno shook his head. "Crescent Hills has a long way to go before its crime can come any where near Chicago's statistics."

"Well, I think when you get married, you should transfer to the force here. Then, when you have bambinos, I can help you with them." Angie grimaced. Five minutes into dinner and she had already broken her promise to herself. "I'm sorry. I wasn't going to bring up the subject."

Dana smiled at her. "It's okay, Angie. When I have bambinos, I'll need all the help I can get."

Bruno started to make a comment, but fortunately for Dana, the waiter appeared to take their order. Angie and Dana both ordered eggplant parmigiana. Bruno ordered lasagna.

"The eggplant here is good," Angie told Dana.

"But not as good as yours," Dana replied.

"No. Have you tried to make it yet?"

"I'm afraid not. I've been too busy to cook anything lately."

"Next time I come for a visit, we'll make it together."

"Yes, you will," Bruno said. "It'll be a lot safer than the last thing you two did together."

Dana and Angie exchanged a look. Bruno had still not gotten over the fact that he could have lost the two people he loved most in the world. He was also a little disgruntled at the crazy way they had saved themselves.

"That was a once in a lifetime thing," his mother told him. "We are not planning on doing it ever again. Although it was very exciting."

This time Dana and Angie smiled at each other, but Dana was facing the front door of the restaurant and the smile froze on her face when she saw Marko Senese and a woman come through it.

Dana grabbed Bruno's hand. "Don't turn around but Marko Senese and some woman just came in."

"Are you kidding?"

"I wouldn't kid about that…oh, oh, the waiter is bringing them this way."

The waiter led the woman who looked like a Barbie Doll with black hair and Marko towards them. Dana tried to decide if she should ignore him or say hello. After all, the man had sent her flowers, but perhaps he wouldn't want that to be acknowledged especially when she was with Bruno.

Marko looked at her and smiled. "Just a minute," he said to the woman and the waiter. "I have a friend to greet."

Both the woman and the waiter turned as Marko held out his hand to Dana. She had no choice but to smile and offer her hand to him.

"Miss Sloan, what a pleasure to see you again. What are you doing here?"

"Just having dinner," Dana said lamely. "This is Al Bruno and his mother, Angelina." Dana was pretty sure that Marko knew who Bruno was, but she introduced them anyway. They didn't bother shaking hands.

Marko bowed slightly in deference to Angie. "A pleasure to meet you, madam," he said softly, then turned back to Dana. "I hope you enjoyed the flowers, Miss Sloan."

Dana had no choice but to respond. "Yes. Thank you. They are lovely."

The raven haired "Barbie" took hold of Senese's arm to remind him of her presence. "This is my wife, Giada. Miss Dana Sloan, Detective Bruno and his mother, Angelina."

Giada nodded briefly at Bruno and Angie and turned her eyes on Dana. Her eyes were dark like her husband's and her look was as menacing as a panther ready to strike down its prey.

"How do you know my husband?" she asked.

Before Dana could reply, Marko grabbed Giada's arm and pulled her back from the table. "We don't want to keep you from your dinner," he said coolly. "Good evening."

Marko motioned for the waiter to move, pushed his wife in front of him and the trio continued their trek to a private booth in the back of the restaurant. Dana watched them go, feeling another pair of eyes boring into the back of her head.

She turned around and picked up her wine glass and took a drink.

"He is the son of Carlo Senese," Angie whispered. "They are the bosses of this city. How do you know such a man? And why would he send you flowers?"

Dana looked at Bruno who was drinking his ice water. The waiter would have to bring a pitcher of it now.

"He showed up at my office yesterday to give me information about a case I'm working on. A woman he was interested in has disappeared." Dana replied in an equally soft voice.

"That girl disappeared and may be dead," Bruno said. "So, now it seems he's interested in Dana."

Dana glanced towards the door. The big guy that had accompanied Marko to her office yesterday was standing guard there.

"His bodyguard is standing at the front door," she said lightly, trying to change the subject. "I guess he doesn't get to eat."

"When did you get flowers?" Bruno set the empty water glass down on the table carefully.

"They were delivered while I was having dinner with you last night. Mrs. Walters accepted them for me. She thought they were from you."

"We've been together all day today. Why didn't you mention it?"

"Because I knew it would upset you and because it upset me and I didn't want to talk about it."

Angie placed her hand on Bruno's arm. "It is not Dana's fault the man sent her flowers."

Bruno turned and looked at her. "I didn't say it was her fault, Mama. I just asked why she didn't tell me about it."

"And she just explained the reason to you. Accept it and let's talk about something else. Your sister, Maria, is getting a new job."

"What kind of a job?" Dana asked, anxious to steer the conversation away from Marko Senese and the flowers.

"She will be tutoring students in math. Maria taught math at the high school before she was married. This job will allow her to earn some extra money and still be home in the afternoon when the kids come from school."

"That's great," Dana said. "I'm not very good at math. Maybe I should have her tutor me."

Angie and Dana laughed. Bruno sighed and shook his head.

THIRTEEN

THANKS TO AN excellent dinner and Angelina's talent for keeping the conversation light and humorous, Bruno's mood had improved immensely by the time they dropped Angie off at her house.

He and Dana were on the expressway headed back to Crescent Hills before he spoke of Marko Senese again.

"I'm sorry if I over-reacted to the flowers," he said.

"I'm sorry he mentioned the flowers. It was very awkward. I know you were upset, but his wife was livid. If looks could kill I would have been face down in my eggplant."

Bruno grinned. "She's very attractive, if you like the type that looks like she's ready to jump off a ledge."

"I'm sure being married to a man like Senese is incredibly stressful."

"She should be used to it. Her father and brothers are mob bosses in Vegas. Rumor has it that they are going to take over the Chicago area from Carlo and Marko."

"Really?" Dana said as if she hadn't heard it before.

"Carlo is retiring and Marko will be reassigned. The rumor also says the Vegas boys don't think Crescent Hills is worth much in terms of their business ventures. Since his wife mainly lives in Vegas with her family, I'm betting Marko will be sent there so they can all keep an eye on him."

"How did you find all this out?"

"We've got a guy undercover at the pool hall where Marko and his guys hang out."

"Anyone I know?"

"No."

"I thought maybe you'd chase after Marko and question him about Victoria Romero. He is the one that gave me her name and address."

"If I tried to approach him in the restaurant, I would have had to do battle with his bodyguard."

"I'm assuming his being in Chicago made it impossible for Jack to question him either."

"We'll catch up with him tomorrow. First I'm going to talk to Carlson again."

"That reminds me," Dana said reaching into her purse. "I have that C/D of the show Beth was in. Let's listen to it."

Dana slipped the C/D into the player and the music began. The music was lively and jazzy indicative of the prohibition era that spawned bathtub gin and illegal nightclubs. The first few songs were performed by people other than Beth, but on the fourth song, Beth sang a duet with one of the male leads in the show.

"Wow," Dana said as the song ended. "She does have a beautiful voice."

The next song, *When Nothing Else Was Right,* began. It was a solo for Beth. As the music and her lovely voice filled the car, Dana and Bruno listened together in silence. Both of them were struck by the words of the song that seemed to have been written especially for them.

Sometimes you find the one you've searched for through the years at a time and place when you can hardly keep back tears.
It takes a while to realize after all that you've been through, that special certain someone is looking at you. Why did this happen when nothing else was

right? How can love break through this heart that
still just wants to fight?
Who is this man that loves me just the way I am?
And holds my heart and soul so gently in his hands…

The song continued and Bruno reached over and covered Dana's hand with his. "Sounds a lot like our relationship," Bruno said as the song ended and another upbeat
tune began. "Do you think the composer knows us?"

Dana shook her head. "It certainly fits us. We did meet
when nothing else was right in the middle of a triple homicide."

"I was the one with the tears. You just wanted to fight."

"I don't recall any tears on your part. You gave me a
hard time from the beginning."

"And you gave it right back to me."

Dana sighed and nodded. Some of the battles had torn
them apart, but somehow they always found a way to move
past the rough patches and stay together. "You still try to
bully me," Dana said.

"Like that ever worked. You just tell me to take my big
fat ego for a swim in Lake Michigan."

"I've never used the word, fat. Over-sized, inflated,
enormous…"

"Okay, you win. And now that you've managed to get
my own mother to take your side in everything, you'll
win every time. By the way, I like what you said to Mama
about having bambinos and I think it's time we got started
on that."

Dana laughed. "So, now you're going to skip the wedding and fast forward to having babies?"

"You're the one who doesn't want to change her name
to Mrs. Al Bruno."

"Oh, that reminds me," Dana said. "Did you remember

to ask the Chicago cops to check on the passenger named Elizabeth Stratton?"

"I did. They'll check and get back to me tomorrow."

"Great. I didn't tell you, but I talked to Sam and told him about the name on the passenger list and he got upset and said he had to talk to Richard Stratton about it. I asked what was going on, but he just said he'd explain everything to me in the morning."

"So, cookie, are you going to change your name to Bruno in the near future?"

"I'll make a deal with you," Dana said in an impish tone. "Let's find Beth Carlson and the person who murdered Victoria Romero and then I promise we can talk about a wedding."

"Our wedding?"

Dana laughed. "Yes."

"That song must have really gotten to you."

FOURTEEN

DANA ARRIVED IN her editor's office at eight the next morning. She was surprised to find Richard Stratton there. He stood when she came through the door.

"Good morning, Dana," he said stiffly.

"Good morning."

Dana sat down in the other chair and looked at Sam who posed the first question. "Did Bruno get any more information about the passenger named Elizabeth Stratton?"

"I don't think so," Dana replied. "He promised to call me as soon as he heard anything."

Richard shook his head. "I don't need any more information from the airline. Beth Carlson handled the office files and the mail. Elizabeth's file had a copy of her birth certificate and her social security card. I checked it this morning. Both items are missing. It's all anyone would need to steal her identity. She could have gotten a passport or a drivers license issued in the name of Elizabeth Stratton with her own photo on it easily enough."

"Excuse me, Richard," Dana said softly. "Who is Elizabeth Stratton?"

"My daughter. She disappeared when she was seven years old.

She would be twenty-six now, just a year or so younger than Beth Carlson."

"And your daughter was never found?"

"No. She is presumed dead, but her body was never recovered. My mother-in-law is Beth Carlson's aunt so I'm sure she learned about Elizabeth from her. My mother-in-law is the one who asked me to give Beth a job in my office."

"Yes, I know that," Dana told him. "I spoke to her yesterday. She told me she has no idea where Beth is."

"Right. I'd forgotten you asked for her contact information."

"Dana, I told Richard that you will remain on this case until Beth Carlson is found," Sam announced, notifying Dana that this case would take priority over any others that came into her office.

Richard spoke directly to Dana. "I understand her husband is in jail and he has confessed to murdering her."

"Yes, but Jake is also in trouble with his boss, Marko Senese, so we think that he confessed just to get away from him."

"Are the police going to release him?" Sam asked.

"I don't think so." Dana explained about the unidentified murder victim that had now been linked to Jake Carlson.

"I'd like to speak to Carlson," Richard said. "Does he have an attorney?"

"Yes and no. Michael Dominic showed up when he was being interviewed, but Bruno said Jake wasn't happy about that."

"Obviously Dominic was sent there by Senese," Sam said. "I heard that Marko Senese was in your office yesterday. What did he tell you?"

"Money that Jake collected for Senese's various business enterprises went missing at the same time Beth did. I think she took the money and left her husband here to face the music."

"I would never have believed it," Richard said shaking his head sadly. "Beth always seemed like such a lovely person."

"Her husband abused her and Marko Senese was romancing her," Dana told him. "I think she just wanted to get away from both of them."

"She committed a crime and if she's found alive I will prosecute her," Stratton declared. "I'll get one of my staff to start checking with hospitals and clinics in the LA area. Beth is pregnant and should have to seek care within the next few weeks."

"That's the other thing," Dana replied. "I don't think she was pregnant. I think it was something she made up to keep her husband and Marko Senese at arm's length."

"One lie upon another," Sam said.

The meeting ended with Dana promising to keep Sam and Richard apprised of any information she received regarding Beth Carlson.

Dana entered the reception area of her office to find Marianne opening the morning mail. She stopped what she was doing and looked up at Dana. "That must have been a tough meeting. You look upset."

"I am," Dana admitted. "Bring that mail in my office and I'll tell you about it while you finish sorting."

Dana went in, got a cup of coffee and sat down at the conference table. Marianne followed a few seconds later carrying the mail and her letter opener. She saw Dana's coffee and decided to get a cup for herself.

When they were both settled at the table, Dana filled Marianne in on everything that had happened the day before in Chicago and then told her about the meeting with Richard Stratton in Sam's office.

"When you get done with the mail, I want you to help me find Beth Carlson," Dana said.

Before Marianne could comment the telephone rang. Marianne answered the extra phone that was placed on the end of the conference table. "Good morning, Globe Investigations," she listened for a moment and then grinned.

"It's the father of your future children calling. His words, not mine," Marianne said, handing the phone to Dana.

"Who is calling?" Dana asked.

"How can you say that after last night?"

"I'm having a bad morning. Do you have any information on Beth Carlson?"

"Chicago just faxed me a copy of the ticket Elizabeth Stratton purchased. It was a one way, purchased at the ticket counter and paid for in cash about an hour before the plane took off. The I.D. used to verify the name on the ticket was a passport."

"That fits," Dana told him. "I just met with Richard Stratton. Elizabeth Stratton is his daughter who disappeared without a trace nineteen years ago. He had a file in his office that Beth Carlson had access to with his daughter's birth certificate and social security card. That's all Beth would have needed to get a passport. Oh, and Elizabeth Stratton would be around the same age now that Carlson is."

"Pretty clever," Bruno said. "If the girl was never found there would be no death certificate on file and I'm sure her parents wouldn't have the heart to declare her legally dead."

"Right. Did you question Jake yet? Maybe you can ask him if his wife ever mentioned Stratton's daughter."

"I haven't talked to him yet. I'm waiting for Waters. Jack took him out to the crime scene and when he gets back here we're going to talk to Carlson together."

"What about Senese?"

"I'll pay him a visit after I talk to Carlson and see what he has to say about Victoria Romero."

"Sounds like you'll be working through lunch."

"And supper too. I'll catch you later, sweets."

Dana hung up and looked at Marianne but before they could speak the telephone rang again. Marianne answered it. "Yes, this is she." As she listened, Marianne frowned, "I'm sorry, I have an exclusive relationship with someone, but thank you for thinking of me." She listened for a few more seconds. "No. Lunch is not possible either. Good-bye."

"Who was that?"

"Oh, my God," Marianne said shaking her head in disbelief. "It was that man who came in here with Marko Senese. He asked me out."

"Well, I'm not surprised," Dana said. "I thought his eyes would bug out of his head, the way he was staring at you."

"He is one scary dude," Marianne said with a shudder.

"So is his boss. Maybe he thinks we could double date?"

This got them both laughing.

"I can't believe Senese would mention sending you flowers right in front of his wife."

"And Bruno and his mother. It was a nightmare. And by the way, your new admirer was there too, but he had to stand guard at the door while Mr. & Mrs. Senese had dinner."

Marianne finished opening the mail and she and Dana sorted it together. "I can take care of these," Marianne said indicating a small pile of requests that required Internet research.

"Are Casey and Bob out together this morning?" Dana asked.

"I don't think so. They split up the cases you left for them and went their separate ways."

"I haven't seen Casey much since last week. How is she doing?"

"Not much better. I asked her to meet me for lunch at the mall. Why don't you come along?"

"Thanks, I will unless something earth-shattering comes up."

ACROSS THE STREET, Detective Bill Waters from the Chicago precinct was meeting with Bruno and Jack O'Brien. Just as Bruno had determined, the crime scene held no real clues.

"You want me to pick up Senese for questioning?" Jack asked, always eager to volunteer for jobs that gave him a chance to flaunt his own importance.

"Not yet," Bruno told him. "Bill and I are going to question Jake Carlson now. You sit tight and field the phone calls until we get back."

Jack wasn't too happy to be kept on the bench but Bruno was his superior and he had to comply.

Jake was waiting in one of the interview rooms. "What about his lawyer?" Bruno asked the officer standing guard at the door.

"He said he doesn't want Dominic within two miles of him. One of the public defenders is in there with him."

"Which one?"

"Hastings."

"Do you know him?" Bill Waters asked Bruno.

"Yeah. He's young, but he's a smart kid."

Lance Hastings stood up when Bruno and Waters entered the room. Bruno introduced Hastings to Waters and the men sat down. Jake Carlson, looking sullen, remained in his chair. His right hand was shackled to a ring on the metal table in the interview room.

"My client says he's in trouble with Marko Senese and feared for his life which is why he said he killed his wife. It was simply a way to get away from the guy that Marko assigned to watch him. He has retracted his confession again and Mr. Dominic has been informed that my office is now representing Mr. Carlson."

"Does Jake want to admit that he works for Senese?"

"He is or was employed by Senese," Hastings said.

"Why is he in trouble with Senese?"

"It seems that a large sum of money that my client was supposed to deliver to Senese is missing."

"Beth took it." Jake said loudly. "She ran off with the money. That's the truth."

"Okay, Jake. We are searching for your wife. Does the name Elizabeth Stratton mean anything to you?"

"No...oh wait...she worked for a guy named Stratton... yeah...that's the name of one of the lawyers she worked for."

"Did your wife ever mention the name Elizabeth Stratton?"

"No."

Bill Waters took over. "Mr. Carlson, do you know a woman named Victoria Romero?"

"Yeah. I know her. Why?"

"What is your relationship to Miss Romero?"

"We're friends. We used to work together at a club in Chicago."

"When was the last time you saw her?"

"I don't know."

Waters took out the photo that Bruno had taken from Romero's apartment. "When was this photo of you and Miss Romero taken?"

Jake stared at the photo. "I don't remember. Where'd you get that?"

"From her apartment on Lake Shore Drive. What did Miss Romero do for a living that she could afford the rent there?"

"How should I know?"

"Cut the crap, Jake," Bruno said sternly. "Sources tell us that you and Miss Romero were having an affair and you always met at the Riverside Motel."

"Bull shit. That's not true. Vicki and I were just friends, that's all. I remember now. That photo was taken down at

Navy Pier a long time ago, when we worked together. Ask Vicki. She'll tell you we are just friends."

"We'd like to ask her," Bruno said quietly. "But it's impossible."

"Why? Did something happen to her?"

"She's dead, Jake," Bruno told him.

"Oh, no. Shit. Not Vicki." Jake was visibly shaken. Either he didn't know that Romero was dead or he was an excellent actor.

"Do you have any idea of who might want to harm Miss Romero?" Waters asked.

"Only one person I can think of," Jake replied. "The guy she was having an affair with since we worked the club together, the guy who kept her in that fancy apartment."

"And who would that be?"

"I want to confer with my lawyer," Jake said suddenly. "We need to talk privately."

Hastings turned to Jake. "Just tell them who you suspect, Jake. That's your best shot at getting out of here."

Jake's face drained of color. The thought of leaving the safely of his jail cell was terrifying. Marko's goons were probably hanging around outside just waiting for him to walk out into the street.

"On one condition. I stay here in protective custody."

Bruno and Waters looked at each other. "It's your call, Bruno," Waters said.

"If you didn't kill your wife and you didn't kill Miss Romero, we have nothing to hold you on," Bruno said. "Of course if you want to confess to the illegal activities you've been performing for Marko Senese over the years, it'll give us another reason to keep you here."

"Do you think I'm crazy?" Jake yelled. "No way. I didn't kill Vicki, but I did kill my wife. I buried her in the woods along the lake front."

DANA HAD INSTRUCTED Marianne to start checking with hotels in the Los Angeles area to see if a woman named Elizabeth Stratton was registered.

"Should I start with the small inexpensive ones or the high class ones?" Marianne asked.

"Considering the amount of money I think she has, start with the high class ones," Dana said as she left the office.

Dana drove to Greta Malone's house and Greta pulled the door open as soon as Dana parked her Mustang at the curb. Greta rushed down the walkway to meet Dana. Dana had told Greta on the telephone that they had reason to believe that Beth might have gone to Los Angeles. Greta said she didn't know anyone there and doubted if Beth did either.

"Do you really think Beth is alive?" Greta asked anxiously as they walked to the house.

"I do, but locating her in a city as large as Los Angeles isn't going to be easy."

Once they were settled in the living room, Dana asked Greta if the name Elizabeth Stratton meant anything to her. "Yes, of course. My husband's older sister was her grandmother. Dorothy and I have never gotten on well, and after Artie died we didn't bother trying, but my heart broke for her when Elizabeth disappeared. She was just a little younger than Beth."

"Yes, I know that," Dana said. "How much did Beth know about her cousin?"

"Nothing really, until Dorothy got her the job at Stratton's office. Then she and I talked about the tragedy of it. Beth wanted to know what I thought happened to the girl. Of course I don't know any more than anyone else."

"According to the newspaper accounts I looked up, she was playing in her front yard and when her mother went to call her in for lunch she was gone."

"Someone snatched her," Greta said firmly. "Snatched her and killed her."

"Extensive searches were conducted for weeks, but her body was never recovered. There were no ransom demands. No witnesses came forward. The child's disappearance remains a mystery."

"What does this tragedy from the past have to do with Beth?" Greta asked.

"I'm afraid that Beth may have used Elizabeth's birth certificate and social security number to obtain a passport that she used to purchase a plane ticket and travel to Los Angeles."

Greta's eyes grew wide. "How could she do that?"

"The documents were in a file that Richard Stratton keeps in his office. Beth had access to the file."

"And people named Elizabeth are often called Beth," Greta said in a sad, weak voice. Then, she brightened. "But if that's true, it means that Beth is alive. That's wonderful."

Dana's cell phone rang and Dana looked at the caller ID. "Excuse me. I have to take this call," she said.

"Where are you?" Bruno asked when she answered his call.

"I'm with Beth Carlson's mother. Do you have news?"

"Her husband confessed to killing her again and said he buried her body in the woods along the lake front."

"Do you believe him?"

"No, but we're going to search the area anyway. He denied any knowledge of Romero's murder and insinuated that she was having an affair with Marko Senese, but wouldn't actually give up his name. He's scared out of his wits that we'll release him and Marko will nab him again. I think he's confessing to killing his wife because he didn't and he knows we won't be able to come up with a body. In the meantime, Waters and I are going to question your other boyfriend."

"Not funny," Dana said.

"Sorry. This case has me breathing fire."

"I have Marianne checking all the hotels in Los Angeles to see if Elizabeth Stratton is registered at any of them. I'll let you know."

"I'll call you later," Bruno said as he clicked off.

"Was there news about Beth?" Greta asked anxiously.

"Not really," Dana said. She thought it best not to repeat Jake's latest confession to Beth's mother.

"You said someone was checking the hotels in Los Angeles?"

"That's right. I'll let you know if we find Beth. In the meantime, if you should hear from her, please call me immediately."

"Yes, yes, I will. If Beth used that missing child's identity she is in trouble isn't she?"

"From what I've learned, Beth was in a terrible situation. I don't think people will fault her for doing what she had to do to escape." Even as she said it, Dana knew that her statement did not apply to the parents of Elizabeth Stratton.

FIFTEEN

IT WAS CLOSE to noon when Dana got back to her office.
The shopping mall where they were meeting Casey for
lunch was just a few blocks from the newspaper, so Dana
parked her car in the newspaper's lot and went upstairs to
get Marianne.

"I've got good news and bad news," Marianne said as
Dana walked through the door.

"About Beth Carlson?"

"Aka Elizabeth Stratton who was registered at the La
Maison Hotel in West Hollywood from Monday morning
until this morning when she checked out."

Dana pulled out her cell phone and called Bruno, but
his phone was turned off and her call went directly to message mode. The next best thing was to call the station and
speak to Harrison or O'Brien. She would have preferred
Harrison, but she had to settle for Jack O'Brien. When she
got him on the phone she told him about the West Hollywood hotel where they suspected Beth Carlson had spent
Monday and Tuesday night.

"So how does that help us?" O'Brien wanted to know.
"LA's a big city. If she checked out, she could be anywhere.
Besides, her old man confessed to killing her and burying
her body in the woods. We have to check that out first."

"I know that Jack," Dana said patiently. "But you can
fax her photo to the station nearest the hotel and ask that
someone go over and question the desk clerk, the bell boys,

and the maids. Maybe she left a clue as to where she was going next."

"Bruno told you her husband confessed again?"

"Right."

"He shouldn't be sharing that kind of information with a reporter, even if you are his girlfriend."

"We are working this case together, Jack. And it's important that the hotel staff be questioned right away before any crucial information is lost or forgotten. Bruno will be very upset if you drop the ball on this."

"Okay, okay. I'll do it. The gal's photo is right here. She's a really good-lookin' chick. I may go to LA and look for her myself."

"Just call LA and fax the photo, please."

"Yes, madam," Jack said sarcastically and hung up on her.

"That guy is such a jerk," Dana told Marianne.

"Is he going to do what you asked?"

"I hope so. Let's go to lunch. Casey will be waiting for us."

MARKO SENESE HAD just arrived at his office at the pool hall when Bruno and Detective Waters confronted him. A guy as big as Turk moved towards the detectives as they entered the office, then recognized Bruno. Harry stopped in his tracks.

"Mr. Senese," Bruno said, ignoring Harry and addressing his boss. "We'd like to have a few words with you?"

"Do I need to call my lawyer?" Senese asked with a polite smile.

"That's up to you. We can talk here or you can call your attorney and have him meet us at the station."

"We'll talk here for the moment. Harry, get another chair and then make yourself scarce."

Harry hurried over and got a folding chair from the

corner and placed it next to the visitor's chair in front
of Marko's desk. "I'll be right outside if you need me,"
Harry said as he left the office closing the door firmly
behind him.

Bruno and Waters sat down. Waters removed a small
notebook and a pen from his pocket and set them both on
the front of Marko's desk.

"I didn't expect to see you again so soon, Detective
Bruno," Marko said smoothly. "How was your dinner last
night?"

"Fine. How was yours?"

"Mine was good. My wife didn't like hers, but Giada
always complains. So why are you here with my old friend,
Detective Waters."

Waters pulled the photo of Romero and Carlson out
of his pocket and placed it on the desk in front of Marko.
"You know this woman?"

"Yes. It's Vicki Romero. She used to work in one of my
clubs in Chicago. Why?"

"She was found murdered in a room at the Riverview
Motel."

This time the news of Victoria Romero's death didn't
seem to come as a surprise to the man who heard it.

"I'm sorry to hear that," he said smoothly. "She was a
nice girl."

Bruno spoke up again. "You gave her name to Dana
Sloan in connection with the missing persons case she's
working on. You said that Romero and Jake Carlson were
having an affair."

"That's correct. This photograph shows them together."

Waters was shorter than Bruno but twice as bulky. He
adjusted himself in the uncomfortable folding chair he
had taken and gazed intently at Senese. "You and I go
way back, Marko, so don't lie to me. One of my investigators showed your photo to people at Romero's apartment

building and they all said you were a frequent visitor there. No one recognized Carlson's mug."

"You just said she was found in the Riverview Motel. Obviously, she was here to visit Jake."

"The coroner fixes the time of death as sometime Saturday. Where were you on Saturday?" Waters asked.

"In Chicago with my wife, all day and all night."

"We'd like to speak to your wife," Waters said.

"You know perfectly well that Giada lives and works in Las Vegas. She returned there last night after our dinner at Dolce Vita where we saw Detective Bruno and his charming girlfriend."

Bruno was sitting in the visitor's chair that had arms on it, so he was able to grab hold of them and keep himself from getting up to wipe the leer from Senese's face.

"I'll need her number in Las Vegas," Waters said coolly.

"You can reach Giada at the Majestic Casino Hotel. She's there most weekdays."

Waters made a note on his pad. "Okay, Marko. I guess that's it for now, but we'll probably have more questions for you later."

"Always happy to help," Marko told him, then turned to Bruno. "Give my regards to Dana. You're a very lucky man."

Bruno stood up and leaned over the desk to speak to Marko. "If you have any more information for me, deliver it yourself. Miss Sloan is not a messenger. Understand?"

Marko Senese was like a snake, cunning and dangerous, but he was smart enough not to challenge Bruno. "I understand perfectly," he replied with a smirk.

CASEY WAS WAITING for Marianne and Dana in Donovan's Bar & Grill. They had chosen Donovan's because it didn't do a huge lunch business. It was more of a happy hour/ dinner place.

The three girls ordered the special of the day, a turkey club sandwich with a side salad. With their orders on the way to the kitchen, Dana asked Casey about one of the cases she had taken that morning. It involved two complaints that had come in about an organization that was selling coupon books for discounts at various business establishments in town. Two people who had purchased the books tried to use the coupons and the businesses had refused to honor them.

"I interviewed both the clients," Casey said. "The woman selling the books said the money went to her son's school for athletic equipment. While only two people complained so far, I think we will get a lot more in the next few weeks. I visited the school in question and they denied any knowledge of such a fund raiser."

"So, someone is printing up phony coupons and selling them door to door?" Marianne asked.

"It looks that way. I've got one of the books and I'll spend the afternoon contacting the businesses on the coupons before I write up my report and my story for the evening edition."

"Did you get a description of the woman who was selling the books?"

"Yes, but I'll bet she's long gone by now, probably working another neighborhood."

"Can I see the coupon book?" Marianne asked.

"They are pretty authentic looking," Casey said as she pulled one out of her purse and handed it to Marianne.

Marianne started looking through the coupons. "These look pretty good. It's amazing how people will put so much work into a scam like this." Marianne stopped at one of the coupons and turned it around to show to Dana and Casey. "Hey, isn't this Bob's friend, the garage guy who helped with that case earlier this year?"

Casey glanced at the coupon. "Yeah. That's him."

"Didn't he ask you out?"

"Not really. Bob told me he wanted to, but I'm not ready to date anyone right now. I can't inflict my screwed up life on a nice guy like that."

"Your life is not screwed up, Casey. You fell in love with the wrong guy and it ended badly. It wasn't your fault."

Casey laughed cynically. "It was my fault. Our relationship was based on lies and deceptions. I pretended to be something I'm not or he would never have been interested in me."

"Most relationships are initially based on deceptions. It's only after you get to know each other that you let your guard down and show your true self to each other," Dana told her.

"Look, I know you two are trying to help, but this is something I have to work through on my own. Let's change the subject. What's going on with that missing person's case you're working on?"

Dana and Marianne exchanged a look and a nod. They had both tried to talk Casey out of the depressed state she had been in since her marriage ended in tragedy. It only seemed to make her feel worse.

"I think we tracked her to Los Angeles," Dana said. "Marianne found a person registered at the La Maison Hotel in West Hollywood under the name we believe she's using."

"Is someone there checking it out?"

"Bruno wasn't available so I called Jack and he promised to call LA and get someone there to go to the hotel and question the staff. I'm not sure if he did it or not."

The waitress delivered their lunch orders and as they ate, they changed the subject again.

"Dana and I are going to check out the sale at Logan's after lunch. Want to come along?"

"No. I'd better go back to the office and get the phone

calls done on this coupon book scam. I don't need any new clothes anyway."

"I always need new clothes," Marianne declared.

After lunch Casey went to the mall lot where her car was parked and found that it wouldn't start. Exasperated, she walked to the office. Casey and Bob didn't have offices or desks. They each had laptop computers that they used to write up reports and cell phones paid for by Globe Investigations. When they had office work to do, they used the conference table and telephone in Dana's office.

Casey settled herself at the conference table and used the phone there to call Bob's friend at the garage he owned.

The phone rang several times before it was picked up. "Clark's Auto Repair, Damien."

"Hi Damien," Casey said. "This is Casey Jordan. I don't know if you remember me, but…"

"Hey Casey, you're the gal that works with my buddy, Bob Farrell."

"Right."

"What can I do for you?"

"My car is stalled at the Crescent Hills Shopping Mall. I think I need a tow."

"No problem. Give me the info."

Casey gave him the license number, make, model and color of her car and explained where it was parked in the mall lot. "How soon can you get to it?" she asked.

"My driver and my receptionist are both out to lunch, but they'll be back within the hour. I'll send him right over to get your car. What number can I reach you at?"

Casey gave him her cell phone number. "I'm at the office, but I may not be here long. Oh, do you have another minute to answer a question for me?"

"Sure."

"I'm investigating a scam involving a coupon book with

bogus coupons in it. Your garage is in it, offering a big discount on a tune up."

"Yeah, I know about it," Damien told her. "I've had a few people come in to redeem it. I didn't want to chase away potential customers so I honored it."

"That was nice of you."

"I'm a nice guy. Hasn't Bob listed all my good qualities for you?"

Casey couldn't help but laugh. "Actually, he has, more than once."

"But you still don't want to go out with me?"

"I'm just not in a good place right now," Casey replied softly.

"Sure. I understand. I didn't mean to pressure you."

"Thanks. Do you have any idea who might have made up these phony coupons?"

"Not a clue," Damien answered. "Sorry."

"It's okay. I didn't expect you to know." Casey could hear a phone ringing. "I'd better let you go so you can get your other line. Call me when you know something about my car?"

"Will do. Bye, Casey."

Casey clicked off and turned the coupon book to the first page and dialed the phone number on it. She was still at the conference table making calls when Dana and Marianne returned each carrying a bag with Logan's printed across it.

"What did you guys buy?" Casey asked.

Marianne had purchased a white cotton dress with a scooped neck and full skirt. It had come with a cloth belt that had variegated shades of blue and green. "I won't be able to wear it until next summer, but it was half-off."

"I like it," Casey told her.

Dana pulled a bolero-style sweater from her bag. It was dark green with three-quarter length sleeves and no buttons. "I bought it to go with that green dress I have. I think it will give me a few extra months of wear with this over it."

"The dress is a lighter shade of green so I think it will look great," Marianne added.

"Our resident fashion expert," Dana said.

Marianne folded her dress and put it back in the bag and then hurried out to her desk to check for phone messages and e-mails.

Casey went back to her phone calls. Dana went to her desk and began to review the cases that had yet to be assigned, trying to organize them in order of importance. Marianne came back in and handed Dana the phone messages she had gotten from the answering service and walked over to the table and handed Casey a copy of an e-mail she had printed out.

"For me?" Casey asked.

"It's another complaint about the coupon books."

One of Dana's messages was from Bruno asking her to call his cell phone. She did.

"Hi, sweets," Bruno said sounding very far away. "I'm out in the woods so reception isn't too good. If I lose you, I'll call you right back."

"Are you searching for Carlson's body?"

"Yeah, we got the search team with the dogs. So far, nada."

"What happened with Senese?" Dana asked.

"He has an alibi for the entire weekend, his wife. Waters is checking it anyway. We're sure he already knew that Romero was dead. He still claims she was Jake's girl and probably gave you her name to get Jake in more trouble by providing another motive for him to have murdered his wife. That photo in her apartment probably gave him the idea. The staff at her building said Senese was a frequent visitor."

"I guess that makes sense, but why would he do that?"

"To keep Jake in jail while he hunts down Beth and his money."

"I have a news flash for you," Dana said. "Marianne tracked Elizabeth Stratton to a hotel in West Hollywood. She spent two nights there and checked out this morning. I couldn't get you so I called Jack and he promised to fax her photo to the West Hollywood police and request that someone go over to the hotel and question the staff about Elizabeth Stratton. Do you know if he did it?"

"I haven't talked to Jack. Waters went back to Chicago and I came out to the woods on this waste of taxpayers' money." Static on the line warned them that the call would soon be lost.

"Call me when you get back to civilization," Dana said.

"I will," Bruno replied just before the connection died.

Dana shrugged and hung up. Casey had left the conference table and was sitting in one of the leather chairs holding the e-mail she had gotten from Marianne.

"This e-mail is from another person who purchased the phony coupon books. Says she thinks she knows who is behind the scam. I just talked to her on the phone and she said two of her neighbors also got taken. I'd like to go out and speak to them in person, but my car isn't running."

"Where is it?"

"I had to leave it in the mall parking lot. I called Bob's friend, Damien, and he's going to tow it to his garage and check it out for me. In the meantime, I have no wheels."

"You can use my car," Dana said. "I'm going to stay in the office and try to catch up on some paperwork. Marianne finished all her reports."

"Sometimes she makes the rest of us look bad," Casey said.

Dana retrieved her car keys from her purse and handed them to Casey.

ACROSS THE STREET in the detective division, Jack O'Brien was on the phone talking to an officer from West Hollywood. Jack was listening and taking notes in his own form of shorthand.

"Okay. I got it," Jack said. "Thanks for your help."

Jack hung up the phone and reviewed his notes. It appeared to be a dead end in the search for Beth Carlson. The woman at the hotel had short reddish brown hair and was definitely not pregnant. The maid had found a copy of *Daily Variety* in the woman's room after she checked out but that didn't prove anything. Jack wasn't surprised. He believed that Jake Carlson had murdered his wife. Any minute now, Bruno would call in and say they discovered the girl's body in the woods.

In the meantime, Jack decided to walk over to Globe Investigations and give Bruno's girlfriend the report he had taken from West Hollywood in person. It was a good excuse to get out of the office for a while and get a look at Dana's hot redheaded secretary.

As Jack crossed the street, he saw Casey Jordan come out of the newspaper building and walk towards the parking lot. Casey was tall and slim with an athletic body. She wasn't what you'd call gorgeous but she was attractive and he liked the way she moved her hips so he decided to walk behind her and enjoy the view.

Unaware that Jack was following her, Casey strode into the parking lot and found Dana's car in its assigned space near the entrance. She was about to click the door open when she noticed the button was up and the car was unlocked. That was a little strange as everyone who worked at the paper locked their cars and set alarms. You needed a key card to get in and out of the lot, but most people just left those in their cars, giving a thief easy access to them.

Casey shrugged and pulled the door open. Maybe Dana had been in a hurry this morning when she parked. Casey slid into the car and had to move the seat back to accommodate her legs which were a lot longer than Dana's.

Jack stood a few feet away watching Casey get into the car and adjust her skirt, getting a good look at one of her shapely legs. Most people shut the car door before making adjustments and turning the key in the ignition, but Casey didn't do that so Jack kept standing there staring at her legs.

Finally, Casey shut the car door, and turned the key. The front of the car exploded. The air bag deployed pinning Casey between it and the seat as the front of the car was engulfed in flames.

SIXTEEN

JACK HAD BEEN about to turn away when he heard the explosion and saw the Mustang shudder with such force it moved back a few feet. The flames began at the front of the car and were licking at the shattered windshield. Jack ran towards the car.

Inside, Casey was stunned and dazed. She screamed and inhaled the smoke from the fire that caused her to cough and sputter. She struggled to remain conscious and release the seat belt and reach for the door handle. She knew if she didn't get out of the car in the next few seconds she would die, but she was losing consciousness.

Prayers formed silently on her lips and tears slid down her face. It was hopeless; she was trapped.

Then she heard someone yelling her name, and a second later the car door was wrenched open. Strong arms reached into the car as the deflated airbag allowed Jack to release the seat belt, grab Casey's shoulders and pull her from the car. She stumbled and fell against her rescuer but he held on keeping her upright and half-carrying, half-dragging her away from the flaming auto.

Looking back, Jack saw the flames dance over the roof of the car. He pushed Casey to the ground and threw himself on top of her as the fire reached the gas tank and the back end of it blew up sending metal and debris sailing through the air. Flying metal crashed through car windows setting off alarms.

Jack got to his feet. Casey had passed out. He scooped

her up into his arms and ran from the blazing inferno of Dana's car that had also ignited the car parked next to hers.

Within seconds the street in front of the newspaper was a tangled web of cars and people. Jack managed to get Casey and himself to safety. He gazed down at her face blackened by smoke and tears and shouted her name.

"Casey, Casey, can you hear me?"

Casey's eyes fluttered open. She nodded and then passed out again. The welcome sound of sirens could be heard in the distance.

Sam McGowan and a few others emerged from the newspaper building. Sam saw Jack holding Casey limp in his arms and sprinted towards them. "What happened?" he shouted. "Is she okay?"

"I don't know," Jack answered. "I saw her getting into Dana's car and the next thing I knew it was in flames. Casey was knocked silly and couldn't get out of the car."

Sam took Casey's hand and began rubbing it and calling her name. Once again, her eyes fluttered open and then closed again.

The fire engines arrived first and crashed through the parking lot gate to get to the fire. Then, the ambulance and the paramedics arrived. Some of the uniformed cops who had run from the station were out on the street, directing cars and pedestrians away from the chaos and clearing a path for the paramedics and the cart they pushed onto the sidewalk.

One of the paramedics gave Casey a cursory exam and then took her from Jack's arms and placed her on the cart. "We need to get her to the hospital," he said. Then looking at Jack added. "You look like hell, you'd better come along too."

"Go on, Jack," Sam ordered. "You need to get checked out."

Jack shook his head. "I'm fine, but I'll go along to be

with Casey." He let the paramedic lead him away following behind the cart where Casey lay still and silent.

Dana and Marianne finally came out of the building. They had heard the explosion and the commotion but the elevators were jammed with panicked people and they had to take the stairs and were both out of breath.

The girls ran right into Sam who quickly explained what happened. "We'll go to the hospital together," he told Dana. "But we'll have to take a cab, my car was parked next to yours and it's destroyed too."

One of the uniformed cops approached them. "Miss Sloan, I understand it was your car that blew up. I'll need to file a report."

"Not now," Dana said firmly. She turned to Marianne. "Go back to the office. Someone has to field the phone calls. Bruno's cell phone number is on my rolodex, please call him and tell him what happened."

Dana didn't have her purse or her cell phone, but she didn't have time to go and get them. Sam shouted for all the Globe employees to get back in the building. Then, he grabbed Dana's arm and the two of them ran down the street to the cab stand on the next corner.

As Dana and Sam got into a cab, Marianne turned and ran back into the building to manage the phone lines in the office and call Greg, Bruno, and Bob Farrell in that order.

DANA WAS SO worried about Casey she wasn't thinking about anything else. She was pacing the floor of the waiting room next to the emergency department. Sam had gone to the admittance counter to inquire about Casey and give them her insurance information.

Dana heard someone approaching and looked at the doorway as Jack O'Brien came through it. His reddish blond hair was sticking to his scalp, a result of the perspiration that had soaked his body from the fire, the exertion of pulling Casey from the car, and the adrenaline that was still pumping through him.

"The doc thinks Casey is okay," Jack said. "She doesn't have a concussion, but they're sending her to radiology for an MRI and stuff to make sure she doesn't have any internal injuries or broken bones."

Relief flooded over Dana and she collapsed in the nearest chair. "Thanks, Jack. Sam said you pulled her from the car. We're so lucky you were there."

"Yeah." His ruddy complexion was pale. "It scared the hell out of me. Who hates you, Dana?"

The question took Dana by surprise. "I don't know." It was the first time she had thought about the fact that it was her car that had been booby-trapped. It sent a chill racing through her slim body.

"You think it has something to do with the Carlson case?"

"I don't know," she said again. "I'm too upset to think right now."

"I think the Carlson dame is dead. Her old man killed her," Jack said in a callous tone. "I was coming across the street to give you the report I got from the West Hollywood guys you had me send to that fancy hotel. The woman there had dark, short hair and was definitely not pregnant."

"Okay, thanks." Dana didn't want to argue with him about Beth Carlson although she had already surmised the girl was not really pregnant and knew that any woman could easily dye and cut her hair to change her appearance. Jack O'Brien had just saved Casey's life so no matter how much he aggravated her in the future she would always be nice to him.

"I'm going to go back to the station," Jack told her. "I'll start writing up the report. You start thinking about who wants you dead."

Jack left and Sam came in. "They sent Casey for more

tests, but I talked to the doctor and he said there was no sign of head injury or internal bleeding. The tests are just precautionary."

"Jack told me that," Dana replied. "Thank God, he was there or Casey…" Dana couldn't finish the sentence. Tears formed in Dana's eyes and Sam walked over and sat down next to her.

Sam took a handkerchief from his pocket and handed it to his star reporter. "I've always thought Jack was a horse's ass, but he really came through for us this time. What was he doing in our parking lot anyway?"

"He just told me he came across the street to give me a report on something I asked him to check on." Dana dried her eyes and told Sam that Marianne had traced Elizabeth Stratton to the hotel in West Hollywood and Jack asked the police there to question the staff about the girl.

"Jack says the girl doesn't match Beth's description, but I still think it was her. The problem is she could be anywhere in the LA area now."

"Well they didn't find her in the woods where her husband said he buried her."

Dana looked at him. "How did you know that?"

Sam chuckled. "You know I've got spies everywhere, especially at the police station."

"I wonder if Marianne was able to reach Bruno. We got cut off when I talked to him earlier."

As if on cue, Bruno's broad frame suddenly filled the doorway. "I just saw Jack outside," he said. "He told me what happened."

Bruno came across the room. Dana stood up and Bruno put his arms around her. She leaned into him, grateful for his physical strength and support. "You okay?" Bruno asked.

Dana nodded. "Did Marianne call you?"

"Yes, but the connection was so bad, she just said Casey got hurt and you were here with her."

Sam stood up. "Okay, now that Bruno's here to take care of my reporters, I'm going back to the paper. Call me if you need me."

Bruno released Dana and they both sat down. She stared across the room at a painting of a lake with sailboats on it. "Did you find anything in the woods?" she asked Bruno after Sam left the waiting area.

"Not a thing. We were getting ready to give it up when Marianne called. I left and came directly here."

"Did Waters check on Senese's alibi?"

"I don't know."

"Marianne traced Elizabeth Stratton to a fancy hotel in West Hollywood, but she'd already checked out. I asked Jack to fax her photo there and ask someone to question the hotel staff."

Bruno grabbed her shoulders and turned her to face him. "I don't care about Beth Carlson or her crazy husband right now. It was your car that blew up. We need to talk about that."

"Casey was almost killed. I'll never say another bad word about Jack O'Brien. If he hadn't been there…" Dana's voice trailed off.

"He's sworn to serve and protect and that's what he did today."

"I'm so worried about Casey."

"I asked about her condition when I came in and they said she was okay."

"Physically, yes. But you know she's been depressed for months. I'm worried about what this is going to do to her mental state."

"Why was she in your car anyway?"

"Her car wouldn't start so she left it at the mall and called the garage to have it towed. Then, some witnesses in a case she's been investigating contacted the paper and she wanted to go out and talk to them. I told her to use my car and I almost got her killed."

"Stop saying that, Dana. It wasn't your fault. You have to face the big issue here."

"I know, Bruno. Jack told me earlier. Someone wants me dead."

"The only person you've been in contact with lately that would do this or hire someone to do it is Marko Senese."

"I know, but it doesn't make sense. Why would he want me dead? I'm trying to help him find Beth Carlson."

"Guys like Marko do a lot of things that don't make sense."

WHILE HE WAS waiting for his flight to be called, Marko Senese used his cell phone to call his father. Carlo's bodyguard answered the phone and brought it to the old man who was sitting in his back yard, communing with nature.

"Marko, where are you?"

"I'm at O'Hare. I'm flying to Vegas to meet with Joseph. There's been a bit of trouble and I need to talk to him before it gets blown out of proportion."

"Victoria Romero?"

"Right."

"It's already in the news here, but your name is not mentioned."

"Good."

"Did you have something to do with it?"

"No, papa. I didn't know anything about it until Monday morning when I got to the office. You know I was with Giada all weekend. The cops will question her today too to verify my alibi. That's why I need to go there and make sure it doesn't make waves with her family."

"Buy her something nice before you go to the house."

"Of course. How are you doing?"

"I'm good today."

"I'm glad. I'll call you tomorrow after I talk to my father-in-law."

Marko turned off his cell phone. He wouldn't turn it on again until he landed in Vegas. Harry was standing a few feet away near the lounge and Marko walked over to him.

"Let's get a drink," Marko suggested.

Harry felt naked without his gun, but there was no way he could get it through airport security. Mr. Verano would have one waiting for him in the limo at the Vegas airport. Marko sat down at the end of the bar out of earshot of the few people at the other end. Harry stood directly behind him.

Marko ordered a scotch and soda for himself and a ginger ale for Harry. On the television set behind the bar, a pretty Asian news reporter was announcing breaking news.

"A car bomb detonated in the parking lot of *The Globe* newspaper in downtown Crescent Hills this afternoon. Reporter, Casey Jordan, was in the car when it burst into flames, but was pulled from the car by Homicide Detective Jack O'Brien," the girl reported.

Marko glanced at the screen but was lost in his own thoughts and wasn't paying much attention until he heard the reporter say that the booby-trapped car belonged to the head of Globe Investigations, Dana Sloan.

Marko cursed and turned to Harry who was staring at the TV screen. "Did you hear that? Someone tried to kill Dana Sloan."

Harry nodded. "Yes, sir."

"You know anything about that?"

"No, sir, I don't."

"Damn it." Marko pulled out his cell phone again, turned it on and dialed a number.

Vinnie who was in charge of things when Marko was gone answered. "Yo!"

"Did you hear the news about Dana Sloan?"

"Yeah. It was on the radio. Relax, boss, she's okay. Some other broad started the car, but she's okay too. Some cop was there and got her out."

"I know that," Marko said. "What I want to know is who is responsible for it. Find out. I won't stand for someone coming into my territory and doing things without my okay."

The airline announced that Marko's flight was about to board. He turned off the phone again, drank down his cocktail and slipped off the stool.

Harry took a few more sips of his ginger ale and laid money on the bar to pay for their drinks before he followed Marko to the gate. In the past no one had dared commit a crime in Marko's territory without Marko's blessings. Anyone who got out of line was quickly and severely dealt with, but now Joseph Verano and his sons were about to take over Marko's territory and banish him to some flunky job in Las Vegas. The rules were changing for Marko and he wasn't going to like it one bit.

SEVENTEEN

WHEN DANA REALIZED that the incident with her car might make the national news, she borrowed Bruno's cell phone and called her parents. Luckily, they had been busy with the fall harvest and had not heard the report.

Linda and Warren Sloan lived in a small community of farms and country estates. They had raised their three sons and their only daughter there. When the kids first moved out, the house seemed too big and empty and the farmland too vast to work by themselves. So, they sold off some of the property, keeping the house and just enough land to keep themselves in fresh fruits and vegetables. Once Dana's three older brothers married and began having children, the old farmhouse was again filled with children and was almost too small to accommodate them all.

"I'm so glad you called, Dana. We would have panicked if we heard it on the news," Dana's mom told her.

"Call my brothers and let them know I'm all right," Dana said. "I'm at the hospital waiting to see if Casey will be released. Bruno's here with me."

"That's good. When are you two coming for another visit? It's been weeks since we've seen you."

"Soon, Mom. I promise."

While Dana was talking to her parents, Bruno was building a case in his mind against Marko Senese. He was convinced that Senese was involved in the attempt on Dana's life. He had questioned Senese earlier this afternoon and a few hours later Dana's car blew up. It was the type of thing Marko would do. Bruno had rattled Marko's cage, but he couldn't put a hit out on a cop. So, he tried to get even with Bruno by killing Dana and if Casey hadn't been the one to start the car, he might have succeeded. Although Marko claimed to have an alibi, Bruno also suspected that he was the one who had Victoria Romero executed. Of course, Marko's wife would say she was with him all weekend. Giada was Joseph Verano's daughter; she knew what her father and her husband expected of her.

All of this was going through Bruno's head, but when Dana came back and sat down next to him again, he didn't share these thoughts with her. He often told her that getting involved in police cases was dangerous, but being involved with him could also put her life in jeopardy. He knew he wouldn't have to tell her that because once she calmed down about Casey's mental and physical state, Dana would figure it out for herself.

"I think we should visit your folks this weekend," Bruno said as Dana handed his cell phone back to him.

"My mom just asked when we were coming down again."

"I think you should stay there with them for a few weeks."

"You know I can't do that." Dana replied, not bothering to reiterate the fact that she was working on a case. Bruno knew that Dana was not one to ever give up on any investigation she started. She always saw them through to the end.

"I'd better call my mom," Bruno said. "It may be on the Chicago news by now."

Marianne and Bob came into the waiting room. "Any news?" Marianne asked as she came over and sat on the other side of Dana. She handed Dana the purse and cell phone that Dana had left at the office in her rush to get to the hospital.

"No. They sent her for some precautionary tests, and we're still waiting to hear something."

"It's after five, that's when the emergency room starts to fill up with the day's casualties," Bob said.

Marianne gave Dana a report of the calls she had made that afternoon. "I talked to Casey's mom. She's visiting her sister in Denver. She wanted to come back here, but I told her that Casey was all right and I'd have her call her there. Also, Damien Clark called the office just before I left," Marianne said. "He was trying to call Casey's cell phone. Of course it burned up in the car so it didn't answer. He finally tried the office number. I told him what happened and he was very upset. He said Casey's car just needed a new battery and he was fixing it free of charge."

"He's really a nice guy," Bob said. "I wish Casey would go out with him."

"Don't you dare say anything like that to her," Marianne warned. "I mentioned it at lunch and she got upset."

"Okay, okay," Bob agreed. "But I think getting into a new relationship will help heal the scars she has from the last one."

Before anyone could argue with Bob's statement, a nurse entered the room. "I'm looking for Dana Sloan?" she said.

Dana jumped to her feet. "I'm Dana."

"Miss Jordan is back from radiology and would like to speak to you. Follow me, please."

Dana put her purse over her shoulder and hurried after the nurse who had already started off towards the area where Casey was awaiting the results of her tests. The emergency room now buzzed with activity. Bob was right, after five o'clock it got busier.

The nurse delivered Dana to Casey and left them alone.

Dana was relieved to see Casey sitting up in the hospital bed studying her face in a mirror.

"Hi," Dana said softly. "How are you doing?"

Casey lowered the mirror and sighed. "Same old face," she said. "I was hoping it had been shocked into looking better."

"You look beautiful," Dana said as she rushed forward to hug her friend. "I am so sorry."

"I knew you'd be feeling guilty. That's why I asked the nurse to send you in here. Besides, I have something important to tell you, so listen up."

"Okay."

"When the device attached to your car went off, I got a huge jolt. I was dazed and disoriented and smoke was filling the car. I knew it was just a matter of seconds before the fire would reach the gas tank and explode, but I couldn't function. I was certain I was going to die in that car. And after all these months of being depressed and thinking I didn't care about living any more, it made me realize what an ass I've been. It made me realize how much time I've wasted feeling sorry for myself. I have fabulous friends who have stuck by me, waiting for me to stop being a mope and get on with my life."

Tears formed in Dana's eyes again. "I never called you a mope."

Casey laughed. "Bob did. Anyway, my mother always says that everything happens for a reason. So, I know that using your car and getting trapped inside of it happened to get me out of the funk I've been in so I could get on with whatever I'm supposed to do with the rest of my life. My car not starting this afternoon was all part of it too. It gave me a reason to call Damien Clark and believe it or not, he's still interested in me."

"Of course he is. He called the office and said he fixed your car for free. You just needed a new battery."

"He really is a nice guy," Casey admitted. "And when I

asked him about those bogus coupons he said a few people had brought them to the garage and he honored them."

"Maybe I'll dump Bruno and go out with him myself," Dana said.

"No way. I saw him first." Casey grinned and then turned serious. "I do have one big question to ask you."

"What's that?"

"A man pulled me out of the car and shielded me with his own body when the gas tank exploded. I was only semiconscious but I think it might have been Jack O'Brien."

"It was Jack O'Brien. I had asked him to check out a lead we got on Beth Carlson and he was coming to the office to give me a report on it. He was in the parking lot and saw you get into the car just before it caught fire."

"Wow! I really dislike Jack. Now I'm going to have to be nice to him."

"We all are," Dana said. "He saved your life. He's a hero."

"Is he here?"

"No. He went back to the station to file a report. But Bruno, Marianne and Bob are here. Sam was here too, but when they said you were okay, he went back to the paper. We've all been worried sick."

"Well," Casey said firmly. "I'm fine. The radiologist told me he saw no sign of broken bones or other injuries."

"That's good news."

"For me, yes. But what about you? That bomb was attached to your car. You're the one someone is trying to kill. One of the things that saved me is that I'm so much taller than you are and I had to move the seat way back."

WHEN MARKO AND Harry arrived in Las Vegas, a limo was waiting for them. Harry got into the front passenger seat while the driver opened the back door for Marko. Giada was sitting in the back seat.

"Giada," Marko said sliding into the car next to her. "What are you doing here?"

"Daddy said you were coming. I came to meet you. Aren't you happy to see me?" Her tone was cold.

Marko kissed her cheek. "Of course, I am. I just thought you would still be at work."

"How was your flight?"

"Fine."

"Good."

"You seem upset. What's wrong?"

"My father and brothers are angry at you and that makes me worry. If you weren't my husband, they would deal with you very harshly."

Marko stiffened. "I don't understand. What have I done to anger them?"

"Several things, my love." She turned her head away from him so that he was looking at the back of her freshly coiffed hair. Giada had a beautician who came in every morning and braided her long black hair and then worked it into an elegant twist down the back of her head. The woman also did her makeup, so Giada always looked as perfect as a porcelain doll. Her clothes were expensive and elegant and with her willowy figure she could have been a fashion model had she been five inches taller.

"Don't play games with me, Giada," Marko said softly. "Tell me exactly what is going on."

She turned and faced him again. "They feel you are losing control of your territory. Money has been taken and one of your women has been murdered."

Marko looked at her. "What woman is that?"

"Don't you play games with me, Marko. I know about your affair with Romero."

Now Marko turned his head away from her. She was right, he had lost control of his territory. Someone had told Giada about Vicki and someone had told Joseph about the money Beth had run off with. Both Turk and Harry were originally Joseph's boys. It could have been either of them.

"Do you want me dead, Giada?" he asked, moving close to her and stroking her face with his fingertips.

She grabbed his hand and brought it to her lips, shaking her head in a negative reply.

"Then tell me who is filling your head with lies."

"It was Jake Carlson. He called me at the casino one night. I think he was drunk, but he told me that you were after his wife and that you had been cheating on me with Vicki Romero. He said Vicki lived in Chicago, but came to Crescent Hills every few weeks to meet you at the Riverview Motel."

"Why didn't you come to me?"

"Because I didn't believe him, but today daddy told me that Vicki was murdered in the Riverview Motel in Crescent Hills and that you had lost a large amount of money."

"May I remind you, Giada, the lost money does not yet belong to Joseph. It is my father's money that is lost."

"Daddy doesn't care. He says it shows that you have lost control of your territory."

"Yes, that is exactly what Joseph would think. That's why I'm here, to talk to him and let him know that I am doing what is necessary to correct the problems and make sure they do not happen again. Vicki was having an affair with Jake Carlson. His wife found out. That's why she ran away with the money Jake collected for me. I think Jake killed Romero and he would be dead too, but he is in jail, out of my reach for the moment."

"Why is he in jail?"

"He confessed to murdering his wife."

"Then she is dead?"

"No one knows for sure. I think Jake just said it to get himself arrested and away from Turk who was watching him for me."

"Was he telling the truth about you and his wife? Were you after her?" she asked.

"Of course not. Jake abused her. I simply stepped in and warned him to stop hurting her. You are the only woman I love, Giada, the only woman I will ever love."

Giada smiled and slipped her arms around his neck and kissed him. "I'm so sorry, *cara.* Forgive me for doubting you."

Marko held his wife in his arms as he contemplated the latest incident in Crescent Hills. "Do you remember the woman we met at the restaurant in Chicago on Tuesday night?"

"The one you sent flowers to?" she asked pulling away from him.

"She is an investigator and the girlfriend of the big cop who was with her. She passed information to him for me. She is also helping me find Beth Carlson and the missing money. I told you that is why I sent flowers to her."

"Yes, I remember. What about her?"

"This afternoon there was an attempt on her life. No doubt Joseph has heard about that too. It will be another reason for him to be angry with me."

"Don't worry, darling," Giada whispered pushing herself against him again. "I will go with you to talk to my family. Together we will convince them that the problems in Crescent Hills are being dealt with properly."

CASEY USED DANA'S cell phone to call her mom in Denver. By the time she got off the telephone, the doctor came in and said she could go home.

Dana went back to the waiting room and reported on Casey. "Her clothes are a mess, but she says she's starving and wants to go out and eat."

"That's a great idea. I'm starving too," Bob said.

"You can only come with us if you promise to stay on your diet," Marianne told him.

"Don't you have to meet Greg or something?" Bob asked pointedly.

"No. He's working tonight."

Suddenly, Dana realized that Bruno was gone. "Where's Bruno?"

"He got a call from O'Brien and had to leave," Bob told her. "But he made me promise to watch you and keep you safe. He said he'd hook up with us again at the Aztec Club, so I guess that's where we should go for dinner."

"That's fine with me," Dana replied. "But it's not a good place for someone on a diet."

"My wife has been talking to you too, hasn't she?"

"I'm afraid so," Dana said.

Bob pulled out his cell phone and dialed his home number. "Hi Jason. Let me talk to your mother." Bob waited while his son went to get Cynthia. "Hi, Honey. Casey is being released, but she still needs some moral support. We are taking her to dinner at the Aztec Club. Do you want to join us?" He paused while his wife answered. "Oh, that's too bad. Listen, the stress of almost losing Casey made me lose ten pounds this afternoon, so I'm going to have pizza for dinner." Bob picked up a magazine and crumpled the cover into the phone. "What? I can't hear you, honey. Bad connection. I'll call you later." Bob hung up the phone and then turned it off so Cynthia couldn't call him back.

Marianne and Dana looked at each other and shook their heads.

"Let's go and collect Casey," Dana said. "She has something she wants to share with both of you."

EIGHTEEN

DANA AND HER staff had already finished an extra large pizza by the time Bruno showed up at the Aztec Club. Bruno dragged a chair over to the table and joined them.

The waitress came over and Bruno ordered a soft drink and a meatball sandwich with fries, then he turned to Casey.

"You look okay. How are you feeling?" he asked.

"A little sore, but no permanent damage," she answered. "But now that I've eaten, I'm exhausted."

"She's going to come home with me," Marianne said. "I don't think she should be alone tonight." She stood up and some of the guys sitting at the bar twisted around to get a better look at her.

"We need to stop at my place so I can get some clothes," Casey said. "In the morning, you can drive me over to the garage to get my car."

"No problem," Marianne agreed.

Casey rose to her feet. "Is Jack still at the station?" she asked Bruno.

"No, he went home, but he's going to take any calls that might come in tonight so I can stay with Dana."

"I guess I'll track him down tomorrow to thank him for what he did today," Casey said.

Bob pushed himself away from the table. "I'd better get home."

"Do you think Cynthia will let you in?" Dana asked.

"Of course she'll let me in. She'll want to be face-to-face when she gives me lecture number six."

"I assume that's the one that has to do with staying on your diet," Dana said.

"No, that's lecture number one, six is the one about pretending I can't hear her when she's yelling at me."

"Cynthia is a saint for putting up with you all these years," Marianne said.

"Cynthia is a wonderful person," Bob agreed. "And soon thanks to me, you'll be related to her by marriage."

"Greg and I are not talking about marriage."

Bob just grinned, waved and hurried out of the Aztec Club with Casey and Marianne right behind him.

"Alone at last," Bruno said putting his arm around Dana and kissing her cheek. "Casey seems good. Are you feeling less guilty?"

Dana nodded and told Bruno what Casey had said about nearly losing her life shocking her out of the depression she had been in. "I suppose Jack is feeling pretty proud of himself," she added.

"Jack is more angry than anything. Now that he's had time to think about it, he's convinced that Marko Senese or someone in his organization is responsible for booby-trapping your car. This type of attack is something Carlo Senese did on a regular basis in Chicago. Jack says, 'like father, like son'."

Dana bit her lip. "I don't know, Bruno. Why would Senese send me flowers one day and try to kill me the next?"

Bruno sighed and shared the thoughts he had been reluctant to express at the hospital. "When I questioned him today he brought up your name and I warned him to stay away from you. Senese doesn't like to take orders especially from a cop. I'm afraid he ordered a hit on you just to show me how powerful he is."

"Now who's feeling guilty?"

"Me with a capital G." The waitress delivered Bruno's sandwich and drink and he released his hold on Dana so he could eat.

"I don't think it was Senese," Dana told him. "He's in love with Beth Carlson and he knows that his best chance of finding her is me."

Bruno swallowed and looked at her quizzically. "Where did you get the idea he was in love with the Carlson woman?"

"From the look in Marko's eyes when he talked about Beth. And because he told me if Beth had run off with the mob's money, it was okay with him. She could keep it."

"And you believed him?"

"Yes, I did. When he first came in my office, he was more interested in trying to find out if you were going to keep Jake in jail, out of his reach. He thought Jake had killed his wife and stolen the money. I was sure if he had been able to get his hands on Jake, he would have tortured him to death. Then, I told him I thought Beth was alive and his whole demeanor changed. He was relieved and happy. And then, he told me that Jake was having an affair with Victoria Romero. I've decided that was to keep Jake in jail and give himself a clear field with Beth."

"You're making a lot of assumptions about a guy who has a reputation for being as cunning as the snake that convinced Eve to bite that apple. Marko is not the kind of guy to ever let his guard down, Dana. He was conning you."

"Okay. He was conning me."

Bruno finished his sandwich and started on the fries. "Yes, he was."

"You're right."

"You know I hate it when you agree with me just to shut me up," Bruno told her.

"I'm sorry. I've had a rather traumatic day and I don't

want to argue. So, is Jack going to question Senese about the car bomb?"

"He wanted to. He sent two uniforms over to the pool hall to bring Senese in, but Marko left town just before they got there. He talked to our undercover guy later and he told Jack that Marko's in trouble with his father-in-law and went to Las Vegas to smooth things over with him."

"Why is Senese in trouble?"

"Mob bosses expect their underlings to manage the territories assigned to them with an iron hand. Money has gone missing, a girl associated with the organization has been murdered and Joseph Verano doesn't like surprises. That's another thing, the attempt on your life could have been Marko's way of showing his father-in-law that he's still in control of this area."

"By killing me?"

"Killing you would be his way of getting back at the cop who had the nerve to question him about Victoria Romero, insinuate that he was the one having an affair with her, and then warn him to stay away from you."

"Why wouldn't he just put the bomb in your car?"

"Because Carlo Senese and Joseph Verano have a rule against killing cops."

"So they kill me, hoping it will disable you. I don't buy it."

"You don't think losing you would destroy me?" Bruno asked putting his arm around her again.

"Temporarily, but then you'd find the people responsible and tear them apart. Wouldn't you?"

"Yes, I would."

"You and Senese have had run-ins before and I think he's smart enough to know that about you. That's why I don't think he would order a hit on me. And he definitely was not conning me. He's in love with Beth Carlson and he won't rest until he finds her."

Bruno lifted her chin and looked into the hazel eyes that looked blue in the dim light of the club. "I know you never give up on a case but I hope you are as frightened as I am about this attempt on your life. You're going to have to be on guard every minute of every day until we find out who is after you."

"I know. Sam is hiring extra security for the building and the parking lot. Bob said he'd watch over me when you're not around."

"That's good. Bob looks like a Cupie Doll, but he's trained in martial arts."

BETH COULDN'T BELIEVE that she was packing a bag to leave her new apartment in the Hollywood hills within twenty-four hours of moving in. Having so much cash at her disposal had made renting the furnished apartment easy. She had paid the security deposit and six months rent in advance and the manager hadn't seemed the least bit surprised or impressed by receiving so much cash.

Beth Carlson was establishing herself as Elizabeth Stratton, resident of Hollywood, California and an actress who had just landed a small role on the soap opera, *Forever Love*.

Knowing that she was going to appear on television screens across the country was a little frightening, but Beth convinced herself that people like Jake and Marko Senese wouldn't be caught dead watching a soap opera and with her new look it was doubtful anyone else who knew her would recognize her either.

Besides, Beth was only to appear in one scene filling in for an actress who had been injured in an auto accident.

Beth closed the small bag she had packed and looked at the clock. The show had booked her on a ten p.m. flight to Las Vegas where the episode she was appearing in was to be taped. A studio car was scheduled to pick her up and take her to the airport in an hour. The rest of the cast and crew of *Forever Love* were already in Las Vegas at the MGM Grand Hotel where they had been taping for the last few weeks.

Perhaps if Beth had known what had transpired that evening when Marko and Giada met with Joseph Verano, she would have unpacked and remained hidden in her new apartment. Instead she sat down to wait for the studio car to arrive and thought back on the series of events that had resulted in her first really professional acting role.

This morning, Beth had seen an ad in Daily Variety for an open audition being conducted at Coldwater Studio where the show, *Forever Love,* was produced. They were looking for an actress who could also sing. Beth had never auditioned for anything other than stage productions and she thought this audition would be good practice for her. Since she hadn't yet tried to get an agent who would send her on auditions, she knew that open calls were the only way she could be seen by any industry people.

Beth arrived at the studio to find a long line of girls waiting to audition. She registered and was assigned a time slot in the middle of the afternoon. She was also asked if she had a song prepared to sing and if she had brought the music for it along with her.

"Yes, of course," Beth said thinking quickly. "I have several I can sing. What type of song are they looking for?"

"A torch song," the woman at the registration desk replied. "But let me give you a word of advice. Make it something different; something they haven't heard before."

"Thanks," Beth said trying not show how flustered she was. She had not thought to bring any music with her at all.

"Sign here for permission to tape you," the woman said shoving a form at Beth.

"They're going to tape me?"

"They tape everyone who auditions. This is a television

show and they choose the actress based on how well she comes across on the screen."

Beth nodded and signed the form. She looked at her watch. She had more than two hours before her scheduled audition time and hurried off in search of a music store. Beth saw a public phone booth and slipped inside to look at the phone directory hanging by a chain attached to the small shelf under the telephone. The directory was battered and torn, but it had the yellow pages for that area. Beth looked up sheet music and found a listing for the Norman Maine store. As soon as she saw the name, Beth remembered that Norman Maine was a play publisher. Better yet, Beth knew that they had published the small musical she had starred in at Center Stage Playhouse. Beth called the store and asked if they had the play script and music for it in stock.

"You're in luck, lady," the clerk said when he came back on the line. "Some theater in West Hollywood ordered it a few months ago and then never came here to pick it up. I think they went belly-up. How many copies you want?"

"Just one with the sheet music," Beth said not believing her good fortune. "I'll be right over to get it." Beth told the clerk where she was and he gave her directions to the store. More good fortune as the store was just a few blocks away.

When it was Beth's turn to audition she handed the piano player a copy of the music for *When Nothing Else Was Right*.

"Never heard of this one," the middle-aged female accompanist told her. "You'd better introduce it to the producers along with yourself before you sing."

Beth stepped up to the microphone and looked at the camera that was already video-taping her. "Hi, my name is Elizabeth Stratton. Everyone calls me, Beth. The song I'm going to sing is one you may not have heard before.

The song is *When Nothing Else Was Right*. It's from a musical I performed in once called *The Last Decent Crooks*."

Beth couldn't see the producers behind the camera because of the light they had focused on her, but the music began and she sang the song with as much heart and feeling as she could put into it. When it ended, she turned to leave, but a voice called out to her.

"Thanks, Miss Stratton. Please wait in the next room."

A young guy escorted her into a small room adjacent to the audition area. Three other girls were already there waiting.

"Congratulations," one of the girls, a petite blond said as Beth sat down. "You're one of the chosen few."

The auditions went on for another two hours, but only one other girl was sent to wait in the room. They all sat quietly, exchanging nervous glances and a few whispered words until the door finally opened and the young guy who had escorted Beth into the room stuck his head in.

"Elizabeth Stratton, come with me, please."

Beth jumped up so quickly she dumped her bag on the floor and had to bend down and retrieve it and some of its contents. They're probably just going to send me home, she thought as she followed the young man down a corridor to another room. This one had a conference table where a man and two women were seated. The man rose as Beth entered the room and held out a chair for her.

"Can you be ready to leave for Las Vegas tonight?" one of the women asked, flipping her long black hair behind her shoulder. "We'll be taping the segment tomorrow morning."

"You mean I got the job?" Beth said incredulously.

All three producers nodded. "It was the song that sealed it," the man said. "In fact we liked it so much we're going to use it instead of the one we originally planned on. Do you belong to AFTRA?"

"No, sir," Beth replied. She did belong to Actors Equity, but not under the name of Elizabeth Stratton.

"Then you've got some additional forms to fill out. You know what AFTRA is, don't you?"

"The union for television actors," Beth replied.

"Ordinarily we don't audition anyone who is not a member of the union, but this is an emergency situation. Stay put and my secretary will help you fill out the necessary papers and make your plane reservations. We're taping at the MGM Grand Hotel and that's where you'll be staying. This is very short term, so don't pack a lot. Your costume for the segment will be provided."

Without another word, the three producers rose and left the room, leaving Beth feeling like she'd just stepped off a cliff and was floating in thin air.

NINETEEN

BRUNO SPENT THE night on Dana's sofa so he'd be between the front and back doors of her apartment. Dana had a restless night, dreaming of exploding cars and screaming people.

Dana awoke to find Bruno standing next to her bed with a breakfast tray. "You're kidding?" she said as she sat up and ran a hand through her tousled curls. "You've never brought me breakfast in bed before."

"I'm pampering you this morning. You had a rough night."

"Funny how your fears manifest themselves in your dreams, or should I say nightmares."

"I hope that means you're properly scared."

"Yes, Bruno," she replied in an agitated tone. "I am properly scared." She swung her feet over the side of the bed and padded off to the master bathroom. "Bring that tray into the kitchen. I don't like breakfast in bed," she called out as she closed the bathroom door.

They had breakfast at the counter in Dana's cheery kitchen. After Dana had showered and dressed in a conservative blue pants suit, they drove over to Bruno's apartment where he showered and dressed in fresh clothes that had not been slept in the night before.

It was almost ten when Bruno parked in the police lot and walked Dana across the street to the newspaper building where Dana went directly to Sam's office.

"I told Richard that Marianne traced Elizabeth Stratton

to the hotel in West Hollywood. He's hiring a private detective to try and track her down there," Sam told Dana as soon as she sat down.

"You'd better call him again and tell him that she's changed her appearance. She's dyed her hair a darker color and cut it short. And as I suspected, she is definitely not pregnant."

"How did you find that out?"

"I asked Jack to contact the California police and have them send someone to the hotel to question the staff. That and the fact that she left a copy of *Variety* in her room is all they got. Jack was coming across the street to deliver the report in person. That's why he was in the parking lot when Casey got into my car."

"Thank God for that," Sam said voicing Dana's own feelings.

"I'll call Richard and give him this new information. In view of what happened yesterday, I think you should let him and the detectives he's hired handle this case. I'm not even sure you should be here today."

Dana shook her head. "Now you sound like Bruno. He wants me to go and hide out with my folks on the farm."

"Good idea."

"Maybe," she admitted. "Bruno's going to try and get tomorrow off and if he can swing it, we'll drive to the farm for a three-day weekend, but that's it. On Monday morning, it's back to work as usual."

"Look, Dana, we're all worried about you and you need to be worried about yourself."

"I am worried about myself," she said defiantly. "But I can't let some maniac run my life. I'll be careful, but I'm not going to lie down and play dead."

"Have they brought Senese in for questioning yet?"

"I don't know. Bruno said he'd call me after they talked

to him. In the meantime, I'm going to go to my office and get some work done."

"You'll find an additional security guard on duty there. I already introduced him to the rest of your staff."

"Okay, thanks," she said.

"I'll walk you to the elevator."

"I don't need to be escorted everywhere I go," Dana told him.

"Probably not, but I'm going to walk you anyway."

Dana was already annoyed by the men in her life who insisted on monitoring her every move. Going to visit her folks on the farm suddenly sounded like a great idea. She just hoped that Bruno's overprotective attitude wouldn't alarm her family.

Dana found the new security guard stationed outside her office door. He nodded and opened it for her. She heard laughter coming from her office and found Casey and Marianne at the conference table having coffee and eating donuts.

"What's so funny?" Dana asked.

Casey spun around to face her. She was dressed in a pretty pale blue knit top that hung loose over a pair of tight fitting jeans. Her hair and her make-up had been done and once again she looked like the girl who had announced her engagement at a staff meeting last winter. "You won't believe it," she said. "You'd better sit down."

Dana slipped into a vacant chair and Marianne poured her a cup of coffee which Dana ignored waiting for Casey to tell her the joke.

"I'm waiting," Dana prompted.

"I saw Jack's car in the parking lot this morning, so I stopped in there to talk to him. I thought it was only proper that I thank him for saving my life yesterday." Casey paused and took a deep breath. "So, I thanked him for what he did and I no sooner got it out of my mouth, when he said, 'I was following you because I like that swing on your back porch. I've been thinking about how you could repay me. Your place, or mine?'"

Dana put a hand over her mouth to stifle her scream. "He is unbelievable."

"You know what they say, leopards don't change their spots," Marianne added. "Leave it to Jack to turn a heroic deed into a proposition."

"What did you say to him?" Dana asked Casey.

"I said I'd think about it and got out of there fast. I don't know if I can keep being civil to him even if he did save my life."

Bob came in munching on another stalk of celery. The girls stopped talking and looked up at him. He pulled a plastic bag from his jacket pocket. It was filled with celery and carrots.

"My lunch for today," he told them. "My punishment for eating that pizza last night." Bob sat down at the table with them. "Is this a staff meeting?"

"Not really, but we'll make it one," Dana said.

"I already opened today's mail," Marianne announced. "I'll get it."

Casey turned to Dana. "I picked up my car this morning and I called the woman I was on my way to interview yesterday. I've got another appointment with her in an hour."

"What about your laptop?" Dana asked

"I had left it in the trunk of my car so all my notes are safe."

"That's good."

"Damien said he could help you get another car if you're interested, Dana."

"Forget the cars and laptops," Bob said impatiently. "Did Damien ask you out?"

"No. When I talked to him on the phone yesterday I told him I wasn't ready to begin a new relationship."

"But that was before you almost died. Didn't you tell him all that stuff about your life flashing before your eyes and shaking you out of your mope mood."

"There were lots of people dropping their cars off there. He was busy and we didn't talk about personal things."

"Okay. I'll call him. We can double-date Saturday night. I promised Cynthia I'd take her to some chick flick she wants to see."

"What makes you think Damien wants to see a chick flick?" Casey asked.

"Look, I'm going because my wife is mad at me. Damien will want to go because it will be your first date and he'll want to impress you with his feminine side."

"I don't like guys with a feminine side and I'd rather see an action movie."

"All the better for me," Bob said with a grin. "Cynthia will agree because she'll want to be there to support you on your first date with Damien and I won't have to endure the chick flick."

"Forget it, Bob. I don't need your matchmaking services."

Dana got up and walked into the reception area where Marianne was standing with the morning mail in her hand and a brilliant smile on her face. "Isn't it wonderful," she whispered to Dana. "They're arguing just like old times."

Dana and Marianne came back into the office in time to hear Bob's next ploy. "Listen to me, Casey. Damien is a really good catch. He's an ace mechanic and women are always asking him out so you'd better make your move before some other gal snatches him away from you."

"All right," Casey said. "I'll go out with him. Then, I can tell Jack O'Brien I'm already in a relationship."

"He propositioned you already, huh?" Bob said smugly. "Don't worry. I'll take care of him. I have the perfect woman for him."

"Who?" all three girls asked at once.

"She works at the nursing home I investigated a few weeks ago. She's just what O'Brien needs to keep him in line."

"Is it the woman who got arrested for dealing drugs?" Marianne asked.

"No, but now that you mention it, she could be an alternative for him. She's out on bail."

They all laughed and then Dana called for order and they got down to business. Within an hour, all the cases were assigned. Fortunately, there had been nothing pressing that Dana needed to handle herself, so with the Beth Carlson case in the hands of Richard Stratton and the LA detective he was hiring, Dana was free to visit her parents for the weekend.

After Bob and Casey left the office and Marianne went to her computer to research the requests she had been assigned to handle, Dana went to her own computer. A year or so ago, the newspaper had put all the past issues of the paper on the computer. Dana brought up the archives for the year and the month that Elizabeth Stratton had disappeared and began to study all she could find about the girl's case.

The fact that Beth Carlson had assumed Elizabeth's identity had given Dana an idea for a story. She couldn't publish it until Beth Carlson was found, but working on it now would give Dana something to think about rather than the fact that someone might be lurking outside her office waiting for another chance to kill her.

BETH WAS IN the make-up chair getting the finishing touches on her face. Having only worked in small theaters with small budgets, she had never had professional people to help her get ready for a performance. A long cape was covering the slinky black gown Beth was supposed to wear in her scene. On the table in front of her, the costume woman had placed the jewelry Beth was supposed to wear in the scene. Long sparkling earrings with a matching bracelet glittered in the lights from the mirror. Beth didn't know if the set contained real diamonds, but they sure looked good.

"This is so exciting," Beth told the make-up artist. "I hope my voice doesn't crack from nervousness."

"If it does, they'll just do another take," the girl told her. "Some of these actors never study their lines and have to have dozens of takes."

"When does today's taping air?" Beth asked.

"Tomorrow. This is the last segment we're doing here. After they wrap today, everyone goes back to LA so they can tape Monday's episode at the studio tomorrow."

"I used to watch soap operas when I was a kid," Beth said. "My mother liked them."

"Then you know that Friday's shows always have a cliff-hanger to keep the audience in suspense over the weekend."

"According to the script they gave me, I'm part of the cliff-hanger."

"You are?"

"I think so," Beth told her. "I'm supposed to be a lounge singer that someone named Barton sees and becomes infatuated with."

"Oh, right. Barton is the sex maniac on the show. He seduces everyone."

"I don't even get to play hard to get." Beth laughed. "I sing the song and in the next scene I'm in a hotel room in bed with Barton until his wife walks in on us. I memorized my lines but I hope I get to rehearse the scene a few times with the other actors."

"You will. They're using the hotel's show lounge to tape

the scene where you sing, but they won't tape the other scene until later today."

"You seem to know exactly what's going on," Beth said.

"That's because I have a schedule to follow. I do the actors in the order of their appearance in the scenes and you and Barton aren't due to come back to my chair until later this afternoon."

"Good," Beth said. "I'm going to take it one scene at a time. First I get through the song and then I'll worry about the other scene. I met Barton at breakfast this morning and he seems very nice."

"He is nothing like the stinker he plays on the show. You'll do fine with him."

The cast and crew were all staying in rooms at the MGM Grand, but most were already asleep by the time Beth's plane had arrived last night and a limo delivered her to the hotel. Beth had gotten her key and brought her bag up to the room. She was too excited to sleep, so she went back down to the casino and walked around for a while and then went outside into the warm night air.

It was well after midnight, yet the Las Vegas strip was filled with people. Another large hotel/casino was next door to the MGM Grand. It was New York, New York. Beth went outside and stood on the walkway outside of the casino and gazed up at the replica of the Statue of Liberty outside of New York, New York.

Beth went inside the casino and saw that it was designed to look like well-known places in New York City. She had never actually been there, but living in New York and working on Broadway had been her dream since she was a little girl. She had walked around New York, New York for an hour or so and then returned to the MGM Grand and went straight to her room to get some sleep.

One of the assistant directors came into the make-up room. His name was Henry and he was short and stout with long hair and a gold earring in his left ear. "We're ready for you, Miss Stratton."

"She's ready for you," the make-up artist said, removing the cape that covered Beth's costume.

Beth slipped out of the chair and picked up the jewelry. She put it on as she walked behind Henry to the show lounge where she was to perform.

"Let us run through the song once," the piano player, who was an older man dressed in a tuxedo, told Henry. "I've never played this one before."

Beth stood behind the accompanist and sang the song softly as he played it. It went well, so Henry said they were ready to tape and spent a few minutes explaining the scene to Beth and positioning her in front of a microphone on the stage.

"We're only going to tape Barton and the few extras that are at the other tables." Henry said. "As you sing you focus your attention on Barton. You're singing the song to him."

Beth nodded her understanding and took her place. Barton and the extras were already at the front tables. When everyone was ready to begin, the director came in and looked everything over and then called for quiet on the set, then lights, camera, action.

The music began and Beth began to sing. "Sometimes you find the one you've searched for through the years at a time and place when you can hardly keep back tears." Her voice was clear and lovely and Beth directed her gaze at the actor playing the part of Barton pretending that he was the man who held her heart so gently in his hands. The song ended and Beth smiled and bowed as she had been instructed to do.

The director yelled, "Cut."

Barton and the extras began to stand up to leave the set, but Beth stayed on the stage unable to move. With the lights out, Beth was able to see a man standing in the back of the lounge staring at her. She was paralyzed with fear by the sight of him. It was Marko Senese.

TWENTY

DANA STAYED AT her desk reading everything she could find about the disappearance of Elizabeth Stratton. A babysitter who had worked for the Stratton's caring for Elizabeth and her older brother had been fired for stealing a few weeks before the girl went missing. The woman, Darlene Smith, had been tracked down and questioned but she had moved to Chicago and was working as a waitress there the day that Elizabeth disappeared. Her alibi had been verified by her employer.

There were really no other suspects. The neighbors had all been questioned but no one recalled seeing any strangers or strange cars in the area at any time before the alleged kidnapping.

The girl disappeared on August 20th just two weeks before she was to begin second grade at St. Michael's Catholic School.

An intense search of Crescent Hills and the surrounding communities yielded no sign of Elizabeth and no clues as to how or why Elizabeth had gone missing.

Dana found that the story stayed in the news for more than a month after the disappearance moving from the front page of *The Globe* to the back pages before finally being replaced by more current happenings.

After printing out as much about the story as she felt was relevant, Dana went out to talk to Marianne. The fact that Darlene Smith had such a common name would make it difficult to trace her, especially after all these years, but

Dana asked Marianne to try anyway. She gave her the name of the restaurant where Darlene worked and the age the woman would be now.

"I'll try," Marianne promised. "What's this for?"

"A story I'm thinking about writing about the disappearance of Elizabeth Stratton."

"The girl Beth Carlson is now pretending to be?"

"Right. Of course I won't do anything until Beth Carlson is found and we determine that she did indeed assume Elizabeth's identity. I'll also have to run it by Sam and Richard Stratton. I don't want to dredge up painful memories but I'm thinking that it wouldn't hurt to run a side-story with a computerized photo showing how Elizabeth would look now."

The door opened and Bruno came in carrying two brown paper sacks. "Lunch anyone?" he said holding up the bags.

"Not for me," Marianne said. "I have errands to run." She looked at her watch. "It's after noon. I didn't realize it was so late." She got up and reached for her jacket and purse.

Dana smelled the aroma of hamburgers and French fries and suddenly realized she was hungry. "Come on in my office, Bruno. We can eat at the conference table."

"I see Sam got you a rent-a-cop," Bruno said as he followed Dana's shapely figure into her office.

After they were settled at the table eating their lunch and sipping icy cold colas, Dana asked Bruno for an update on the Victoria Romero case.

"Waters is supposed to be notifying her next of kin, but he called and said he's having a problem locating her."

"Who is her next of kin?"

"A younger sister, Roxanne Romero, but she moved from the address Waters found in Victoria's address book and he hasn't been able to track her down yet."

"Is Romero still in our city morgue?"

"Yes. Dr. Vic did the autopsy, but nothing interesting turned up. She died just as it appeared from a gunshot to the head."

"What about Jake Carlson? Have you talked to him again?"

"No. The newspaper found in Beth Carlson aka Elizabeth Stratton's room at the hotel is being sent through the fingerprint lab to see if we can pull any usable prints from it. The room had already been cleaned by the maid, so they couldn't get anything else from it."

"What can you compare it to? Beth Carlson was probably never fingerprinted."

"I thought maybe you could call her mother and ask that question. Some parents have their kids fingerprinted for security reasons."

"I'll check with her this afternoon," Dana promised. "What about Marko Senese? Did Jack bring him in for questioning?"

"We think that Marko Senese has been permanently transferred to Las Vegas. In fact, the entire operation in Crescent Hills has been shut down. Our undercover guy went to the pool hall this morning and found out that three of Joseph Verano's boys showed up late last night and carried out everything that wasn't nailed down. Word is that Marko's people have all been reassigned to other areas."

"Who did he talk to?"

"One of the bartenders was there with a cleaning crew. The guy was pretty upset about losing his job. He told our guy that the building was going to be demolished."

"And he told your guy that Marko was transferred to Las Vegas."

"That's what he assumed. Jack wants to go to Las Vegas next week and check it out for sure."

"Can he do that?"

"Not officially, but he has time coming and says he'll fly there on Wednesday and see if he can track Marko down in the casino Verano and his family run there."

"Did you get tomorrow off?"

"Yes, I did. We'll leave early. Tell your mom to expect us for lunch."

"Okay, but now that Senese and company are gone, maybe the threat to me is over."

"Maybe, but a weekend at the farm sounds like a good way for both of us to relax and unwind."

The door in the reception area opened and Marianne called out to Dana.

"In my office," Dana called back.

Marianne came rushing in, her green eyes wide. "Something is going on at the station. I just saw an ambulance pull up and two paramedics rush inside."

Marianne had no sooner delivered this news when Bruno's cell phone rang. "Detective Bruno," he answered, then listened to the information the caller was giving him. "Okay, thanks. I'll be right over." Bruno clicked off the phone.

"Who got hurt?" Dana asked.

"Jake Carlson. A guard found him unconscious in his cell. "I'll call you later."

Marianne sank into the chair that Bruno had just vacated. Her creamy complexion looked paler than usual.

Dana looked at her with concern. "Did something else happen when you were out?"

Marianne nodded. "I saw Turk lurking in a doorway down the street from the police station."

"Do you think he was looking for you?"

"I hope not."

"That's strange," Dana told her. "Bruno just said Marko and his people had all left Crescent Hills. I never saw Marko without Turk. I wonder if Turk had something to do with Jake Carlson needing medical care." Dana thought about it for a minute and then decided to call Bruno. He answered his cell phone after three rings and Dana told him about Turk.

"Thanks, sweets. I'll see if I can find him. By the way, Carlson is dead."

"How?"

"Don't know yet. Thanks for the tip." He hung up without saying good-bye.

THE NEXT MORNING, Bruno drove Dana to the station and made sure she got on the train. Jake Carlson's death had canceled Bruno's day-off. Dana's dad picked Dana up at the station and drove to the farm where her mom was waiting on the porch that wrapped around the front of the farmhouse.

The trees surrounding the two-story white farmhouse were beginning to turn wonderful shades of orange and gold and the fields next to the house were green with healthy stalks of corn and tomato plants weighed down with their plumb yields. The lovely familiar setting instantly dispelled the anxious thoughts and apprehension Dana had carried with her from the city.

It seemed that her parents' hugs were longer and stronger today. "Are you okay, honey?" her dad asked as he held her close to his chest.

"I'm fine, dad. Casey was the one who got hurt."

Warren released Dana. "I'm sorry Bruno couldn't come with you. We saw the news report last night."

"And we're not going to talk about that or anything else unpleasant," Linda Sloan said firmly, putting an arm around her daughter's shoulder and leading her into the house. "Did you have breakfast?"

"Yes, with Bruno at the train station," Dana told her.

"I made a loaf of homemade bread for lunch and last night I baked an apple pie for dinner."

"What time is lunch?" Warren asked.

"At noon," Linda answered. "It will just be us this afternoon, but the boys and their families are all coming for dinner tonight. They can't wait to see their baby sister."

Dana grinned. "And I can't wait to see them."

After lunch, Warren went outside to do some chores. Dana and her mom cleared up the lunch dishes, chatting about the family news. Dana's three brothers were all married with children so there was always a lot going on with them.

"Do you mind if we watch my soap opera?" Linda asked glancing at the kitchen clock.

"I didn't know you watched soap operas," Dana said.

"Only one, *Forever Love*. I got hooked on it last winter when I had the flu."

Dana followed her mother into the den where the big screen television set was located. It was a comfortable room decorated in browns and beiges with casual sofas and chairs and oak tables spread around the room to hold books for the grandchildren and magazines for the adults.

In front of a window that looked out on the back yard was her father's favorite chair with wide arms and a deep seat that faced the television. When Dana and her brothers were young, they used to fight over who would sit there. Since her brothers weren't there to challenge her Dana settled herself into the chair while her mom turned on the television and found the station she wanted.

"They've been taping the show in Las Vegas this week from the MGM Grand Hotel. I'd love to go there sometime," Linda told her daughter.

"Well, maybe we should arrange a trip for you and dad. Don't you have an anniversary coming up soon?"

"We do, but I doubt if I could talk your dad into spending it in Las Vegas."

"Then I'll have to help you," Dana replied.

Forever Love began with a scene of a couple arguing in a hotel room. Dana picked up a magazine from the table next to her dad's chair and began looking through it while her mother focused all her attention on the soap opera.

While the commercial was running, Linda explained that the girl Barton was in Las Vegas to see was a singer, but the girl who was supposed to play the part had been injured in an accident. "They had the whole story on one of those entertainment news shows last night and showed a tape of the girl that is replacing her."

Dana nodded and turned back to her magazine as the show resumed. Music began to play and Dana closed the magazine and looked at the television screen. She knew that song. A girl with short dark hair took her place at the microphone and began to sing.

"Sometimes you meet the one you've search through the years," the girl sang in a lovely vibrant voice and Dana dropped the magazine and scooted forward in the chair to get a better look. The actress continued to sing and Dana jumped to her feet.

Jack had said that the girl who had checked out of the West Hollywood hotel had short dark hair and was not pregnant. Although Dana had only seen Beth Carlson once in person, she had studied the photo Greta Malone had given her enough to recognize the facial features of the girl. In addition, the song and the voice were the same as those recorded on the CD Bruno had in his car. They had listened to it again on the way to the train station this morning.

"Oh my, God," Dana said as the song ended. "That's Beth Carlson. I'd bet my life on it."

Another commercial was on and Linda turned and looked at Dana. "You know her?"

"She's the girl who went missing in Crescent Hills last Sunday. When do they run the credits for this show?"

"At the end of the show."

Dana was practically jumping out of her skin. Beth Carlson was the girl who had replaced the injured actress in the show. "How long are they going to be taping this show in Las Vegas?" Dana asked her mother.

"I don't know."

A few scenes later, Beth Carlson was on the screen again. This time she was in a hotel room with the actor who had been on camera several times when she was singing the song. Dana ignored the dialogue and kept her eyes fixed on Beth the whole time. Finally, the show ended and the credits began to roll. Dana moved as close to the screen as she could get to read them.

One of the last names to roll past on the credits was Elizabeth Stratton. As soon as Dana saw the name, she rushed from the den into the kitchen to make some phone calls.

It took a few minutes to get the phone number for Coldwater Studios but Dana got it and called the studio and found out that Friday's episode was the last one to be taped in Las Vegas and the cast and crew had returned to Los Angeles on Thursday night. The woman who gave her that information refused to give Dana any personal information about the cast members, but Dana had expected that. She hung up and called her editor.

Fortunately, Sam was in his office and his secretary put Dana's call through to him immediately. "What's up, Dana?" he asked.

"I found Beth Carlson," Dana told him breathlessly. "I just saw her on a soap opera produced in Los Angeles by Coldwater Studios. Beth is using Elizabeth Stratton's name. Has Richard hired that private detective yet?"

"Probably. Richard isn't the type to delay action on anything. Tell me more."

Dana quickly explained that the episode of *Forever Love* had been taped in Las Vegas yesterday at the MGM Grand Hotel. "I called the studio and found out that was the last taping in Las Vegas. Beth should be back in Los Angeles. I'm going there to try and locate her. I'll need the name and number of the detective Richard hired. We can work together on this."

"I'll get in touch with Richard immediately. Are you going to call Bruno?"

"No, I don't want him to know yet. I want an opportunity to talk to Beth before the police get involved. Call me back on my cell phone after you talk to Richard."

Dana hung up and turned to look at her mother who was sitting at the kitchen table listening to Dana's end of the phone conversation.

"You're going to Los Angeles?" her mother asked.

"Yes. I'll need a ride to the airport." Dana's purse was still sitting on top of the suitcase in the hallway outside the kitchen. She had not yet carried it upstairs to her room. She retrieved her cell phone from the purse and handed it to her mom. "Answer this if it rings, please."

While her mom sat staring at the cell phone Dana had placed on the table in front of her, Dana used the house phone to call the airlines and arrange for a flight leaving the local airport at nine o'clock that night. Then, Dana booked a room at a hotel near the airport. She had stayed there with her family last year when they took her brother's kids to Disneyland.

A few minutes after she got off the house phone, Dana's cell phone rang. Dana answered it expecting it to be Sam, but it was Bruno. "Hi, Sweets. How are things there?"

"Fine. How are things there?"

"A total mess. The autopsy confirmed that Jake Carlson died of poison probably in the food he was served for lunch."

"Where did the food come from?"

"Our regular food service outlet. However, a new person made the delivery, told the lock-up guy the regular delivery man was out sick."

"Obviously that wasn't true. What happened to the regular guy?"

"He was conveniently delayed by car trouble."

"Did you pick up Turk?"

"Couldn't find him. For someone so large, he did a great disappearing act. So what is your mom cooking for the dinner I'm going to miss tonight?"

"Chicken and dumplings and apple pie."

Bruno groaned his disappointment. "What train are you taking back Sunday night?"

"I don't know. I'll have to call you."

"Okay. I'm glad you're there with your folks. At least I don't have to worry about you for a few days."

"Right. I'm sorry you couldn't come with me."

"Me too, babe. My landline is ringing, probably another catastrophe. I'll call you later."

Dana clicked off the phone and it rang again. This time it was Sam. "Richard hired a guy named, Craig Collier. He's an ex-cop turned private eye and has worked for some of the movie studios. He's already talked to him and given him the name of the studio. Collier was pretty sure he could get an address for the girl. Richard also instructed him to meet up with you and have you go to see Carlson with him. Richard feels seeing someone she knows with Collier will make it easier to reason with her. Collier's number is 555-323-3998. He's waiting for your call."

Dana jotted the number down. "Okay. Listen I just

talked to Bruno and he thinks I'm going to be here all weekend. Don't tell him differently if you see him or speak to him."

"I'm going to avoid him like the plague. Keep in touch, Dana."

"Will do."

Dana hung up and dialed the number for Craig Collier. A deep, gruff voice answered and identified himself as the private detective. Collier said he already had an address for the girl posing as Elizabeth Stratton.

"That was quick," Dana said in an admiring tone.

"I've done some work for Coldwater and have some good contacts there. Stratton said he wants you to go with me to see the girl. When are you getting here?"

"Not until tonight, probably after ten. We should probably wait until tomorrow to go to the address. I'm staying at the Holiday Inn at the airport. Should I rent a car?"

"No need to do that. I can pick you up there. How about an early breakfast meeting?"

"Sounds good."

They set a time and Collier said he'd ring Dana's room when he got to the hotel. With all her plans made, Dana ended the call and sat down at the table where her mom was still waiting to talk to her.

"Bruno is going to be really upset with you, isn't he?" Linda Sloan asked.

"Maybe."

"But you're going to do this without telling him anyway?"

"Yes, Mom. I have to do it. Beth's mother, my editor, and the father of the girl whose identity she's using have all asked me to find her."

"What am I going to tell Bruno if he calls here?"

"He probably won't call here. He'll call my cell phone."

"If he calls here, don't expect me to lie to him for you."

"No, of course not."

"Tell me the truth, Dana. Will you be in danger doing this?"

Dana placed her hand over her mother's. "Mom, I'm not going to be in any danger. Besides, I'll be with a trained police officer."

"You date a trained police officer, but that didn't stop someone from putting a bomb in your car."

"Mom, I'll be on the other side of the country. No one except Sam, Richard Stratton and you will even know where I am."

Linda Sloan nodded her head, causing the blond curls she had passed onto her only daughter to bounce slightly. "Okay, I'll try not to worry, but having a daughter who chases down felons and other criminals isn't an easy thing for a mother to deal with."

"I know. I'm sorry."

Her mother sighed. "Don't be sorry, honey. We taught you to be brave and independent and we're really very proud of all the good you do."

"Thanks."

Warren Sloan came in through the kitchen door. "What's going on in here? Looks like bad news."

Dana turned to face him. "Nothing serious, Dad. I just located a missing person and have to go to Los Angeles tonight. Good thing I haven't unpacked my bag yet."

"You leaving before or after dinner?"

"After."

"Good. I hate to be late for chicken and dumplings."

TWENTY-ONE

CRAIG COLLIER TURNED out to be a well-built man in his late fifties with a full head of white hair and light blue eyes. At 5' 11" he was three inches shorter than Bruno but he had the same imposing presence.

Seated at a table in the hotel dining room, he and Dana talked easily over breakfast about their respective backgrounds and the case they were going to work on today.

"How did Richard Stratton find you?" Dana asked.

"I was recommended to him by a Judge he knows here. I was about to start working another case, but when I heard Mr. Stratton's story about his daughter disappearing and this woman stealing her identity, I turned the other case over to an associate so I could work on this one for him. Damn shame that he lost his girl like that."

"It's a terrible tragedy, but I don't think Beth Carlson meant to cause Richard any pain. She was in a desperate situation and did what she thought she had to do to escape from it."

"I understand she ran off with money belonging to the mob?"

"We're not sure about that. Her husband was a collector for them and that's what he claimed, but no one knows for sure. He could have taken it himself and just blamed it on her."

"Richard said he was being held in the city jail for her murder and was poisoned there."

"That's right and I doubt if Beth Carlson knows she's a widow."

"Are we going to tell her?"

"I'm not sure what the protocol is on something like this."

"It's been in your local newspaper so we can tell her without your boyfriend feeling that we're stepping on his toes." Reading the surprise on Dana's face, Craig smiled at her. "Richard told me your boyfriend is a Homicide Detective."

"I see."

"Does he know what you're doing here today?"

"No. He doesn't even know I'm here. I'm supposed to be visiting my parents." Dana told him about the bomb in her car and Bruno's insistence that she get out of Crescent Hills for a few days.

"He was right. So, when's he going to find out you didn't stay with your parents?"

"After I talk to Beth Carlson."

An hour later, Craig and Dana arrived at the address Coldwater Studio had given the detective for the actress they knew as Elizabeth Stratton. It was ten-thirty on Saturday morning and the street in front of the apartment complex was filled with parked cars, but devoid of people.

Craig parked down on the next block and he and Dana walked back to the address. The complex consisted of a dozen small apartments situated around a courtyard with a garden area and sparkling pool in the center of it.

Craig and Dana walked through the wrought-iron gate that separated the courtyard from the sidewalk. Craig was busy looking at the apartment numbers when Dana saw a dark haired girl emerge from one in the very center of the complex. She pulled the door shut behind her and hurried through the courtyard pulling a suitcase and struggling to keep a large purse from slipping off her shoulder.

Dana grabbed Craig's arm as the girl walked swiftly through the courtyard towards them. With the trees around the pool area, she hadn't yet seen them.

"There she is," Dana whispered urgently to Craig Collier.

"Looks like she's running again."

Craig and Dana left the cover of the trees. Beth saw them and tried to run, but Craig was too fast for her.

"Elizabeth Stratton?" he asked as he grabbed her arm and halted her flight.

Dana stepped in front of her reading the look of pure terror in the girl's eyes. "Beth, I'm Dana Sloan. Your mother asked me to find you."

"Please, leave me alone," she pleaded. "Let go of me."

Beth struggled to free herself from Craig's grasp, but she was no match for his determination and strength. Suddenly she stopped struggling and burst into tears.

"What happened, Beth?" Dana asked kindly. "Why are you running away again?"

"It's Marko Senese. He found me. I have to get away from here."

"Where is he?" Dana asked.

"In my apartment."

"That's the guy her husband worked for, right?" Craig asked.

"Yes. He's a dangerous man. Maybe we should get her away from here," Dana replied.

Keeping his hold on Beth, Craig pulled out a gun. "What is Senese doing in your apartment?" he asked. "Does he know you're running away?"

"He doesn't know anything anymore." Beth sobbed. She doubled over and would have collapsed on the sidewalk if Craig hadn't been holding onto her. "He's dead."

By the time the police arrived at the complex, Beth's neighbors were out and milling around the courtyard. Dana and Craig had taken Beth over to a round glass table shaded by an umbrella rising from its middle adjacent to the swimming pool.

Craig had put his gun out of sight but kept hold of Beth's arm as she had the look of a scared, cornered animal ready to bolt the first chance she got. Craig had used his cell phone to call a detective he knew to report the homicide.

Dana sat quietly on the other side of Beth Carlson speaking soft words of reassurance that Beth didn't seem to hear. Detective Manny Rodriquez showed up with two uniformed officers.

"Where's the crime scene?" he asked Craig.

"Apartment G right in the middle of the complex."

"Who are these ladies?"

"The girl in the middle is Elizabeth Stratton aka Beth Carlson. She lives in Apartment G. My colleague on the other side of her is Dana Sloan from Illinois. She's been investigating Carlson's disappearance from her area. We tracked her to this complex and were about to go and talk to her when she came running out of the apartment, attempting to flee the scene."

"Where do you come into this?" Manny asked.

"I was hired by a former employer of Mrs. Carlson to find her."

"Why?"

"Because Dana here found out that Mrs. Carlson assumed the identity of the lawyer's daughter who disappeared several years ago."

"Okay, enough. This sounds too complicated to sort out right now." Rodriguez turned to one of his officers. "Jimmy, you stay here and help Miss Sloan take care of Mrs. Carlson. Robert, you come with me and Mr. Collier to take a look at the crime scene." He turned back to Craig. "By the way, do we know who the victim is?"

"The young lady says it's Marko Senese."

"Holy Crap," Rodriguez said. "What the hell is he doing here?"

Dana was a little surprised that Marko's name was so well known on the other side of the country, but then she reasoned that the son of a mobster as famous as Carlo Senese would be known to law enforcement people everywhere.

Craig rose to his feet and the cop named, Jimmy, took his place next to Beth Carlson and placed a tentative restraining hand on her arm.

"Jimmy, don't talk to her. I want to question her myself," Rodriguez said as he walked away.

The neighbors that were outside moved away as the trio of men passed by them. Dana saw them approach the door to Apartment G, try the doorknob and turn around to look in her direction.

"Did you lock the door when you left the apartment?" Dana asked Beth.

Beth nodded.

"Where's the key?"

Beth pointed towards the purse that was sitting on the ground between herself and Dana.

"Can I bring it to the detective?"

Beth nodded her assent and Dana gingerly picked up the purse by its straps, got up and carried it to the front door of Apartment G. Detective Rodriguez had already pulled on plastic gloves, so he took the purse from Dana and pulled it open.

"Holy crap," he said for the second time that morning. He held the purse open so Dana and Craig could see the gun that was inside of Beth's purse. He removed the single key that was on a yellow plastic key ring next to the gun and held the purse out to the other officer and ordered him to hold on to it.

Rodriguez used the key to open the door and the three men stepped inside the apartment. Dana stayed on the threshold, but was able to see Marko Senese clad in dark gray slacks and a light gray dress shirt laying face up on the floor of the small living room. The front of the shirt was full of blood.

"Shot in the chest," Rodriguez said. "Probably died pretty quickly." He turned to the other officer. "Robert, check out the rest of the apartment and make sure no one is hiding in a closet or under the bed, but tread lightly."

Dana scurried out of the way as Craig and Rodriquez backed out of the apartment. Craig looked at her. "Dana, did you get a look at him?"

"Yes."

"You know Senese. Was that him?"

"Yes, it was him."

Rodriguez smiled at her. "How do two pretty young ladies like you and your friend over there know a scumbag like Marko Senese?"

"He was running an operation in Crescent Hills where we live. Beth's husband worked for him."

"She's got a husband?"

Dana shook her head. "Not anymore," she told him. "He died a few days ago."

"Was he shot?" the detective asked referring to the presence of the gun in Beth's handbag.

"No. He was poisoned while he was in custody at our local police station."

"Dana's good friend is a Homicide Detective in Crescent Hills. Dana is an investigator for the city's primary newspaper."

"I see."

Robert came out of the apartment. "It's empty except for the victim," he announced.

"Good." Rodriguez pulled a cell phone from his shirt pocket and dialed a number. "I'll get the lab boys over here. Robert, stay here and guard the door while I go and talk to Mrs. Carlson." Craig, Dana, and the detective walked back to the table where Beth sat with the other officer. "Does she know that her husband is dead?" Rodriquez asked his two companions.

"We don't know. We never really got a chance to talk to her," Craig answered.

Detective Rodriguez sat down next to Beth and began to recite the Miranda warning to her. The words seemed to bring Beth out of the stupor she'd been in.

"Wait a minute," she shouted. "I didn't kill him. I was almost killed myself."

"Okay, miss, calm down," Rodriguez told her. "Let me finish reading you your rights and then you can request an attorney."

Beth looked up at Dana. "The only attorneys I know are in Crescent Hills, Mr. Cauthorne and Mr. Stratton."

"We'll call Richard for you," Dana offered. "He'll get in touch with someone here to help you."

Beth shut up again. Rodriguez started his recitation of the Miranda rights over again and this time got all the way through it. Craig and Dana walked away and went out the wrought iron gate that surrounded the complex to speak to each other privately.

"I'll call Richard and fill him in on what's happened here. If he doesn't want to recommend someone to help her, I'll get a lawyer for her."

"Thanks," Dana said.

"You'd better call your detective friend and tell him what's happened here before he hears it from someone else."

Dana nodded, reached in her purse and removed the

cell phone she had kept shut off since she got to the airport the night before. She turned it on and saw that she had six messages, all sent this morning, and all from Bruno.

The phone rang as she was about to call him back. "Hello."

"Where are you?" Bruno said.

"I'm in Los Angeles."

"I know that. I talked to your mom this morning and she told me where you went and why you went there. Did you find her?"

"Yes. I'm at her apartment complex now."

"Did you tell her about Jake?"

"No. I wasn't sure if I should and as it turned out we caught her just as she was leaving and never got a chance to tell her."

"Who's we?" Bruno asked, his tone was the one he used when he was very upset and making a supreme effort not to show it.

"I'm with the private detective Richard Stratton hired to find Beth. I saw her on a soap opera singing that song we like on the CD. Craig, that's Richard's detective, called the studio that produces the soap and got her address. I met him here this morning and we came together to talk to Beth."

"Why didn't you call me?"

"Because I knew you were tied up there and I didn't think I needed your assistance. Richard asked me to find Beth, who is by the way, definitely using the identity of his daughter, and wanted me to go with Craig to talk to her and bring her back to Crescent Hills."

There was a silence and Dana was pretty sure that Bruno was counting to ten in Italian. His mother spoke the language fluently but other than numbers and a few common phrases her son didn't speak it. However, counting in Italian seemed to have a calming effect on him. "Okay," he finally said. "What did you talk about?"

"We didn't. There was a problem."

"Of course there was a problem. You and trouble are best friends."

"Do you want to know what happened here?" Dana said, losing patience with him. "Or do you want to hear it on the news?"

"The news? Oh, no. What happened? Are you okay?"

"I'm fine. It's Marko Senese. He was murdered in Beth's apartment. That's why she was trying to run." Dana paused unsure if she should tell him about the gun, then decided she would. "We called the police and they found a gun in Beth's purse. Craig is on the phone now trying to get a lawyer for her."

"Marko Senese is dead?"

"Yes. I saw him myself."

"Can I talk to the detective who responded to the call?"

"Sure. I'll get him."

Dana walked back through the gate. Detective Rodriguez was still sitting at the table next to Beth Carlson who now had her face buried in her hands sobbing her heart out. She told Rodriguez who was on the phone and he nodded and took it from her, standing up and walking away from table. Dana reclaimed the seat next to Beth and put her arm around her.

"I'm so sorry, Beth. I know you had good reasons for running away. Your mother called me frantic with worry and asked me to look for you. Now that I've found you, I'm going to do everything I can to help you."

Beth stopped crying and uncovered her tear-stained face. "I just wanted to get away from Jake. I was going to call my mother when I was sure it was safe."

"Of course you were."

"I can't go back to Jake."

"You won't have to," Dana assured her.

"How did you find me?"

"I saw you on the soap opera yesterday and recognized the song you were singing. I went to the theater where you used to work and the director gave me a CD of the show the song came from."

"I should never have used it. I should never have gone to Las Vegas. If I'd known that Marko was there…" Beth stopped talking as Rodriguez came back and looked at her sharply.

"I wasn't asking her anything about the murder," Dana said quickly. "We were talking about why she left Crescent Hills."

"Sure. Your friend wants to speak to you again," he said holding out the cell phone to her.

Dana got up and took the phone as she walked away to talk to Bruno privately, she heard Detective Rodriguez tell Beth that her husband was dead.

Dana turned around to see Beth's reaction. She didn't say anything but she smiled, then realizing how that looked quickly put her hands over her face again.

"Hi," Dana said into the phone. "Rodriguez just notified Jake's next of kin."

"I asked him to do it. They're taking her to the homicide division there. I'm going to get the next flight out of here and should be there late this afternoon."

"Why are you coming here?"

"Because you're there and I know you'll want to stay there and do all you can to help the primary suspect in Senese's murder."

"She didn't murder anyone, Bruno."

"Maybe it was self-defense. Rodriguez told me the gun in Carlson's handbag is a .45 caliber Ruger. The bullet that killed Victoria Romero was a .45. We'll compare bullets and see if they came from the same gun. At any rate, I want to question Beth Carlson and I don't think the LA cops will send her to Crescent Hills to accommodate me. Rodriguez did say he'd send a car to the airport for me."

"Okay. I'll see you later then," Dana told him.

"Yes, you will. In the meantime, try to stay out of trouble."

Dana hung up without saying good-bye. Craig had come over to stand next to her. "Richard Stratton is coming here himself. He says the LA police won't let her return to Crescent Hills and he's desperate to talk to her."

"Will he be able to represent her?"

"No. He's not licensed in California. I called a guy I know. He'll take care of her."

"Damn," Dana whispered. "Rodriguez came back before I had a chance to ask her if she had the mob's money."

"This little complex is right in the heart of the studio district. Rents are a minimum of $2500. a month. Let's see if we can find out who the landlord is and find out how much she paid to move in here."

"What about Beth?"

"They're going to take her in and book her on suspicion of murder. Her lawyer will be there to represent her when she gets there. We'll catch up with her later."

TWENTY-TWO

As it turned out, Bruno and Richard Stratton were on the same flight from Midway Airport to Los Angeles International. Although they had never officially met, both men knew the other on sight and by reputation.

Detective Rodriguez had a car waiting for Bruno at the terminal exit and Bruno offered Richard a ride to the police station with him.

Dana was standing on the steps outside the back entrance of the station talking to Sam on her cell phone for the fifth time since she learned of Marko Senese's demise when the pair arrived. Dana's reports to her editor about Marko's murder had provided the headline and the lead story for the evening edition of The Globe that had already hit the streets in Crescent Hills. It was two hours earlier in California.

"Bruno and Richard just got out of a patrol car here," Dana told Sam. "Do you want to speak to Richard?"

"Not now. Call me later when you have an update," Sam replied.

Dana turned off her phone and greeted Bruno and Richard. "Have they questioned Carlson yet?" Bruno asked.

"I think that's happening now, and I know they ran a GSR test." Dana replied.

"What's that?" Richard asked.

"Gun Shot Residue test," Bruno told him. "I don't suppose you know the results of that?" he asked Dana.

"No, but they'll probably tell you."

"Where is Craig?" Richard asked.

"He's inside talking to some of the people he knows trying to find out what else is going on. I think there's going to be a press conference soon. The news media got wind of Senese's death and have been showing up here in droves."

"Yes," Bruno said. "We saw them gathered at the front entrance. That's why we came in this way."

Richard nodded and walked up the stairs. Bruno took Dana's arm and they walked behind the lawyer whose steps seemed heavy and labored. Dana knew that this situation was probably a painful reminder of the loss of his daughter.

Bruno checked in with the desk sergeant and was escorted back to the interview room where Beth Carlson was being questioned by Manny Rodriguez. Richard and Dana were escorted to another room to wait and were soon joined by Craig Collier.

"Do you have any new information?" Richard asked Craig.

"The GSR test was negative, but the fingerprint lab has matched the girl's fingerprints to prints found on the gun. The victim is in the morgue and they are doing a post-mortem examination as we speak. However, the big news is that when they moved Senese's body they found another gun underneath it. It hadn't been fired recently, but it could give the girl a reason to plead self-defense."

"That's probably what happened," Richard said. "I can't see Beth as a cold-blooded killer even if she did steal Elizabeth's identity."

Dana turned to Richard. "I had to call the story into Sam. It's running in the evening edition, but we held back the information that Beth was using your daughter's identity."

"I understand she appeared on a television show using my daughter's name."

"Right, but we don't know if the news media has made that connection yet."

Richard sighed. "It will soon and that part of the story will come out. Who knows? Maybe the publicity will do some good. Maybe someone will come forward with information on Elizabeth."

"You know, Richard," Dana said softly. "I've been thinking the same thing and I wouldn't do this without your permission, but I'd like to write an updated story about your daughter's disappearance and run one of those computerized photos that would show what Elizabeth might look like today."

"It would be fine with me," he said. "But I'll have to speak to my wife about it."

"Of course. I understand completely."

"Do you have a way of making a positive identification if someone comes forward claiming to be your daughter?"

"Yes. When our children were small I insisted that both of them be fingerprinted. A copy of Elizabeth's fingerprints should still be in her old case file."

The three of them then discussed the effect Marko's death would have on his wife and her family. "Do you know if his family has been notified?" Dana asked.

"I think the police in Chicago and Las Vegas have been contacted and asked to make the notifications."

"I met Marko's wife briefly earlier this week when Bruno and I were in Chicago. She's a pretty girl, but from what I've learned Marko didn't take his marriage vows too seriously." Dana shook her head and looked at the two men. "It hasn't even been a week since Beth Carlson disappeared. I can't believe all that has happened in so short a time."

"Including an attempt on your life." Richard said. "I hope that Senese's death puts an end to that worry. Senese had a reputation for killing anyone who looked at him cross-eyed. I'm sure he was behind the death of Jake Carlson."

"My secretary saw one of Marko's body guards lurking around the station around the time that happened. He could have been carrying out one of Marko's orders."

"I assume they haven't been able to find the guy to question," Craig said.

"That's right. Maybe he's in Las Vegas now."

The door opened and Bruno walked in. "We're finished for the moment. The girl didn't give us much, but she denies killing Senese. Of course Rodriguez doesn't believe her."

"What about the GSR test?" Dana asked.

"Negative, but her prints are on the gun."

Everyone nodded like they hadn't heard that information before.

"I'd like to talk to Beth," Richard said. "Can that be arranged?"

"I'm afraid not. She doesn't want to face you right now, but she agreed to have her lawyer talk to you on her behalf."

"Good enough," Richard said. "When?"

"In about five minutes. He's going to come here to speak to you," Bruno turned to Dana. "Beth did ask to speak to you, Dana."

"Is that allowed?"

Bruno nodded. "Only because she agreed to speak to you in the interview room where everything will be video-taped. Come on, I'll take you there."

Dana rose to her feet. "Craig? Will I see you again?"

"Sure. I'm going to hang out here in case Richard needs something. I'll see you later."

Bruno opened the door and he and Dana left the room. "Did you ask her if she had Senese's money?" Dana asked when she was sure they were alone in the corridor.

"She admitted taking it, said that was why Senese was in her apartment."

"Craig and I checked with her landlord and she paid more than $15,000. in cash to move into that apartment complex."

"I know. She told us that."

"So, why does she want to talk to me?"

"Because you told her you'd do whatever you could to help her out of the trouble she's in."

"Did she tell you that?"

"She didn't have to, sweets. I know you and that's the kind of promises you make to everyone but me."

"Not everyone," Dana replied. "Just people who can't help themselves. You're not in that category."

Bruno smiled down at her and put his arm around her shoulder. "If I ever am, you'll be the first person I call."

Dana returned his smile and then grew serious again. "I called Greta Malone. It was the good news, bad news thing. Your daughter is alive and well. Your daughter has been arrested for murdering one of the biggest mobsters in the Midwest."

"Like I said, Carlson didn't tell Rodriguez much except that she was innocent. When I questioned her, she denied any knowledge of Victoria Romero. See what story you can get out of her."

Dana nodded. "Where are you going to be?"

"I'm waiting here for the lab to remove the bullet that killed Senese so they can run it through ballistics. Then I'll know if the gun is the same one that killed Victoria Romero."

"And Beth will be suspected of that too?"

"Here we are," Bruno said as they approached a door where a uniformed officer stood guard. "I'll see you later."

Bruno turned and walked back down the corridor without answering Dana's question. It didn't make any difference, she knew that if the gun that killed Senese was the same one that killed Victoria Romero, Beth would be in even more trouble.

Dana showed her ID to the officer at the door and he unlocked it and allowed her to enter the interview room. Beth was sitting at a table with her arms wrapped around herself like she was very cold and trying to get warm.

"Hi, Beth," Dana said softly. The girl started to speak and Dana held up a hand to stop her. "Listen, before you say anything I have to tell you that our conversation is being video taped. and the detectives are monitoring every word we say."

Beth smiled sadly. "I know. This is my week for being video-taped," she whispered. "Only I don't think it's going to do anything for my acting career."

"You were very good on the soap opera. You have a beautiful singing voice," Dana told her as she sat down across from her.

"Thanks."

"Do want to tell me your version of what happened?" Dana asked.

Beth nodded. "I'm going to tell you everything that happened, Dana. I didn't tell most of this to my lawyer or to the cops. Men wouldn't understand why I did the things that I did, but I hope that you will and be able to find some way to help me. I never meant to hurt anyone. I just wanted to get away from Jake and start over again somewhere else. I just wanted to follow my dream and when I got chosen for the soap opera I was so happy, I didn't check it out. If I'd known Marko was in Las Vegas I would never have gone there. You've got to believe that."

"I do believe that, Beth," Dana told her. "Marko was a dangerous man. A few days ago someone put a bomb in my car. One of my investigators was almost killed. Detective

Bruno thinks Marko was behind it and we're pretty sure that Marko ordered one of his men to kill your husband."

Beth smiled. "That's the only bright spot in this whole thing. I know this sounds terrible, but Jake made my life a living hell. I'm glad he's dead."

"How do you feel about Marko Senese?"

"I'm sorry that Marko is dead. Believe it or not, he was always nice to me and he stopped Jake from abusing me. Not only that, this morning, Marko saved my life."

Dana nodded. "I think you'd better start at the beginning."

Beth nodded in agreement and began to talk. She explained some of what Dana had uncovered in her investigation. How Marko had been romancing her and how Beth feared that his attentions would ruin the plan she had to get away from Jake.

"The only way I could think of to discourage Marko was to tell him I was pregnant. I did and he believed me so, I decided that Jake would too. Jake didn't think I knew where he kept the money he collected for Marko, but I did and one night when he came home drunk, I took his keys and made a copy of the one that opened the floor safe.

"When I first started working on the files in the law office, I found the one that Richard kept on his daughter. Her birth certificate and social security card were in it. When I saw that our names and ages were similar, I took the documents from the file and used them to get a passport in her name with my photo on it. I'm really ashamed of doing that. My aunt got me the job at the law firm and Mr. Stratton was always very nice to me, but I knew if I ran using my own name, I could be traced pretty easily."

Beth stopped talking and looked at Dana hoping to find some hint of sympathy and understanding in her face or demeanor. Dana didn't disappoint her. She reached across the table and patted Beth's hand.

"I know you were in a terrible situation, Beth, and did what you thought you had to do to get away."

"You said my mother asked you to look for me, but given the way Jake had treated me over the years, I hoped that everyone would think I was dead, that Jake killed me."

"Detective Bruno and I were at the convenience store the afternoon you gave Jake the slip. I did think maybe the whole thing was an act on his part, that you had never actually been in that store at all. Then, your mother called me and I remembered a woman who was arguing with Jake when Bruno and I drove up. She was a big woman and I found her pretty easily. She told me that she had seen you in the store going into the bathroom."

"Oh, right. I forgot about her."

"That made me think you had somehow slipped past Jake without him knowing it was you."

"That's exactly what I did. I had gone to the store earlier in the day and hid my disguise in the bathroom. While Jake was taking his afternoon nap, I got the money and stuffed it in the prosthesis I was using to fake my pregnancy and put the newspaper I had been stuffing it with each week in Jake's bag. I got him to take me to the convenience store, changed into my disguise in the bathroom and walked right past Jake without him giving me a second glance."

"My investigator found the cab driver who picked you up near the store and took you to Midway Airport." Dana went on to explain how they had checked the passenger lists and found the name Elizabeth Stratton and connected it with Richard and traced Beth to the hotel in Los Angeles.

"I only stayed at that ritzy place for two nights and then I rented the apartment. I had changed my appearance and my name and I thought I was safe and that's when I got careless."

"So you ended up on the show and traveled to Las Vegas. I assume that's where Marko saw you."

"I should never have used that song from *The Last Decent Crooks,* but the people at the studio said I would have a better chance of getting the part if I had a different song to sing."

"I might not have recognized you except for the song," Dana told her. "When I went to the theater looking for information on you, I got the CD from the show and had been listening to it."

"I told myself the people who were looking for me weren't the type to watch soap operas. I convinced myself that I was safe, that's why I went to Las Vegas to do the show."

"I never watch soap operas, but I was at my mother's house and she is a fan of *Forever Love.* You said you didn't know that Marko was in Las Vegas or you wouldn't have gone there. Tell me how he found you."

"He said a local entertainment news show did a spot about me taking over for the injured actress. They showed a brief clip of my audition tape and Marko recognized the song and my voice. He had seen me in the show in Chicago. He went to the MGM Grand and watched me tape the scene. When I looked across the room and saw him standing there I almost passed out." Beth put her head down as the memory of the fear she had experienced took hold of her.

"But you were able to tape your next scene?"

"Yes. When I came off the stage, Marko approached me and told the director we were old friends. Of course they believed him. He stuck with me like glue, through the rehearsal and the next scene. Then he took me back to my room to get my things and hustled me out of the hotel to his car. I was scared out of my wits. I thought he was going to take me out into the desert and kill me."

"But he didn't?"

"No. He said he loved me and wanted to be with me.

He said we could get the money I'd taken and use it to leave the country."

"Did he say anything about Jake?"

"He said Jake was in jail and that I would never have to worry about him again."

"We think that Marko had Jake killed. Did he say anything about that or about the murder of a woman named Victoria Romero?"

"He didn't say anything else about Jake but said a woman he knew had been murdered and that there had been an attempt on your life. He swore he didn't have anything to do with either of those things, but said they were a part of a plot to disgrace him with his father-in-law and it was just a matter of time before his father-in-law would force him out of the organization. That's why he wanted me to get the money and leave the country with him."

"All right. Then, what happened?"

"We drove to Los Angeles and went to my apartment. On Friday morning, we went to the bank and got the money. Marko wired most of the cash to some secret account he has in the Cayman Islands or some place like that. Then, we went to a travel agent and bought tickets to Rome. Our flight was supposed to leave this afternoon."

"What about the documents you took from Elizabeth Stratton's file?"

"They're in my purse, along with my airline ticket. I was going to use them to escape again, this time to another country. The police have my purse, you can verify that what I'm telling you about that is true."

"What about Marko's ticket?"

"I left it in the apartment."

"Okay. The police should have found that too." Dana had a question she wanted to ask, but was afraid of making her angry and stopping the information she was giving Dana. Finally, she decided to try to broach the subject anyway. "You said Marko professed his love for you. You spent two nights alone with him."

"Nothing happened. He tied me up and let me sleep in the bed. He slept in a chair next to the bed with his gun in hand."

"Is that the same gun the police found in your purse?"

"I don't know."

"You said Marko saved your life this morning. Can you tell me exactly what happened?"

Beth nodded. "I packed my suitcase and took a shower. The bathroom window is glass blocks and doesn't open, so Marko gave me some privacy. He seemed very nervous and wanted to leave the apartment and get to the airport as soon as possible. We called a taxi and Marko was watching through the window for it when he saw someone he recognized coming through the courtyard towards the apartment. He took his gun out and told me to run out the back door and find someplace to hide."

"Did you ask him why?"

"No. He was very angry and I was afraid to say anything, so I ran into the kitchen and out the back door. I didn't have my purse or anything with me or I would have just kept going and never looked back."

"Where did you go?"

"I ran to the apartment complex that backs into mine and sat in the laundry room there."

"Did anyone see you there?"

Beth's face suddenly brightened. "Yes. There was a young couple in there doing laundry. I was so upset I just sat frozen in the corner and didn't speak to them, but I know they saw me there."

"That's good, Beth. They could be your alibi."

"I was in there with them for over an hour. Then, I went back to my apartment. I looked through the window in the kitchen and saw Marko sprawled on the floor. It took me about twenty more minutes to get up the nerve to open the door and go inside."

"Didn't you think of calling the police?"

Beth shook her head vigorously. "No. All I could think of was running away again and in order to do that I had to get my purse with the airline ticket and some money. Finally, I crept inside. Marko was dead and the gun was on the floor near his body. I picked it up thinking that whoever killed him could be outside waiting for me. I got my purse and my suitcase and ran out of the apartment. That's when you and that guy saw me and stopped me from leaving."

"That guy is a private detective Richard Stratton hired to find you."

"Yeah, I know. I sent my lawyer to talk to Richard and apologize for me. Maybe the cops will give him back his daughter's papers. Obviously, I won't need them any more."

TWENTY-THREE

THE STORY BETH shared with Dana was verified by the airline ticket in her purse and the one for Marko found in Beth's apartment. The couple who were doing laundry in the room where Beth hid verified that she had been there at the time the woman living next door to Beth remembered hearing what she thought was a firecracker going off in Beth's apartment.

These accounts coupled with the fact that the GSR tests on Beth's hands and clothing were negative led Detective Rodriguez and his superiors to decide she was not the person who shot Marko Senese. Beth was released into Bruno's custody.

The two detectives reasoned that the Ruger was Beth's and had been taken from her by Marko and had somehow discharged during a struggle with the person who confronted him in the apartment that morning. This led to further speculation that the gun found underneath Marko's body had been carried into the apartment by his killer who dropped it during the struggle.

Dana thought the two detectives were jumping to some rather bad conclusions, but she didn't argue with Bruno about it. They were momentarily on good terms and she wanted to keep it that way.

By Monday morning, Beth Carlson was in jail in Crescent Hills as the primary suspect in the Victoria Romero murder. Richard Stratton had also filed charges against her for identity theft.

At the morning staff meeting at Globe Investigations, Dana was relating everything that had occurred in Los Angeles. "The theory Bruno and Detective Rodriguez worked out was that Marko was followed by someone in Joseph Verano's employ from the time he left the Majestic Casino to see Beth Carlson at the MGM Grand. They think it's a case of one mobster killing another mobster and I got the impression that Rodriguez isn't going to lose any sleep over it happening in his jurisdiction."

"I wonder why the killer waited to go to the apartment and kill Senese." Bob said. "If he was following them, he knew that they had gotten the money and bought airline tickets."

Dana shrugged. "I think he lost them somewhere along the way and had to check back and get Beth's address from the studio just like we did."

"That makes sense," Marianne said. "You said Beth told you that Marko denied trying to kill you?"

"That's what she said, but of course Bruno says that you can't believe anything a creep like Marko Senese tells someone who is suspected of a homicide."

"So with Senese dead and the rest of his gang reassigned elsewhere you're no longer in danger." Casey smiled. "That's great news."

Dana returned her smile. "I think so. As soon as my insurance company comes through with a check I'm going to buy another car so I won't have to depend on my friends to drive me around."

"Damien said he knows some good people at the Ford dealership here, if you want another Mustang." Bob told her.

"Hey, I forgot about your big double date Saturday night. How did it go?"

"Cynthia wouldn't let me have any dessert at dinner and we ended up at a chick flick, so it wasn't the best date

I ever had," Bob said. "However, it was worth it to see Casey and Damien together at last."

Dana turned to Casey. "What's your version?"

"I had a very nice time and I will be seeing the gentleman again. The downside to that is that Bob's matchmaking efforts will continue to drive us all crazy."

"I'm thinking of charging people," Bob told them. "Marianne and Greg, now Casey and Damien. I'm hot!"

Dana steered the meeting back to Globe Investigation's business and assigned new cases to Bob and Casey. She didn't take any herself as Richard Stratton had called her this morning and gave Dana permission to write the article on his daughter.

Richard had promised to send a photograph of Elizabeth to Dana with written permission from him and his wife for The Globe to publish the article and have the photo run though the process that would show what the girl might look like now.

The murder of Marko Senese made the national news, and the fact that Beth Carlson had appeared on a popular daytime drama under a false identity was the lead-in story on every celebrity magazine and entertainment news show. Beth Carlson was now famous and that added a bizarre twist to the story that Dana spent the morning drafting on her computer.

A little before noon, Bruno showed up to take Dana to lunch. She was more than ready for a break and they walked the few blocks to Big Lou's Café and were able to get their usual booth in the corner of the restaurant.

"I've got the story drafted, but I would really like to interview the nanny the Stratton's fired before their daughter disappeared before I wrap it up. I'm running an ad in the Chicago papers for her to contact me and one in The Globe as well."

"Good luck with that," Bruno said cynically. "Even if

she sees the ad I doubt if she'll contact you. Why would she want to call attention to herself again after all these years?"

"You're probably right, but I thought I'd try anyway."

Big Lou came over with the coffee pot and filled their cups and took their orders. Dana ordered a Chef's Salad which was the special for the day and Bruno ordered a Ham and Cheese Sandwich on Rye with a side of Cole Slaw.

"I'm going to Chicago tomorrow morning," Bruno told her. "Do you want to come along? Mama wants us to come to her house for lunch."

"Why are you going to Chicago?"

"Waters called. Over the weekend, he found Roxanne Romero and notified her of the sister's death. She made the ID on Sunday morning and arranged for her sister to be picked up and brought to Chicago for a funeral tomorrow morning. Since I wasn't here to question her, I thought I'd go to the funeral and talk to her tomorrow."

"And you're inviting me to come along?"

"Given your interest in our primary suspect and the fact that I'm still not comfortable with you being alone here, yes."

"You know that Beth Carlson didn't kill that woman."

"You know she didn't kill the woman. As far as I'm concerned she may have done it."

"Funny," Dana commented. "How Beth has changed places with her husband in your jail house. I hope you are monitoring the food she's served."

"Jack is bringing her food in personally. He thinks she's a babe."

Dana suppressed the urge to make an unkind remark about Jack, keeping the promise she made to herself after he saved Casey's life. "How much longer can you hold her?"

"Just a day or so longer on the murder charges. We

really don't have enough evidence now to make it stick. A good lawyer will argue that Marko's killer brought the Ruger into the apartment."

"Isn't that a pretty big gun for a woman to handle?"

"Yes, but it's not impossible given the proper motivation."

'I think you're grasping at straws. I assume that Beth doesn't have an alibi for the time Romero was killed."

"She says she was home with Jake finalizing her escape plans for the next day. Too bad Jake can't verify that."

"It doesn't make sense, Bruno. Even if Jake were having an affair with Romero. Why would Beth kill her when she was going to leave him and get him in trouble with his employers?"

"You've got a good point, honey, but I've got to finish my investigation before I let her go."

"Which is why you're going to the funeral tomorrow to question her sister."

"Right. I want to try and make an informed decision before she has to appear in court tomorrow afternoon on the charges Stratton filed against her."

"That'll cause a media frenzy."

"Probably. When are you going to run your story?"

"Tomorrow."

"Stratton's case against her is a slam dunk, but the entertainment reporters are already making the girl a heroine. Abused wife running for her life ends up on a soap opera and is kidnapped by a mobster. I'm surprised she hasn't gotten any movie offers yet."

"It is a sensational story, and it would help her pay her legal fees for the fraud case."

"Except if she's charged with murder, the fraud case will probably be dropped."

"I don't think you're going to be able to charge her, Bruno."

"Maybe. Maybe not. Waters seems to think Romero's sister has some valuable information."

"Why didn't he get it from her?"

"She refused to answer any of his questions."

"And you think she'll answer yours?"

Bruno smiled and reached over and touched her hand. "She might, if I have my lovely, compassionate girlfriend with me."

"Wait a minute, buster," Dana said withdrawing her hand. "You always tell me to butt out of your cases. Now you expect me to help you get information that could hurt someone I believe in."

"Absolutely. You can chalk it up as a credit on your side of the fence and use it against me next time you need my help on one of your cases."

Big Lou delivered their lunch order saving Dana from replying to his sarcastic remark and causing yet another rift in their relationship.

MARKO SENESE'S FUNERAL took place in Chicago on Monday afternoon. It was a private service with only close family and friends in attendance. Carlo Senese had allowed Joseph Verano to take control of his operations because of failing health. Now Carlo wished he had shot Joseph in the heart that day three years ago when he appeared on his doorstep with his daughter suggesting that the two crime families should merge their enterprises.

Giada was attractive and passionate enough that Marko agreed to marry her, thinking that the union would immediately make him more powerful and ensure his future with the Verano family. The fact that Marko would continue to work in the Midwest while his wife maintained their home in Las Vegas was an extra bonus.

"My deepest sympathy," Joseph said bending down and hugging Carlo's frail body as he sat like a statue in the front row of the funeral parlor. "I will not rest until I find out who took our son from us."

Carlo didn't answer. Giada dressed entirely in black with her face covered by a thick black veil fell on her knees at Carlo's feet and sobbed. Carlo patted her shoulder. He believed she had tried to be a good wife to Marko who had not really loved or appreciated her.

Joseph helped his daughter to her feet grateful that Marko's casket was closed and they would not have to look at the corpse of his son-in-law. He placed Giada on the chair next to Carlo and took a seat on the other side of her, supporting her with a strong arm around the middle of her body. Carlo's bodyguards sat behind the old man and Joseph's men, Turk and Harry, took seats behind him and Giada.

Giada had been inconsolable since word of Marko's death had been delivered to her at the casino on Saturday evening. Joseph and his sons had feared the girl would have a total breakdown. That was one of the reasons Joseph had left the funeral arrangements to Carlo. Giada was much too distraught to make any decisions about Marko.

The funeral home near Carlo's residence had handled the services for many of Carlo's relatives, friends, and business associates and always made sure the arrangements were simple and respectful despite the fact that members of Chicago's police force often showed up to monitor the services.

Joseph knew that like the police, Carlo believed that Marko had died as a result of his father-in-law's order. Although Joseph had come to dislike Marko more and more over the years, he had not ordered his death. He had brought Marko to Las Vegas to monitor his actions and make Giada happy.

When Marko suddenly disappeared, Joseph learned that he had taken off with an actress from the soap opera that was filming in Las Vegas. As usual, Giada had sprung to Marko's defense, defusing her father's rage by explaining that this was the woman who had stolen the money from the Crescent Hills operation and promising that Marko would dispose of the girl and return with the money. Instead, someone had murdered Marko.

The priest walked over and blessed the casket and then invited everyone to pray with him. Carlo bowed his head and prayed but not for his dead son. Carlo prayed that he would have the strength to murder Joseph Verano before this day was over.

As the service progressed, Turk kept his eyes on Giada. Her shoulders shook with her sobs and he wished that he could comfort her. Now that he was no longer assigned to watch over Marko, Joseph had assigned Turk to guard Giada. With Marko out of the picture, perhaps the girl would finally notice him and realize the deep feelings he had for her.

While Turk kept his eyes on the young widow, Harry watched Carlo Senese. He was an old man in poor health, but Harry had once worked under Carlo and knew him well. He was like a snake lying in the grass waiting for a chance to strike his prey.

AFTER LUNCH, DANA went back to the office and was at her desk polishing the article she had written about Beth Carlson stealing Elizabeth Stratton's identity. She was about to e-mail it to Sam to review when Marianne buzzed her.

"Yes?" Dana said cheerfully.

"There's a woman on line one who wants to talk to you about Darlene Smith. She says she is her daughter."

Dana immediately picked up the call. "This is Dana Sloan."

"My name is Susan Watkins. I saw your ad in today's paper asking for information about my mother."

"Your mother is Darlene Smith?"

"She was. She died a few months ago."

"I'm sorry."

"Thanks. Your ad said you were interested in talking to her about the Elizabeth Stratton case."

"That's right."

The woman sighed. "I don't know if I can help you or not, but I have some information that's been bothering me."

"I'd appreciate any information you can give me," Dana said. "When can we meet?"

"I work at the shopping mall near the newspaper. I could come to your office when I get off of work this afternoon."

"That would be fine. What time?"

"I get off at three today?"

"I'll look forward to meeting you."

"Look, I'm not sure if this is important or not. I may just be wasting your time."

"Don't worry about that," Dana told her. "I want to hear what you have to say."

Dana hung up the phone and instead of e-mailing the copy she had written to Sam, she printed it out and took it to his office. Sam read through the copy Dana gave him and nodded his approval.

"This is very good, Dana. I'm going to put it out on the AP wire. With all the publicity Beth Carlson is getting other newspapers around the country will pick up the story."

"How soon will the lab be done with Elizabeth's photo?"

"They promised it would be here first thing in the morning."

"Fine. I'll e-mail the final copy to you tonight. I may have more to add to it." She explained about the phone call from Darlene Smith's daughter. "You can format it to show the old photo and the age-enhanced one side by side in the article. I'm going to Chicago to Victoria Romero's funeral with Bruno. He wants to question her sister."

"And he's letting you come along?"

"Strange as it seems, yes. He thinks my presence will encourage the woman to talk to him about Victoria."

"Good luck with that," Sam said.

"Thanks."

Dana returned to her office and reviewed the cases that Marianne had researched that day for the requests that had come in over the weekend. By three o'clock, Dana was pacing back and forth in front of Marianne's desk.

Casey and Bob both called in and reported on the cases they were working on. Both promised to write up their reports and e-mail them to Dana so she could review them before she went home that evening. Dana went back to pacing. Then at three-thirty the door opened and a woman who appeared to be in her thirties with bleached blond hair came in and introduced herself as Susan Watkins.

After they were settled in Dana's office Susan Watkins began to speak about her mother. "As I told you on the phone, she died a few months ago. She was in her sixties and had Alzheimer's and liver cancer. She was in a nursing home for the last six months of her life. She became too erratic for me or my sisters to take care of at home."

"I see." Dana nodded sympathetically. "Did you know Elizabeth Stratton?"

"Not really. I was a teenager when my mother worked for the Stratton family. My father had just died and she took the nanny job because she was really strapped for cash. He had been ill for a long time and she had a lot of unpaid medical bills."

"The Stratton's said that they fired your mother because they suspected her of stealing money from them."

"I don't know if she did steal money from them. It's possible since she was barely supporting us on what they paid her. I do know that she was very angry at being accused and losing her job."

"She moved to Chicago and got a job at a restaurant there."

"That's right." Susan began to fidget in her chair. "She was hounded by the police for weeks after the girl disappeared and after that we were never allowed to speak about the Stratton's or their little girl again. Then, a few weeks before she died, I was visiting my mom at the nursing home. It had been some time since mother recognized me or my sisters or any of our family members, but one of us tried to visit at least once a week. Anyway, we were in the day room and another resident was being visited by her great-granddaughter. The little girl's name was Lilly and she has dark hair and eyes like Elizabeth Stratton."

Dana felt a prickling sensation on the back of her neck and sat forward in her chair. Susan Watkins stopped talking and looked at Dana with tears in her eyes.

"Please, tell me what happened," Dana prompted softly.

"My mother thought that Lilly was Elizabeth and started asking her if she was happy in her new home. Of course Lilly didn't understand and I tried to change the subject, but mother started crying and begging the little girl to tell her that she was happy in her new home. I took mother back to her room and asked her what new home Elizabeth had gone to. She said she didn't know, but that the man had promised that Elizabeth would be loved and taken care of. Then, she said the man had paid her twenty thousand dollars to bring Elizabeth to him."

"Then, it's possible that Elizabeth Stratton may still be alive," Dana said.

Susan Watkins nodded. "It's also possible that my mother took part in her abduction and it's been eating at me since that day."

"Did she ever speak about Elizabeth or the money again?"

"No, but then I remembered that shortly after Elizabeth disappeared my father's medical bills were paid in full."

"How did your mother explain that?"

"She said that my dad's youngest brother had gone to the hospital and negotiated a settlement for a fraction of what she owed. I believed her because since my dad had died, Uncle Turk had done a lot for our family. He was the one who got my mom the job in Chicago and helped us move there."

Dana was almost too stunned to speak. "Your uncle's name is Turk?"

"Actually it's Theodore Smith, but everyone calls him Turk."

"Did you ever ask your uncle about the money or the hospital bills?"

"I did, right after the incident with the little girl at the nursing home. He said he knew someone at the hospital and had been able to help mom negotiate a settlement, but when I told him what she said about Elizabeth he said she was a sick woman and didn't know what she was saying or doing anymore." Susan Watkins got to her feet. "I'm sorry I didn't come forward with this information before my mother died, but I don't think she actually knew where Elizabeth was taken."

"No, she probably didn't," Dana said slowly. "Can you give me the name of the nursing home where your mother was cared for? Perhaps she talked to someone there about Elizabeth and her part in the disappearance."

"If she did, they probably wouldn't have known what she was talking about."

"That's true, but I'd like to check just the same. If you'd prefer, I won't use your name."

"It doesn't matter," Susan Watkins said. "I feel better just having told someone about it."

Susan Watkins left the office as Bob and Casey came running in together.

"I thought you were e-mailing your reports," Marianne said as they ran past her into Dana's office.

Bob was out of breath and flopped into the chair Watkins had just vacated. Casey ran over and turned on the television set on Dana's credenza.

"What's going on?" Dana asked, still reeling from the information she had just received from Darlene Smith's daughter.

Casey backed away from the set and motioned for Dana to watch the news report that was on.

"The grave side services for alleged mobster, Marko Senese, at Chicago's Holy Hope Cemetery ended violently this afternoon when Carlo Senese stabbed Las Vegas casino owner, Joseph Verano, in the stomach, then collapsed. Both men were taken to an area hospital for treatment where Carlo Senese was pronounced dead on arrival. The condition of Joseph Verano is not known at this time. The widow, Mrs. Giada Senese, who is the daughter of Verano accompanied her father to the hospital. Stay tuned to this station for updates on this breaking news story."

Dana sat down so hard on her desk chair that it rolled back and banged against the wall. "Holy Crap," Dana said, borrowing the phrase Detective Rodriguez uttered when he learned of Marko Senese's death. Then, she reached for the telephone and called Sam.

"I already heard," Sam yelled into the phone at Dana. "Get down here now."

"I can't," Dana yelled back. "I just got information about the disappearance of Elizabeth Stratton that I have to check out immediately."

TWENTY-FOUR

BOB TOOK DANA to Helping Hands Nursing Home located in Pine Grove City, a thirty-minute drive from the newspaper office. It was close to five o'clock and some of the residents were being taken to the dining room for supper. Those people who weren't well enough to eat in the dining room were having trays delivered to their rooms.

The young woman on duty at the front desk didn't question Dana's story that she and her husband had just learned of their aunt's death and wanted to talk to someone who had cared for her in her final days. The girl remembered Darlene Smith and was able to give Dana the names of two of the staff who were assigned to the Alzheimer's wing and took care of the Alzheimer's patients. Fortunately, one of them, a male nurse named Rico, was on duty there now.

"This is a good time to talk to Rico," the girl told them. "When the patients are eating, it's pretty quiet."

Bob and Dana went to the Alzheimer unit and found Rico sitting behind the desk playing a hand-held poker game. They introduced themselves and asked Rico about Darlene Smith.

"Sure I remember her. She was in the advanced stages of Alzheimer's when she came here, so communicating with her wasn't easy, but she wasn't violent like some of the patients."

"Did she ever talk about a little girl named, Elizabeth?"

"Yeah, all the time. I thought it was one of her daughters, but it turned out none of them were named Elizabeth."

"Elizabeth was my daughter," Bob said improvising a story. "She spent a lot of time with Aunt Darlene when she was young. Can you remember anything she might have said about Elizabeth?"

"Mostly she would cry and say she was sorry about Elizabeth."

"Did she ever mention the name Turk or Theodore?" Dana asked.

"No, but some big guy that visited her once in a while was named Theodore. In fact he was here the afternoon she died."

Dana's heart rate accelerated. "Really?"

Rico thought for a moment. "Yes. She didn't recognize him but he stayed and visited with her anyway. Nice guy, brought her some candy. Darlene loved candy."

"And how soon after that did Aunt Darlene pass away?" Bob asked.

"One of the staff found her dead the next morning. She had passed peacefully some time during the night."

"Was there an autopsy?"

Rico shook his head. "No need for one. Besides the Alzheimer's Darlene had terminal cancer. We knew it was just a matter of time."

Dana and Bob thanked Rico and left the nursing home. They didn't speak until they reached Bob's car.

"I think Turk killed his sister-in-law," Dana said as Bob drove out of the parking lot. "He probably used the same poison that killed Jake Carlson."

"Are you going to use any of this in your article about Elizabeth Stratton?"

"I don't think I can accuse her or Turk of being involved in the kidnapping, but I will mention Darlene Smith and run a photo of her. I'm sure there's some in our files from the time that Elizabeth disappeared."

"I see," Bob said. "You're hoping that Elizabeth Stratton will see the photo and recognize her old nanny's photo."

"Yes. Elizabeth was seven years old. She must have some memory of the kidnapping."

"You know, Dana. Darlene Smith was a very sick woman, mentally and physically. She could have been talking out of her head, just remembering the little girl she used to care for, and Smith's death could have been a natural passing."

"I could believe that except for the relationship between her and Turk, a man who has worked for gangsters his whole adult life."

"Do you think her family will agree to let the police exhume the body to check it out?"

"I don't know. I'll talk to Bruno about it tomorrow."

By the time Bob and Dana got back to The Globe, the evening edition had hit the streets. Carlo Senese had suffered a stroke, his second that year. His attack on the man who was primed to take over Carlo's operations had left Verano in critical, but stable condition. His daughter remained at the hospital at her father's side, but refused to comment on the death of her husband or what had prompted her father-in-law to attack her father at the cemetery.

Reporters were camped out at North West hospital waiting for further word on Joseph's condition. Sam had already sent a reporter and a photographer to join the vigil in Chicago.

Dana sent her staff home while she stayed in her office and reworked the Elizabeth Stratton story. She was just about finished with it, when Sam came in to talk to her.

"What was the new information you got on Elizabeth Stratton?"

Dana laughed. "I thought you'd never ask."

Sam placed a black and white photograph of a woman

on Dana's desk. The woman looked a lot like Susan Watkins. "Here's the best one they could find," Sam told her.

"It's great. Do you have the one the lab enhanced of Elizabeth?"

"It's ready to be inserted into the article, but I haven't seen it. All hell broke loose when the news came in about Carlo Senese attacking Verano and then dying himself."

"It sounds like Carlo blamed his successor for his son's death."

"Obviously. Are you going to make me read your story to find out why you ran out of here today?"

"No, because I can't include everything I learned." Dana told Sam about her meeting with Susan Watkins and the connection between Darlene Smith and Turk. "The nurse in Smith's ward said that Turk visited Darlene the afternoon before she died and brought her candy."

"Oh, oh," Sam said, nodding. "Isn't Bruno looking for this guy in connection with Jake Carlson's death?"

"That's right, and tomorrow I'm going to ask Romero's sister about him."

"You think he killed her too?"

"I think it's a possibility. Jake Carlson was at the convenience store looking for his wife on Saturday afternoon and Marko Senese was in Chicago with his wife that day. Turk was at the restaurant with Marko and his wife on Tuesday night, but that was three days after Romero was murdered."

"You think Turk is the one who put the bomb in your car?"

"I don't know, but it's possible. It's also possible that he's the one who killed Marko Senese. Apparently, Carlo Senese thought that Verano had something to do with Marko's death and Turk works for Verano now. Beth Carlson told me that Marko thought someone he trusted was reporting on him to Verano."

"Makes sense. What can I do to help with any of this?"

"Darlene Smith was working at a restaurant in Chicago when Elizabeth Stratton disappeared. Her boss verified her alibi. I want to know who owned that restaurant back then." Dana leaned across the desk and handed Sam the slip of paper with the name of the restaurant she had found in one of the old stories about the investigation of the Stratton kidnapping.

"I'll get someone to research this for you tomorrow morning," Sam promised as Bruno walked through the door.

"Investigate what?" Bruno asked.

"I'll tell you over dinner," Dana said brightly. She turned back to her computer and sent the finished copy to Sam's computer in the newsroom.

VICTORIA ROMERO'S FUNERAL was held at a church in the same neighborhood as the theater where Beth Carlson once performed. It was a small gathering of mourners who dispersed quickly after the service. Roxanne had announced that her sister would be cremated and her ashes flown back to Connecticut to be interred in the family plot with her parents.

Bruno had introduced himself and Dana to the girl when they arrived at the church. They had agreed to talk over coffee in a nearby café.

Roxanne Romero didn't look much like her sister and she explained that they had the same mother, but different fathers. "We were still very close," she added. "I'm four years younger and Vicki always took care of me when we were kids."

"I understand that you're a teacher," Bruno said.

She nodded. "Yes. I teach English at the community

college. Most of the people at the funeral are students of mine. They didn't even know Vicki."

"None of Vicki's friends attended the funeral?" Dana asked.

"Since Vicki got involved with Marko Senese, she didn't have any friends who wanted to be seen with her."

"What about Jake Carlson?" Bruno asked. "We found this photo of him and your sister in her apartment."

Roxanne took the photo that Bruno held out to her and looked at it closely. "Oh, right. I know this guy. He and Vicki used to work together in one of Senese's clubs. They dated for awhile, but then he dumped her for some actress and Vicki took up with Marko."

"You know that Marko Senese was murdered a few days ago."

"Everyone knows that. Good riddance. Do you think Marko is the one who killed my sister?"

"He was a suspect, but he had an alibi."

"That doesn't mean a thing. He could have sent any one of his guys to do the job for him," she said bitterly.

"Do you think that's what happened?"

"Yes."

"Do you know which one of Marko's men might have carried out the order?"

"Either Harry or Turk."

"Do you know them?" Dana asked.

"Only by reputation and by what Vicki told me." Roxanne stopped and thought about it for a moment. "You know," she said slowly. "It was probably Turk and he could have acted on his own."

"Why do you think that?" Dana asked as Roxanne was speaking directly to her now. As Bruno had hoped, the presence of another woman had made the girl more comfortable.

"He's been taking care of Giada since she was a little kid and is very protective of her. Her marriage to Marko was arranged by their fathers. Vicki told me that Turk didn't like it and asked Verano to assign him to Marko so he could keep an eye on him for Giada. Marko told Vicki he didn't want Turk to know that he was keeping her in that apartment or meeting her at the motel where she was…" The girl stopped unable to speak the fate that had befallen her sister.

Their conversation continued until their coffee cups were empty. Roxanne didn't really have any information that could positively link Theodore Turk Smith to her sister's death, but the more she talked, the more she was convinced that he was the one who had murdered her sister.

Bruno called a cab for Roxanne and paid the driver to take her home. He and Dana then walked slowly to Bruno's car that was still parked in the church parking lot.

They got in the car and Bruno aimed it in the direction of his mother's house where they were going to have lunch. Dana's cell phone rang. She answered it and it was Sam.

"I found out who owned the restaurant where Darlene Smith worked. It was Joseph Verano and it was run by his oldest son, Salvatore."

"Do we know where Verano was at the time?"

"He was already running the casino in Las Vegas."

"Turk must have gotten his sister-in-law the job there."

"Probably."

"Okay, thanks, Sam. When is the article running?"

"It's on the newsstands now and I understand the Chicago papers are picking it for their afternoon editions."

"Good. Thanks."

Angie was waiting with open arms when Bruno and Dana arrived. "Lunch is ready. Come, sit down."

They ate in the newly remodeled kitchen of Angie's house and lunch was more like a five course dinner.

"Mama, you have enough food here for an army," Bruno told her.

"I cooked for the whole week. Your sisters and their families always drop in two, maybe three nights a week to eat. They work all day and are too tired to cook when they get home."

Dana didn't say anything; she was too busy filling her plate with eggplant parmigiana, her favorite dish. They ate and brought each other up to date on family news. Angie had met Dana's family on a visit to the farm last winter and since then Linda Sloan and Angie had kept in touch. Both women were silently hoping that they would become related by marriage some day soon.

Dana helped Angie store the leftovers and put the dishes in Angie's brand new automatic dishwasher.

"I didn't think I could get used to washing my dishes in a machine, but it is wonderful." Angie told her.

Bruno was in the living room when the afternoon edition of the newspaper was delivered. He heard it thump on the front porch and went outside to retrieve it. When he unrolled the paper, he saw that Dana's story had made the front page and he went into the kitchen to show it to her.

Dana didn't bother reading the copy. She knew what it said, but she was anxious to see if the Chicago paper had picked up the photographs. They had. There were two photos of Elizabeth Stratton, one taken just before her abduction. The other one was an electronically aged copy of the little girl to show what Elizabeth might look like now at twenty-six. Dana stared at the aged likeness of Elizabeth and thought she looked familiar, but it was Angie who recognized the image as someone she had seen before.

"She looks just like the girl we saw in the restaurant that night when we went to dinner. The one with the gangster who sent you flowers."

Bruno took the paper and studied the photo. Dana peered at it again leaning against his side to get a better look.

"I didn't pay much attention to her that night," Dana admitted. "I was more concerned with Marko and what he would do or say."

"Mama's right," Bruno finally said. "She looks a lot like Giada Senese."

"Oh, my God," Dana said sitting down at the kitchen table again. "Do you think that's possible?"

"Sure, it's possible." Angie sat down next to Dana. "I remember her father when he was working here in Chicago. He had two sons and a sick wife. One of the reasons Carlo helped financed the casino in Las Vegas was so Joseph could take his sick wife to live in the desert. My friend, Maria, God rest her soul, knew the wife and said she was always saying her husband and sons ignored her and she wished she had a little girl because girls are always close to their mamas."

Dana and Bruno stared at his mother. "How long ago was this?"

"I'm not sure, eighteen, nineteen years now." Angie replied.

"Wait a minute," Dana said. "If Mrs. Verano didn't have a daughter when she moved to Las Vegas, the girl would have to have been born there and she would only be about nineteen years old now."

Angie shook her head. "Mrs. Verano had trouble delivering her youngest son and almost died. He had a very large head. Anyway, she bled so much they had to do a hysterectomy. She couldn't have had another child."

"How do you know all this?" Bruno asked.

"I told you from my friend, Maria, God rest her soul. Her son worked in the restaurant Verano owned and brought home all the gossip."

Dana got up and began to pace off her excitement so

that she could think more clearly. "It all fits, Bruno," she said slowly. "Turk worked for Verano and his sister-in-law had money problems and was fired as Elizabeth Stratton's nanny. Turk got Darlene Smith to kidnap Elizabeth. She was seven, old enough to know not to go with strangers, but if her nanny came along and took her out of the front yard, she would go willingly. She was too young to understand that the woman had been fired. The nanny turned the child over to Verano who whisked her off to Las Vegas, probably telling his wife that the child was an orphan."

"Her disappearance in Crescent Hills was a big news item locally and maybe even here in Chicago, but I doubt very much if the news traveled across the country to a place like Las Vegas."

"Is Verano's wife still alive?" Dana asked.

"No, she passed a few years before my friend, Maria," Angie replied. "Maybe five years ago now."

Dana's cell phone rang. It was Sam again. "Richard Stratton is in my office. He wants to talk to you."

"Hello, Richard," Dana said when he got on the phone. "I assume you've seen the story."

"The photo of Elizabeth," he said in a choked up voice. "I just showed Sam a photo of my wife at that age and they look identical." He paused and then spoke again, this time in a normal strong voice. "Sam told me about the connection between Darlene Smith and that gangster."

"I couldn't really put those details in my story," Dana said. "They're not substantiated facts."

"I've already contacted a friend who works for the FBI. He's got a file on Carlo Senese and Joseph Verano that goes back years and names all the people who have worked for them. Theodore Smith is one of them. I also had him fax me a photo of Verano's daughter. I believe she is Elizabeth."

"We were just discussing that same possibility."

"I'm going to take immediate action on this, Dana, and I wanted you to know ahead of time."

"What are you going to do?"

"The statue of limitations has run out on the kidnapping crime, but I can still take legal action against the kidnappers. I'm going to sue Joseph Verano and Theodore Turk Smith for kidnapping my daughter."

Dana felt chills running down her spine. What Richard was suggesting could be very dangerous for him. "Don't you think we should interview Giada first and see if she remembers anything about the kidnapping? The evidence is hearsay and circumstantial."

"Yes, but filing the suit will give me a chance to see the girl and find out if she is Elizabeth."

"There may be another way," Dana said. "Give me twenty-four hours to see if I can arrange a meeting for you, please. If you threaten the people she considers her family, especially with Verano in the hospital in critical condition, she may refuse to speak to you or testify against them."

There was a long silence. Finally Richard spoke. "Are you thinking she'll see the story in the newspaper and come forward of her own accord."

"I don't think we can count on that," Dana replied. "But I have an idea for another way we can get to her."

"All right, Dana. It will take me at least twenty-four hours to draw up the papers for the law suit anyway." They said their good-byes and Dana clicked her cell phone off.

Bruno was glaring at her. "This idea of yours is going to get me in big trouble, isn't it?" he asked softly.

"Maybe," Dana admitted. "But it could help you flush Turk out of hiding."

TWENTY-FIVE

DETECTIVE WATERS WAS waiting in the lobby of North West hospital for Bruno and Dana.

"Is the girl in the room with her father?" Bruno asked after they shook hands.

"Yes, she is. I've got one of my guys stationed outside his door and he says the girl left after she knew her father was out of danger last night, but came back this morning and has been there ever since."

"Good." Bruno turned to Dana. "You wait here, sweets. This shouldn't take long."

Dana nodded and took a seat in the lobby near the door where they had entered the hospital. The plan she had come up with to isolate Giada from the rest of her family had not been very hard to sell to Bruno. Bruno in turn had talked to Waters who was more than happy to help out. Bruno was technically out of his jurisdiction and Waters was happy to do anything that might cause Joseph Verano some concern.

Ten minutes later, Giada Senese was brought down to the lobby in handcuffs. She walked silently between Detectives Waters and Bruno. She looked confused and frightened. As they passed by, Dana got up and followed them out of the building. The news media that had been camping out at the hospital waiting for updates on Joseph Verano's condition sprang into action, snapping photos and yelling questions at the group.

Bruno opened the door to the squad car Detective Waters had waiting at the front door of the hospital. Waters pushed Giada into the back seat ahead of him and the officer behind the wheel put the car in gear and took off leaving the news people on the sidewalk still yelling and snapping photos.

"Dana, what the hell is going on?" Buddy Matthews from The Globe's newsroom grabbed her arm.

"Giada Senese has been arrested," Dana said simply.

"For what?"

"At the moment, for the murder of Victoria Romero and Jake Carlson in Crescent Hills, but there will probably be more charges to follow in connection with the murder of Marko Senese in Los Angeles." Dana's words were spoken loud enough for most of the reporters to hear. Then, Bruno pulled her away from Buddy and hustled over to his car that was illegally parked in the driveway leading out of the hospital.

THE RIDE TO Crescent Hills' police station took less than an hour because both the squad car and Bruno's car took advantage of their flashing light to move through traffic quickly.

Michael Dominic was already at the Crescent Hills station when Giada arrived. "I demand a private interview with my client," Dominic shouted as Bruno and Waters passed by him with Giada in tow.

"No problem," Bruno told him. "After she's processed."

Giada was fingerprinted and then taken to an interview room where her attorney was allowed fifteen minutes to talk to her before Bruno barged in and sat down across the table from them.

Dana was allowed to sit next to the computer technician who was video-taping the question and answer session. Whatever Dominic had told Giada had erased some of the fear from her face, but she still looked dazed and confused.

Both Dominic and Giada seemed shocked when instead of asking her questions about the murders she was suspected of committing, Bruno took a copy of The Globe and laid it on the table in front of Giada.

"Have you seen this story?"

She blinked and looked up at him shaking her dark head in a negative reply.

"I suggest you and your attorney here read the article and examine the photographs that accompany it."

"What are you pulling, Bruno?" Dominic shouted. "You accuse this poor girl of murdering two people and then you ask her to read the newspaper."

"Just read the article, Dominic. It relates to the murders."

Dana watched Giada's face as she pulled the paper towards her and looked at the photographs. A flash of recognition seemed to fill her dark eyes as she looked at the photo of Elizabeth Stratton at seven and the photo of Darlene Smith. She turned to Dominic.

"Please be quiet, Mr. Dominic. I want to read this."

Giada read the article and studied the photos again. When she raised her head, she looked directly at Bruno. "Why are you showing this to me? Do you believe that I am this missing girl?"

"Yes, I do," Bruno replied. "The fingerprints we just took were compared to a set of prints that have been in the missing persons file here for nineteen years. Your fingers were smaller then, but your prints are a match to Elizabeth Stratton's."

"Yes," Giada said matter-of-factly. "I know that my name is Elizabeth."

Dominic was outraged. He pounded on the table demanding Bruno to explain his actions.

Bruno smiled. "We have arrested this young woman on

suspicion of two, maybe three homicides, but before we can formally charge her, we have to know her true identity."

Richard Stratton and a woman Dana assumed was Mrs. Stratton came into the room where Dana was observing the interview. Dana had called Sam and Richard on her cell phone from Bruno's car while they were driving from Chicago to Crescent Hills.

"Dana, this is my wife, Meralee," Richard said quickly.

"How do you do," Dana said extending her hand.

Meralee didn't answer or take Dana's hand, she was staring at the video screen at the girl who had been known as Giada for the last nineteen years. Dana looked at Giada's face and the face of Meralee Stratton. The resemblance was remarkable.

"Can I talk to her?" Meralee said suddenly. "Please, let me talk to her."

The technician pushed a button and spoke into the microphone attached to the headset he was wearing. "Mr. & Mrs. Stratton are here. They would like to speak to the girl."

Bruno nodded and looked at Giada. "Would you like to meet with the Stratton's? They may be able to answer any questions you might have."

Giada was looking at the photographs in the newspaper again. Finally, she answered Bruno's question. "Yes. Can I speak to them alone, please?"

"Sure."

"No way," Dominic objected. "I need to stay here with Giada."

Giada turned to the lawyer again. "Please. I want to speak to them privately."

Bruno escorted Dominic out of the room as he allowed Richard and Meralee to enter. The computer technician turned off the audio to the room but left the video running.

Bruno came and stood next to Dana and to Sam Mc-Gowan who had just entered the technician room.

"She looks just like her mother," Sam said softly. "Even more in person than she does in the newspaper article."

INSIDE THE INTERVIEW room, Meralee and Richard sat down across from Giada. Richard pulled out an envelope with some photographs in it and put one down on the table in front of Giada.

"I remember this house," Giada said softly picking it up to look at it more closely. "I used to sleep in this room." She pointed to one of the upstairs windows that faced the yard. "There was a bed with a white headboard that had a big pink elephant on it."

"Yes, darling. That's right," Meralee said reaching across the table to touch Giada's hand.

Richard placed another photograph on the table. It was of a young boy of ten or eleven. He had dark eyes and dark hair. "Do you know this boy?" he asked.

Giada picked up the photo and looked at it. "Benjamin. It's Benjamin," she said excitedly. "Where is he?"

"He lives in New York now. He's works at a big law firm there."

"Benjamin is married and has two children. He named one of them Elizabeth after you," Meralee added.

Giada nodded. "I hope he doesn't tease her like he used to tease me. He used to call me Elizabrat." She smiled at the memory. "He didn't mean it though."

"Do you remember what happened the day you left the yard?" Richard asked.

Giada thought about it for a minute. Then began to tell her parents about her abduction. "Nanny came to the side gate and called me. She said mama told her to take me for ice cream. She said I should bring my doll with me."

Richard placed another photo on the table. "Is this the doll?"

It was obvious that the photo had been taken at a birthday party. Little Elizabeth was dressed in a pink party dress and she was holding up a Cabbage Patch doll that was also wearing a pink dress."

"Yes. Her name is Lucille, but I called her Lucy. I still have her."

A sob tore itself from Meralee's throat, but she quickly gained control again as Giada continued her story.

"Nanny did take me for ice cream and Turk met us at the ice cream shop and then we got into his car to go for a ride. That's when nanny told me that you and daddy were going on a long vacation and I was going to stay at a nice lady's house for awhile. We went to the airport and got on a plane. I was very excited. I'd never been on an airplane before. I fell asleep on the plane and when I woke up I was in a pink and white room with a nice lady who smelled like flowers."

Giada's story continued as she told her parents how she had asked to go home to her mommy and daddy and the nice lady who smelled like flowers told her that her mommy and daddy had been killed in a car accident while they were on vacation and that she was going to live with her from then on.

"They all lied to you," Richard said. "We would never have gone off and left you. We looked for you for months."

"We thought you were dead," her mother added.

"And I thought you were dead," Giada told her. "I accepted the Verano's as my parents and they treated me well."

OUTSIDE THE INTERVIEW room, Dana, Sam, and Bruno continued to watch the video monitor. Although they couldn't hear what was being said, the fingerprints had positively identified Giada Verano Senese as Elizabeth Stratton. The question now was whether Elizabeth Stratton was guilty of murder.

Dana had come up with the idea of arresting Giada in order to get her away from Joseph Verano and his thugs and have her fingerprinted. However, Bruno and Detective Waters believed there was a possibility that she did kill Victoria Romero and Marko Senese. She might even have been behind the attempt on Dana's life. She was after all raised by people who had little regard for the law and had been married to a man who cheated on her every chance he got. Jealousy was often a motive for murder.

Bruno had reminded Dana of the look Giada had given her in the restaurant that night when Marko announced that he had sent Dana flowers.

"If looks could kill I would be face down in my eggplant," Dana had said that night.

"So, Bruno," Sam said pulling him away from the video monitor. "Do you have any evidence linking this girl to the crimes you arrested her for?"

"Not really, but her alibi for the time of Romero's death was her husband, who is now dead himself. If she didn't do it, she could have asked her friend, Turk, or her father to do it for her. I called Detective Rodriguez in LA and asked him to canvass that apartment complex again to see if anyone saw a woman answering to Giada's description around the time that Marko was killed."

"She's Elizabeth Stratton," Sam reminded him. "After all these years the Strattons would be devastated to find their missing daughter, and then see her go to prison."

"Right. So I'm hoping that Dana's theory is correct."

"And that is?"

Before Bruno could answer, the door to the room

opened and Jack O'Brien came rushing in. "Theodore Smith just turned himself in. He's in an interview room now talking to Dominic."

TWENTY-SIX

TURK HAD BEEN delivered to the Crescent Hills' police station, by Harry who was of course following Joseph Verano's orders. Bruno thought Dominic could argue that Turk was confessing under duress. However, once Dominic understood how and why Turk had been taken from his hiding place in Chicago, he shut up and let Turk hang himself.

"Marko was always cheating on Giada and I couldn't stand it. Him and Vicki got it on at the motel at least once a month. She made the mistake of calling the pool hall that Saturday asking for Marko. I answered the phone and read the caller ID so I knew she was in Crescent Hills at the motel. I went there and shot her."

"What kind of a gun did you use?"

"A .45 Ruger. Then, I took her purse and anything else that could identify her and burned them."

"What happened to the gun?"

"You know what happened to it. I used it again to kill Marko when he ran off with that Carlson babe. Giada told us that Marko was just taking her to get the money and he'd be back, but I knew he had the hots for the girl, so I tracked them down in Los Angeles and killed him. I left the gun at the scene hoping the girl who had done another disappearing act would pick it up and get blamed for his death."

"What about the bomb on Dana Sloan's car?"

Turk smiled and nodded smugly. "I learned all about explosives in the army."

"Whose idea was it to kill Dana?"

"Mine. After Marko and Giada met up with her in the restaurant and Marko bragged about sending her flowers, Giada came to me crying. I decided to eliminate the girl Giada saw as a threat to her happiness."

"What type of explosives and detonator did you use on the car?"

Turk laughed. "You want proof that I did it, huh?" He then provided a detailed explanation of how he had rigged Dana's car and it matched the information Bruno had in the report the police bomb squad had prepared.

"Someone saw you hanging around the station the day that Jake Carlson was poisoned. What do you know about that?"

"That little creep. I was in trouble with Marko and Joseph for letting him get away from me. I watched for a few days to see what time his food was delivered. Then I made up a box and hired a kid to deliver it for me."

"What kind of poison did you put into Jake's food?"

"Cyanide. It works real fast."

"As long as you're so talkative," Bruno said smoothly. "Why don't you tell me about the day you visited your sister-in-law at the nursing home. I heard you brought her candy."

For the first time, Turk got nervous. "I used cyanide on her too," he said losing the attitude he had maintained since the questioning had begun.

"Why did you kill Darlene Smith?"

"It was a mercy killing," he said. "She was suffering."

"I think it was because she was remembering details of the kidnapping you and she plotted and carried out nineteen years ago."

"I don't know what you're talking about."

Bruno sighed. "I think that's the one crime that Joseph Verano doesn't want you to confess to, isn't it?"

"Mr. Verano doesn't know anything about it."

"That's strange. Giada just met with her real parents and she remembers a great deal about it. Would you like to know what she had to say?"

Turk turned to Michael Dominic with panic in his eyes. "It's true, Turk. I don't think they ever really suspected that Giada committed any crimes. It was just a clever way of getting her away from the family and an excuse to fingerprint her. Giada's prints match a girl named Elizabeth Stratton, who was abducted nineteen years ago. You want to tell us about your part in that?"

"I swear Mr. Verano didn't know we took someone else's kid," Turk said emotionally. "He would kill me if he knew that I didn't bring him an orphan."

"Well, I don't think you have to worry about that Turk," Bruno told him. "Unless someone puts cyanide in your food while you're in custody here."

Dominic touched Turk's arm. "I think Giada has already told everything she remembers. So, you'd better tell your side of the story and convince Detective Bruno that the Veranos weren't in on it too. Word is that Richard Stratton, the girl's father, is going to file a civil law suit against your boss. You know something like that could cause Joseph to lose control of the casino in Nevada."

"Verano paid you to get him a little girl for his wife," Bruno said angrily. "I don't believe he didn't know how you were going to get one."

Tears appeared in the big man's eyes. "He didn't. I swear he didn't. I had just started working for Mr. Verano. One day he told me that his wife was depressed because him and his sons were so busy getting the new casino and other enterprises going in Las Vegas they didn't spend time with her.

"I told him I could probably find a poor orphan who needed a good home for him to adopt. I thought if I could help him out it would make him like me more and keep me on his payroll. I gave most of the money to Darlene for my brother's hospital bills. The rest went to get phony adoption papers and a new birth certificate for the kid. When I brought her to Mrs. Verano she was so happy no one questioned my story that her mom and dad had gone on vacation and were killed in a car accident."

"He's telling the truth, Detective Bruno," Michael Dominic said. "Joseph Verano may be a lot of things, but he would never take part in a kidnapping. You must convince Richard Stratton of that."

"I'll let you do that," Bruno said. "You can talk to him, lawyer to lawyer."

"There's another thing you should know. When you took Giada out of that hospital room today, Joseph called me immediately. He was sobbing and begging me to help his girl. He loves her very much.

"I told him that if he had any idea who did any of the murders Giada was arrested for, he'd better have the person come forward. As you can see, he did exactly that."

Theodore Smith was booked and brought to a cell. The Crescent Hills' jail facilities were not large, but they did have separate quarters for male and female prisoners. Beth Carlson may not have seen the man who came to Los Angeles to kill her, if not for the fact that Beth was being released on bail and walking down the corridor with an officer when Turk was being taken to his cell.

"You should be dead, lady," Turk said as he passed by her.

Beth shivered at the coldness of his tone and the rage she saw in his eyes.

TWENTY-SEVEN

THE NEXT AFTERNOON, Dana was at her desk when Beth Carlson and Greta Malone came to see her. Sam had driven Dana home from the police station last night after it had become evident that Bruno was going to be there into the wee hours of the morning writing his reports on the crimes committed by Turk.

"We just wanted to thank you for all you did to find Beth," Greta said.

"You're welcome," Dana replied.

"I have some incredible news to share," Beth said, smiling brightly. "Actually two pieces of incredible news."

"I heard that the producers of the soap opera bailed you out of jail last night," Dana said.

"Right. And I'm getting a permanent role on *Forever Love*. They're going to write the character I played into the storyline."

Dana rose to her feet and came around the desk to hug the girl. "That's marvelous, Beth. I'm very happy for you."

"There's more," Greta said, unable to keep quiet any longer. "Richard Stratton is dropping the charges against Beth. He and his wife have agreed that if Beth hadn't stolen her identity, you wouldn't have written the article that brought Elizabeth back to them."

"So," Beth added. "We're leaving for Los Angeles today. The studio wants me to start work right away."

"Actually, I knew that Richard was going to drop the

charges. He told me last night before he left the station with his wife and daughter."

"Is that gangster going to be prosecuted for kidnapping that child?" Greta asked.

"No. The statue of limitations on the kidnapping has run out." Dana didn't tell them there was still a possibility that Richard Stratton would sue Joseph Verano.

Beth and her mom left and Marianne came in to deliver that morning's mail. Dana started to tell her about Beth Carlson's news.

"I already know," Marianne said. "It was the lead story on the morning show I watch. The entertainment reporter said it just goes to show again that there's no such thing as bad publicity. I have a feeling the ratings of *Forever Love* will skyrocket. The media will squeeze every ounce of drama they can out of Beth Carlson's story."

IN CHICAGO, JOSEPH VERANO was dressed and sitting in a chair next to his bed. Harry was with him and they were waiting for Joseph's doctor to release him.

"Can I get you anything, Mr. Verano?" Harry asked.

"No, thanks. I just want to get out of this place."

"Hi, Papa," Giada said from the doorway.

Joseph looked up and smiled at her. He stood and opened his arms and Giada ran to him. "Thank God you're safe," Joseph whispered as he embraced her. "I was so worried."

"I'm fine. I've brought someone to see you and we need to speak privately. Is it okay?"

"Who have you brought?"

"His name is Richard Stratton."

Joseph released her and nodded sadly. "Yes. Michael came last night and explained everything to me. Turk is lucky he is in jail or…"

Giada put a finger to his lips to stop him. "May I bring Mr. Stratton in?"

"Of course." He turned to Harry. "Invite Mr. Stratton to come in here, then close the door and stay outside and make sure we are not disturbed."

"What about the doctor?" Harry asked.

"Tell him to sign the papers and let me out of this place."

"Yes, sir."

Harry hurried to do Joseph's bidding and a few seconds later Richard entered the room. He stood silently looking at Joseph and the daughter they each had a claim on.

Finally, Joseph held out his hand. "Mr. Stratton, I apologize for my part in the pain you have suffered."

Richard shook his hand. "I understand that you did not know that Elizabeth was not an orphan."

Giada ran to get the other chair and pulled it across the room so the two men could sit facing each other. She perched herself on the hospital bed as Richard and Joseph sat down.

"What happens now?" Joseph asked.

"That's up to Giada," Richard said.

"Giada?"

"Yes, Papa. I've decided to continue to use the first name you gave me."

"Your mother, I mean my wife, named you after her own mother." Joseph bowed his head to hide the tears in his eyes. "I'm sorry. This week has been filled with so much I could not foresee or control."

"I understand," Richard told him.

They both looked at Giada again. "Tomorrow I am going with Richard and Meralee to New York to see my brother, Benjamin, and his family."

"So you won't be coming back to Las Vegas with me," Joseph said.

"I would like to stay in Crescent Hills and get to know my parents again. They still live in the house I remember."

"My wife would never leave the house. She wanted to be there in case Elizabeth was ever returned to us," Richard said.

"I see," Joseph replied.

"Mr. Verano, my wife and I want to thank you for taking care of our daughter all these years. You can imagine the fear and worry we had that if she was still alive, she was being mistreated."

"In my heart, she is my daughter and she always will be," Joseph replied. "You must believe that my wife and I had no idea that she was not an orphan. Giada brought much happiness to our family, especially my wife, who had always longed for a daughter. I hope that Mr. Dominic was able to convince you that I had no part in the kidnapping."

"Yes, and Giada has told us she loves you very much. She says you have always put your family first no matter what else happens."

Joseph sighed. "Business is business, but my family is my life. It was the same with Carlo. I am sad that he thought I was the one who took his son's life. Although I often regretted that I arranged for Giada to marry the boy."

"I wanted to marry him," Giada said. "You were just trying to make me happy."

"He was not a good husband to you."

"I still loved him, and I am sorry that Carlo did not live to see his grandchild." Both men looked at the girl sitting so calmly on the hospital bed. Their faces filled with emotion. "That is the other reason I wish to stay in Crescent Hills. I will need my mother's help to get through the pregnancy and birth." She directed her gaze at Richard. "I told Meralee last night and she is very happy." Then, she turned back to Joseph. "I will expect you to come for the birth of your first grandchild and tell Sal and Joey that they are welcome too."

"This is incredible news," Richard finally said.

"It is a miracle," Joseph added.

A few minutes later, Harry opened the door and announced that the doctor had signed Joseph's discharge papers. He was free to leave the hospital.

"I have a plane to catch," Joseph said. "I must go home and try to work out the problems of my business enterprises."

Giada and Joseph embraced and then Joseph embraced Richard Stratton. A man who had upheld the law and fought for justice his whole life and a man who lived above the law now shared a common bond and despite their differences would try to be friends.

TWENTY-EIGHT

A MONTH LATER, Turk was serving the first of the consecu-
tive life sentences that would keep him in prison for the
rest of his days. There had been no trial. Michael Dominic had negotiated a plea bargain with the prosecutor that
allowed Turk to avoid the death penalty.

Giada and Meralee Stratton were happily turning Benjamin's old bedroom into a nursery for the new baby. Joseph
Verano was back in Las Vegas and claimed to be a legitimate businessman with no more ties to organized crime.

Casey was still dating Damien Clark. Damien was very
supportive of Casey's job with Globe Investigations. He
had even helped her close the investigation of the bogus
coupon books. The woman who had perpetuated the scam
had made the mistake of coming into Damien's garage to
have her car serviced and tried to use the phony coupon.

Damien recognized her from the description that Casey
had put together from people who had purchased the coupon books. He called Casey and the police in that order,
and the woman was arrested.

On this cool fall evening, Dana and Bruno were at the
Aztec Club. They had just ordered a large sausage and
mushroom pizza. Dana's new Ford Mustang was parked
at the curb. It was a lovely shade of blue.

An entertainment news show was on the television behind the bar in the restaurant. Beth Carlson was being interviewed about her new hit record, *When Nothing Else
Was Right*.

"There's your friend on TV again," Bruno said looking at the set over Dana's curly head. "Everything she touches turns to gold these days."

"Including her recording of *When Nothing Else Was Right.* She sent me an autographed copy of her album. That's the lead song on it."

"Have you listened to that song lately?"

"How could I not? They play it every time I turn on the radio."

Bruno nodded and looked at her with a scowl. "I'm still waiting."

"For what?"

"For you to keep the promise you made the first time we listened to that song."

"What promise?"

"You promised we'd talk about our wedding. Are you going to break your promise?"

"Of course not, but I need to postpone this conversation until after the holidays. I've got a stack of cases on my desk and I don't have time to think about weddings. So, can I have an extension?"

Bruno was silent for a few minutes. Finally he nodded. "Okay, but only until New Year's Eve. At midnight, we either get engaged or we break up."

"Are you buying me a ring?" she asked with a grin.

"Not until you say yes."

"How are you going to propose without a ring?"

"On my knees with my heart in my hand."

Dana laughed. "That's going to be worth waiting for."

"You're worth waiting for," Bruno said reaching across the table and covering her hand with his. "At least until New Year's eve," he added. "Agreed?"

Dana looked into Bruno's dark eyes. This was the first time he had given her an ultimatum. This was the first time she actually believed that if she didn't commit to him, he would walk out of her life for good.

"I always honor my deadlines," she replied. "New Year's Eve it is."

* * * * *

REQUEST YOUR FREE BOOKS!

2 FREE NOVELS
PLUS 2 FREE GIFTS!

Your Partner in Crime

YES! Please send me 2 FREE novels from the Worldwide Library® series and my 2 FREE gifts (gifts are worth about $10). After receiving them, if I don't wish to receive any more books, I can return the shipping statement marked "cancel." If I don't cancel, I will receive 4 brand-new novels every month and be billed just $5.49 per book in the U.S. or $6.24 per book in Canada. That's a savings of at least 31% off the cover price. It's quite a bargain! Shipping and handling is just 50¢ per book in the U.S. and 75¢ per book in Canada.* I understand that accepting the 2 free books and gifts places me under no obligation to buy anything. I can always return a shipment and cancel at any time. Even if I never buy another book, the two free books and gifts are mine to keep forever.

414/424 WDN F4WY

Name	(PLEASE PRINT)	
Address		Apt. #
City	State/Prov.	Zip/Postal Code

Signature (if under 18, a parent or guardian must sign)

Mail to the **Harlequin® Reader Service:**
IN U.S.A.: P.O. Box 1867, Buffalo, NY 14240-1867
IN CANADA: P.O. Box 609, Fort Erie, Ontario L2A 5X3

Want to try two free books from another line?
Call 1-800-873-8635 or visit www.ReaderService.com.

* Terms and prices subject to change without notice. Prices do not include applicable taxes. Sales tax applicable in N.Y. Canadian residents will be charged applicable taxes. Offer not valid in Quebec. This offer is limited to one order per household. Not valid for current subscribers to the Worldwide Library series. All orders subject to credit approval. Credit or debit balances in a customer's account(s) may be offset by any other outstanding balance owed by or to the customer. Please allow 4 to 6 weeks for delivery. Offer available while quantities last.

Your Privacy—The Harlequin® Reader Service is committed to protecting your privacy. Our Privacy Policy is available online at www.ReaderService.com or upon request from the Harlequin Reader Service.

We make a portion of our mailing list available to reputable third parties that offer products we believe may interest you. If you prefer that we not exchange your name with third parties, or if you wish to clarify or modify your communication preferences, please visit us at www.ReaderService.com/consumerchoice or write to us at Harlequin Reader Service Preference Service, P.O. Box 9062, Buffalo, NY 14269. Include your complete name and address.

WWLI3R

ReaderService.com

Manage your account online!

- Review your order history
- Manage your payments
- Update your address

*We've designed
the Harlequin® Reader Service
website just for you.*

Enjoy all the features!

- Reader excerpts from any series
- Respond to mailings and special monthly offers
- Discover new series available to you
- Browse the Bonus Bucks catalog
- Share your feedback

Visit us at:
ReaderService.com

RS13